New York Times & *USA Today* Bestselling Author

CYNTHIA EDEN

This book is a work of fiction. Any similarities to real people, places, or events are not intentional and are purely the result of coincidence. The characters, places, and events in this story are fictional.

Published by Hocus Pocus Publishing, Inc.

Copy-editing by: J. R. T. Editing

PROLOGUE

Chelsea Ember shifted in her seat and sent an apologetic smile to the hovering waiter. "I'm sure he'll be here any minute," she said. A statement she'd already given five other times.

The waiter didn't look convinced. Probably because he thought she'd been stood up. Chelsea felt red stain her cheeks. This wasn't the first time that her date had kept her waiting. In fact, Colt Easton was starting to make her feel way too much like Lois Lane. Always sitting around, waiting for Clark to show up. But Clark had been a superhero, out saving the day.

Colt was an accountant.

And he was twenty minutes late. Again.

Sighing, Chelsea started to stand—

"So sorry." Colt appeared in front of her. Tall and crazily muscled for a man who spent so much time behind a desk. His skin was a sun-kissed gold, and his apologetic grin held mega wattage as he inclined his head toward her. "Work was killer."

She sent the waiter a quick, *See-I'm-not-alone* glance, then quickly refocused on Colt. "It's okay." But it wasn't. An ache had lodged beneath her heart. He had been late for *most* of their dates. And she honestly did not know why she was putting up with—

"You look beautiful." His lips took hers.

A surge of electricity coursed through her body.

Oh, yes. Right. This would be the reason I put up with his lateness. The man could kiss—she was talking serious talent. He could have her toes curling and her body aching with just a touch of his lips. He kissed with clever, passionate skill. Always controlled, always restrained, but Chelsea swore she could feel a fire blazing beneath his surface.

A fire she wanted to break free.

He slowly eased away. Stared at her with his deep, bold gaze. Brown, with flecks of gold. Such an intense gaze behind the lenses of his glasses. One that seemed to promise...

Passion. Pleasure.

And, okay, fine, with the glasses he did kind of give her a Clark Kent vibe but...

Colt eased into the chair across from her. He issued a quick drink order to the waiter, then eased back to stare at her. As always when Colt's stare lingered on her, Chelsea felt a surge of nervousness. Weird. Her date shouldn't make her nervous, and honestly, it was more a sense of being on edge than actual nerves. It was more like she was being—

Hunted?

No, that was crazy, that was—

"I have something to tell you," Colt announced in his deep, rumbly voice.

She licked her lips. "I have something to tell you, too." *Tonight is the night.* The night they crossed the line. The night she finally went past just a few kisses—kisses that made her need cold showers and that had her fantasizing about him touching her—everywhere. Dreaming about him taking her. Touches that had her waking up in tangled sheets and wanting him. "Tonight, I want us to—"

"Tonight, I have to leave town," he said at the same time.

She blinked. Tilted her head. "Excuse me?"

"I can't stay for dinner."

Her heart hit her stomach. *Uh, then why did you show up?*

"I wanted to see you. Needed to tell you in person..." His gaze drifted over her face. Heated. "Such a fucking tangled mess."

"Excuse me?" Chelsea queried again. It sort of seemed like that was the only thing she was capable of saying in that moment. She swallowed, twice.

His hard jaw—lined by the most careful edge of stubble—clenched. "I'm being called away on business. There's an emergency, and I have to leave immediately."

Her body had gone completely still. "An emergency?" At least she hadn't said 'excuse me' again.

A jerky nod.

"An...accounting emergency?" Just to be clear. He was leaving her—leaving right this instant, rushing away from their big date—for an accounting emergency. It wasn't even tax season.

His gaze shot away. "Yes."

You are lying to me. "I see." She could feel the burn in her cheeks. "And when will you get back?"

"I..." He ran a hand over his face. "Things are complicated."

No, they aren't. In fact, she thought things might be crystal clear. *He's lying, and he's ditching me.*

The pain inside surprised her with its sharp edge. Sort of like a knife stab.

So much for finding a good guy. So much for the silly dreams she'd started to spin about Colt. Talk about feeling foolish. When they'd first met, she'd been almost spellbound by him. When she'd looked into his eyes, she'd experienced such an odd sense of safety. There had just been something that told her she could count on him. That he wouldn't let her down.

And she'd wanted him. The kind of instant, panty-melting attraction that you read about in books or saw in movies, but when it came to real life? *Nope.* When it came to real life, she'd never instantly gotten hot for someone. Until him. Only—

Liar, liar, pants on fire.

Apparently, she was a shit judge of character. *I will not be fooled by any other intense brown eyes.* No more soulful stares.

And to think, she'd worn her sexiest underwear for him. Total waste. Anger bubbled and began to cover the pain inside.

"I'm not sure when I'll be coming back," he added, a little roughly. "But I *will* be back for you, I swear it." His soulful eyes were in full *believe-me* mode.

"Oh, don't do that." She pulled some cash from her bag. That would cover her drink and a tip for the waiter who was surreptitiously watching from close by. "Don't go making a promise that you don't need to keep." Chelsea pasted a smile on her face. It might not hold his mega wattage, but it was good enough.

Colt's gaze darted to her smile, then back up to meet her eyes. "What's happening?"

"Not the amazing sex I had originally put on the agenda, that's for sure."

The waiter dropped the drink he'd been carrying. Yep, he'd definitely been listening. Chelsea lifted her chin. "That's off the table, obviously. Your loss, by the way. Because I had such amazing, mind-blowing plans." Okay. Lie on her part, but so what? Not like he'd ever be finding out. She'd planned for sex. Not exactly big, swinging-from-the-chandelier acrobatic acts, but she'd had high hopes that they'd both leave the night feeling satisfied.

Nope.

A muscle flexed in Colt's jaw. "Chelsea..."

"There is no accounting job out of town." She was certain of it.

"Things are *complicated.*"

Oh, God. "Are you married?" Low. Accusing. "I do *not* get involved with married men. Not ever and—"

"There is no one else. Only you."

"Only me." She paused. "And the lies you tell me."

His lips pressed together. Colt didn't deny lying.

Her stomach dipped and twisted. She'd wanted a denial. A denial would have been amazing. But...He was simply staring at her. Behind the lenses of his glasses, his dark gaze seemed to have gone ice cold. She almost seemed to be looking at a stranger.

Oh, wait. I am. "Goodbye, Colt." Chelsea rose. Stood a little unsteadily on her two-inch heels. Again, she'd been going for sexy by wearing them. So much for that plan.

She took a step forward.

His hand flew out and curled around her wrist. "I will be back." A growl.

Chelsea looked down at his hand. Despite everything, his touch sent awareness and arousal careening through her. It was unnatural to want someone so much. Especially since she now understood he was a man she could not trust. "I will *not* be waiting." She pulled free...

And walked away.

Since she didn't look back, he never saw the tear that streaked down her cheek.

Maybe she should make a new dating rule. From here on out, no more nice guys. Nice guys just broke your heart. She'd only date badasses. At least with them, you could get one hell of a wild ride out of the arrangement.

CHAPTER ONE

The waves crashed into the shore. The ocean breeze slid lightly over her face, and Chelsea stretched a bit on her lounge chair as she soaked in the sun and—

A man—large and muscled—moved to stand in front of her. His broad back was to her as he peered out at the roaring waves.

Frowning, Chelsea sat up. She waited a bit for the man to move along. To be on his merry way and not in her space. The minutes ticked past. His dark hair blew in the breeze.

He didn't move along. And there was something familiar about him...

She pushed her sunglasses up a bit higher on her nose. "Excuse me," she said, voice polite, "but you are in my sun, and I—"

He turned toward her.

Her words stopped.

He was *definitely* familiar.

Chelsea shook her head. "No." *Not happening.* Not possible. Not real. She must be dreaming. Or having a nightmare. Maybe even a hallucination? Had she been out in the sun *that* long?

"Hey, sweetheart." He smiled at her. The gorgeous smile that somehow still slipped into her dreams. He wore sunglasses to shield his gaze.

Dark swim trunks that showed off his toned and seriously muscled body. And he was—

"No." The one word that she kept saying. "You aren't here."

He *couldn't* be there. She'd just escaped to the most amazing tropical paradise in the world. A small island in the Caribbean that promised hours of fun and relaxation. She was far, far away from her life in Atlanta. This could not be happening. *He* could not be there.

Her ex, Colt Easton, could not be standing on the beach in front of her. Blocking her view and her sun. And bringing her amazing vacation plans crashing to a screeching halt.

"Surprise," he said.

She shot out of the chaise lounge chair. Nearly fell into the sand but righted herself quickly. "You were not in the brochure."

A faint furrow appeared between his brows, sliding up over the edge of his sunglasses. "What brochure?"

"The one I was given at the check-in desk. The one that said this place was supposed to be paradise. I was promised massages, free drinks at sunset, and all-you-can-eat buffets." She whipped out her cover up and pulled it over her body because she did not want to have a face-off with him in a bikini. "Nowhere did it say anything about having to see my ex on the beach."

"Ex on the beach." A nod. "Isn't that a drink?"

"No. That's *sex* on the beach."

"I'm down if you are," he murmured, voice dropping even more and taking on a sensual note.

Chelsea sucked in a breath. "I am not down." She was *not*.

Colt stepped closer. Towered over her. Her own reflection stared back at her from the lenses of his sunglasses. "You sure about that? Don't you remember what it was like between us?" His hand lifted. Slid over her cheek. "I miss kissing you. I miss touching you. I miss—"

She jerked back. "What are you doing here?"

"Told you I'd be back."

She could only shake her head. "This isn't Atlanta."

"Nope. Better view." He glanced over his shoulder and gazed at the pounding surf and the bright blue water.

Chelsea got a very, very bad feeling. "You did not follow me here." But her assistant had known where she was going. Had Harvey told Colt?

"I came here for a vacation. Same as you."

That wasn't really an answer as to whether or not he'd followed her.

"There are no distractions this time," Colt told her in the deep and rumbling voice that she would never be able to forget, no matter how hard she tried—and she had tried. *Hard*. "It's you and it's me," he continued darkly, "and I can finally show you—"

"There is no me and you." She grabbed her oversized bag. A pair of shorts and a t-shirt nestled in the bottom of the bag, and she shoved her towel and sunscreen inside, too. "Thought that was clear when we broke up in Atlanta. You know, because you kept being late to our dates—or not showing up," because he'd done that a time or three, "and then suddenly telling me that you had to go out of town." She'd been left hanging too many times. Didn't matter how gorgeous the man was or how great of a kisser he could be...

I moved on.

"I want a second chance."

Oh, no. Her breath stuttered. She shook her head. "Bad idea."

"Chelsea, things will be different this time. I'm not the same man I was before."

What was that supposed to mean? She slung her bag over one shoulder. Her gaze swept over him. Lingered for a moment on what looked like truly lickable abs—she was only human, after all. "You look the same to me." Not exactly the same. Normally, he wore more clothes. Lots more clothes. Business suits. Expensive ties. Polished shoes. She'd never seen him quite like this, and her fingers carefully swiped over her lips to make certain that she wasn't doing anything embarrassing, like drooling.

How is he so built? Accountants should not look like Thor.

"Chelsea, I want to explain—"

"Oh, there he is." She picked a man at random. A fellow about twenty yards away, wearing a white t-shirt and blue swim trunks. Almost as big as Colt, but not quite. "On my way!" Chelsea called cheerily as she waved at the stranger.

"What in the hell?" A growl from Colt. "Who is that?"

"My new boyfriend," she lied without missing a beat. *Have to get away.* Because where Colt was concerned, she had an unfortunate tendency to be weak. "It's been two months, Colt." Two very long months. Not that she'd counted. It was just easy to keep track of time. A natural thing. No big deal. Not like she'd been nursing a broken heart. Or sobbing into her chocolate stash late at night. Nope, not her. "I told you I wasn't waiting."

"New. Boyfriend?" Each word was bitten off.

The man in question—the, ah, boyfriend—looked behind him, as if he expected that Chelsea was waving to someone else. She really hoped that Colt didn't notice that movement. She waved again. Smiled broadly. "Yes. We're here together, and he is extremely jealous."

"Know the fucking feeling," Colt muttered as he glared at the man in the white t-shirt. "I...I didn't realize you were seeing someone new."

I didn't either. Neither did the poor, confused man down the beach. "Enjoy your time on the island," she said briskly. Then she did what she had to do.

She walked away. And with every step...

OhGod, OhGod...he'd come after her. Was that supposed to be romantic? Stalkery? She did not know. Chelsea just knew that she had to get away because when she was around Colt, she didn't always think clearly.

Actually, she tended to stop thinking altogether, and she just wanted to jump the man. *This is a no-jumping vacation. Get away from him.*

Sand kicked up in her wake as she rushed for her "boyfriend" as he waited with a frown on his face.

"Hi," she said softly when she was finally close enough to be able to talk to the stranger. "Ahem. I had you confused with someone else. My apologies." Chelsea darted a look over her shoulder. Found Colt staring at her.

A shiver slid over her body because his expression...

"Confuse me with anyone you want," the stranger invited.

Her head whipped back toward him.

He smiled at her. "Want a drink?"

Um...What she wanted was to get off that beach, but a drink? Yes, she could certainly use one of those. "Sure." They headed for the bar. Probably looked like a couple as they left, and she figured their walking away together would certainly seal the deal in Colt's eyes.

One less worry.

Her fake boyfriend—he introduced himself as Brian—ordered her a tropical knockout. Chelsea had no idea just what that might be, but she made polite conversation with Brian while the bartender—a guy dressed in a colorful, Hawaiian shirt—created the lovely concoction. In moments, the bartender slid her a bright blue drink with a cute little umbrella sticking out of the top. Absolutely adorable. If she'd had her phone, she would have snapped a pic of it. But the phone was in her room because she'd been trying to unplug and relax. Cautiously, she sipped the tropical knockout, and wow, the alcohol content was *strong*. A punch in a pretty package. No wonder it was called a tropical knockout.

She curled her fingers around the drink, thanked him and politely excused herself from Brian, then began her meandering walk back toward her room. It was a walk that took her beneath swaying palm trees and away from the crowd and—

"Not going to cut out on me so soon, are you?"

It was her fake boyfriend. He'd followed her.

She turned to face him. "Ah, I think I got too much sun. I'm heading to my room, but it was nice to meet you, Brian." A polite dismissal. She had no interest in pursuing anything with Brian.

Especially when all she could think about was her very troubling ex.

Colt is on the island. Probably staying in the hotel. What will I do when I see him again?

Brian put his hands on his hips. "You made me."

"Made you?" Made him do what? Order the drink? That had been his choice, and the drink had been free, part of the whole happy hour bonus at the hotel so—

"Should have known the minute you showed me to the bastard on the beach." He heaved out a breath. He didn't look nearly as friendly any longer. "So much for doing this the easy way."

Chelsea scampered back a step. "I do not understand what you're talking about." But she had a very, very bad feeling in her gut. She extended the drink toward him. "Why don't you just take this—"

He reached out. But he didn't grab the drink. He grabbed for *her*. "The deal was that I take *you*."

She screamed and threw the drink in his face.

***

A fucking boyfriend?

Colt jerked on his shirt as he stood on the beach. He'd waited too long. He should have known that a woman like Chelsea would have some asshole sniffing around her.

I used to be said asshole.

From the first moment that he'd seen her, he'd wanted her. He'd broken all of his careful rules to get in her life. But he'd lied to her. He'd been pulled away. He'd have to leave for another case...

I came back for her.

Because there were some things in this world that a man just could not give up. Not without one hell of a fight.

Jealousy burned through him as he left his shirtfront hanging open and started marching back toward the hotel. They'd gone to the bar together. Chelsea and the blond asshole who'd been grinning like a loon at her. What in the hell did she see in that guy?

And has he fucked her?

Colt's back teeth ground together. This was not the time to beat the shit out of some stranger. This was supposed to be the time to charm Chelsea. To let her get to know the *real* Colt.

And the real me wants to beat the shit out of—

Chelsea wasn't at the bar. Neither was the blond jerk. The jealousy inside of Colt flared even hotter and harder. *I should have never left her.* But it had been a life-or-death mission, and he hadn't been clear to tell Chelsea what was really going on. Or who he really was. She thought he was some buttoned-up accountant, and he'd tried his best to play that role with her. He'd held onto his control every time they were together when all he'd wanted to do was grab her, push her up against the nearest wall, and take her until she screamed with pleasure.

Hardly civilized. Hardly gentlemanly.

But it's more like the real me.

He stalked away from the bar. He needed a new game plan, ASAP. Because he had to find a way to get back in Chelsea's life. He wanted a second chance. He wanted—

"Help!" A wild, desperate scream. One that chilled his blood because it was a *familiar* voice doing that screaming. It was Chelsea.

He took off running, lunging down a narrow path shaded by twisting palm trees. He kicked a plastic cup and a little umbrella out of his way and barreled around the curving path to see—

Chelsea. Fighting the blond bastard. Fighting him as that SOB shoved her into the back of a van. She tried to lunge away from him, and the guy—

Hit her.

Oh, the fuck, no. A guttural roar broke from Colt even as Chelsea fell back inside the rear of the van. The blond slammed the rear doors, and his head whipped toward Colt.

You are a dead man. Colt raced forward.

The blond surged toward the front of the van. Jumped inside and took off with a screech of the vehicle's wheels. The scent of burning rubber stung Colt's nose as he reached for the back of the van—for Chelsea—and his fingers scraped over the surface before it shot away. "No!" A snarl.

The van didn't slow. If anything, it sped up even more as it zipped away from the hotel.

Someone had just taken Chelsea. Someone had just taken *his* Chelsea.

That someone had made a fatal mistake.

He immediately ran for the line of cars parked near the hotel's entrance. A guy was just exiting his vehicle, and he saw Colt charging toward him. A look of alarm flashed on the man's pale face. Sunscreen slathered across his nose.

"Valet," Colt snapped. "Park your ride for you?"

"I, uh—"

Colt snatched the keys. "Don't you worry, I'll take care of her. Go have a drink. Maybe four." He jumped into the vehicle. Had that little Jeep growling and rushing away in seconds. He didn't have any time to lose. Not like he could rush around to the other side of the place and get his own car. He'd lose the van if he stopped to do that shit.

That couldn't happen. He could *not* lose Chelsea.

What in the hell was going on? Why would someone take her?

Colt didn't know, but until he had her back, the tight fist would remain around his heart. He shoved the gas pedal into the floorboard. *Hold on, sweetheart. I'm coming.*

Fear and fury flooded through him. He didn't even have a weapon. Sonofabitch. Not like he'd brought his gun to the island with him.

Colt's gaze darted to the glove box. What were the odds...Hell, he knew they were slim to none. But maybe there was *something* in there he could use. A screwdriver, perhaps? But when he jerked open the glove box, there wasn't a damn thing in there.

Sonofabitch. Looked like he'd be doing some serious improvising. Good thing he excelled in that area.

He would do whatever was necessary in order to get Chelsea back.

***

The van finally stopped. Chelsea's breath choked out. As soon as she'd felt the vehicle take off, she'd grabbed for the rear doors only to discover that they wouldn't open. She'd hit every wall in the back of the van, desperately trying to find a way out, but she'd been trapped.

Only we've stopped now. She feared that stopping was a bad—extremely bad—sign.

Like being kidnapped in the first place was a good sign.

Her frantic gaze darted to the left and the right. She still had her bag with her. It had been slung over one shoulder when that jerk Brian had shoved her into the van. *And hit me.* Her jaw ached. That asshole had messed with the wrong woman.

She reached inside the bag. Not like there were a ton of weapon options, but she did have a can of spray sunscreen. And as soon as those back doors opened...

She would attack.

Chelsea crouched close to the rear doors. And waited. Every breath sawed in and out. Felt painful.

What is happening? Oh, God, is this some kind of sex slave thing? Is he trying to make me vanish? Is he a serial killer? Is he going to cut me up and—

One of the back doors opened with a creak. Light trickled inside. "I don't want to have to get physical with you again," Brian declared as he opened the door wider. "So just do what you're told and—"

She leapt at him. Sprayed that sunscreen for all she was worth and screamed gutturally.

His scream was even louder than hers as he clawed at his eyes and stumbled back.

Chelsea kept her grip on the sunscreen and her bag, and she hurtled out of that van. She raced past Brian and—

And slammed right into someone else. Another man. Jet-black hair. Piercings in his left ear. Wearing a Hawaiian shirt. A shirt she remembered. He was...

"The bartender?" Chelsea gasped. Yes, yes, this had been the man who made her drink. "You're partners." She tried to jerk back, but he held her in an unbreakable grip. *Oh, damn. Tropical knockout.* Knockout. Had that been some sort of code? It must have been.

There was a whole lot of swearing going on behind her. She risked a glance back and saw that Brian was glaring at her. His very, very bloodshot eyes streamed with tears, courtesy of her sunscreen attack. “You bitch!”

This was bad. Worse than bad. She was trapped between two men who seemed like they were about to hurt her, and it looked like she was in some kind of old, dusty garage and no one else was around and—

“Is that any way to talk to a lady?”

Her jaw almost hit the ground.

And Colt Easton walked out of the shadows.

She shook her head. She was as stunned to see him in that instant as she’d been on the beach. “What are you doing?” she whispered.

“Saving you,” he replied as his hands remained loose at his sides. He still had on his sunglasses. His shorts. An unbuttoned shirt. He was even wearing flip flops. This did not look like a man who was there to save the day.

Well, except for those abs...

Otherwise, he looked like...

Someone who was about to get hurt.

“You need to get your ass out of here,” the man holding Chelsea snapped to Colt even as the jerk maneuvered her to the side. The new position let her see everyone clearly, and even more terror filled her because...

Brian pulled out a gun. One that had been tucked into the back of his waistband. “*Now,*” Brian thundered at Colt. “Get the hell away because this does not concern you!”

A gun. Her heart slammed hard in her chest. He had a gun pointed at Colt. She'd been kidnapped. Somehow Colt had found her—or followed her—or, or something. And now Colt was about to get shot. "No." She licked desert-dry lips. "Go, Colt. *Go!* Go now." He could go. He could get help. He could live.

Worst vacation ever. And it was only day one. She wished she had never, ever left home.

Colt shook his head. "I'm not going anywhere." His hand lifted.

Brian tensed.

"Easy there, trigger happy," Colt cautioned in a voice that was oddly smooth and easy. As if he didn't realize a gun was pointed at him. "Just taking off my sunglasses." And he did. He slowly lowered them. Tucked them into the pocket of his shirt. His intense, dark gaze swept first over Brian, then over the man who still held her.

The man who—

He jerked her against his body. Looped one arm over her collarbone so that he could grab her shoulder and hold her and with his other hand...

Chelsea felt the edge of something sharp press to her throat. A knife. She didn't even swallow because she feared he'd nick her with the blade. Terror pretty much just froze her.

Colt shook his head. "That's a mistake."

The man holding her shouted, *"Get the fuck out of here!"*

She wanted to scream the same thing at Colt, but Chelsea was too afraid to speak. She'd never had a knife pressed to her throat before.

She *did* still have her trusty sunscreen in her right hand, though. Could she spray it in the bartender's eyes? If she did, would he reflexively let her go? Or would he slice her throat wide open in response? She didn't want to risk the slit throat, so she didn't move.

Colt turned his head so that he was looking at Brian. "You hit her."

Brian took several fast, angry steps toward Colt as he blinked his bleary eyes. "Jackass, I am about to—"

Colt grabbed the gun. Just whipped his hand out in a lightning-fast move and took the weapon away from Brian. Made the movement appear so easy. Like...like taking candy from a baby. For a moment, Brian just gaped. Then he did a double-take when he looked down at his now empty hand and then back up at Colt and—

"Don't ever fucking hit her again." Colt drove his left fist into Brian's face. Brian stumbled back, slipped, then fell. His head hit the cement, and his whole body seemed to go lax.

Is he dead? No, no, his chest rose and fell, so he just had to be unconscious. He had to be. *Maybe?*

"Hey, asshole," Colt called out, voice taunting.

The man holding Chelsea—the, ah, asshole in question—stiffened, and his grip tightened on her even more.

"Let her go, or I will shoot you."

Colt had the gun aimed at the man holding her. Except the man was holding her *extremely close*. As in, only inches separated their bodies.

And if Colt shot, he'd probably shoot her, too. "Don't," Chelsea gasped out.

Colt's eyes narrowed.

"You'll shoot me," she added. This was...quite dramatic. Very impressive. She appreciated the rescue more than she could say. *So much more.* But... "Go call the cops. Let's..." Her voice seemed squeaky. "Let's not shoot anyone."

Colt held her gaze. "Do you trust me?" His voice was low. Growling. Ever so fierce.

And her reply was the same. Low. Growling. Ever so fierce. "No. I do not." That was why they had *broken up.* Because he'd never been there. Because she couldn't count on him. Because she didn't feel like she really knew him and—

The knife nicked her. She felt the blade cut her and because she was staring straight at Colt, she saw the change sweep over his expression. His face went savage. No other word for it. It hardened. Tightened. His eyes blazed as fury stole across his features.

"Mistake," he snapped.

She thought he was talking to the man who'd just cut her, but maybe Colt meant she was making a mistake by not trusting him. Either way, his fingers were tightening on that gun, he was going to shoot, and she didn't want to get hit.

Chelsea screamed, hoping the shriek would distract the man who held her, and then she lifted up her sunscreen. She sprayed it back at him.

"Chelsea!" Colt bellowed.

Her attacker let her go. Just for an instant, and she immediately dropped down. Dropped, fell. Same thing. Then she heard the thunder of a bullet blasting.

She wanted to slap her hands over her ears, but instead, she started crawling forward as fast as she could, still desperately gripping her sunscreen and her bag and just trying to get away—

Colt hauled her to her feet. "Baby?" His fingers curled around her shoulders. "Let me see your neck."

Uh, she'd rather see them both *run*. As in, get out of there. "I'm fine." She thought that was the case, but she could feel blood dripping down her neck. Not a lot, more like a trickle. It was her first knife wound. Ever.

Please, be my first and last.

"Fucking sonofabitch." One of Colt's hands moved under her chin. He tilted her head to the left. The right. "Small slice." His gaze raked her face. "How's the jaw? How is—"

Bam.

She actually felt the heat of that bullet whip past her before it slammed into the nearby wall. As her jaw dropped and renewed horror flooded through her, Chelsea glanced back and saw that Brian wasn't unconscious any longer. His *friend* with the knife was on the floor, and there was blood near the guy—a growing puddle—and she felt nausea well inside of her. Chelsea thought she might have been sick right then, if Brian hadn't lifted his gun and aimed it at—

How did he get a second gun? Where the hell had he been hiding that thing?

Colt fired before Brian could get off another shot. "Fucking amateur mistake," Colt shouted.

What was? And who was the amateur? Her? Him? Their attacker?

Colt's fingers threaded through hers. "Come on." He fired, and Brian ducked for cover. Then Colt was running with her, using his body to shield hers, and blasting off a few more shots as they raced out of the garage. The precious sunscreen bottle fell from her fingers, but when she tried to grab it, Colt just lifted her into his arms and ran faster. A few moments later, he pushed her toward a blue Jeep. "Get in and get down!"

She got in. She got down. Apparently, she didn't get down far enough because as soon as Colt jumped behind the wheel, he pushed her even farther toward the floorboard. Annoyed, she snapped back, "Do you really think that's necessary—"

There was an odd metal *clinking* sound.

Her eyes widened. Her mouth snapped closed. A bullet had just hit the back of the Jeep.

"Very necessary," Colt retorted grimly.

She thought so, too. Chelsea tried to become a ball in the floorboard area as he cranked the engine and raced them away from that terrible place. She heard more gunfire, an angry yell and then...

Silence.

No, her own ragged breathing, her racing, wild heartbeat, and...silence. The kind of silence that meant some madman had stopped firing bullets at them. She peeked up from her position on the floorboard. Swallowed a few times. Touched the nick on her throat. And gaped at Colt.

A Colt who had one hand wrapped around the steering wheel and another still holding a gun. *A gun*. The wind tossed back his hair, and his open shirt flew around him.

He glanced down at her. And *smiled*. His megawatt smile. “Are you glad to see me now?”

CHAPTER TWO

"There has to be some mistake."

Colt crossed his arms over his chest and watched the scene unfold. He already knew this wasn't going to end well. He'd tried to warn her, but Chelsea hadn't listened to him.

Chelsea pointed to the empty garage. "There was a van here!" Her voice notched up as she looked at the police officer in front of her—or, rather, what passed for the police on the tropical island. The man in the rumpled, coffee-stained shirt and knee shorts didn't look very official. A line of grizzled stubble covered his jaw, and Colt was pretty sure the fellow had been sleeping when Chelsea had burst into the island's police station. A teeny, tiny station with one cell in the back.

"There is no van here," Chief Victor Sorenz noted.

"No, not now because the bad guys ran away!" She turned around, searched the ground. "There should be blood on the cement."

On that note, she was correct. There *should* have been blood, but Colt's nose was already twitching from the scent of bleach. Someone had done a fast cleanup job after he'd escaped with Chelsea. Not a good sign.

"Blood," Victor repeated as he rocked back and slid a glance toward Colt. "Because your friend shot one of your would-be kidnappers?"

"Yes!" Chelsea declared. She gave a few vehement nods.

Colt didn't speak. He knew this was one of those times when the less you said, the better. Especially when you didn't exactly trust the person you were speaking with—and in this case, his instincts were screaming a warning to him about Victor. He was just too cool. Too unconcerned. When a tourist came screaming to you about a kidnapping, you should at least pretend a little concern. Chelsea had practically needed to drag the fellow from the little station. For Colt, it all boiled down to one big question. Why did Victor seem to not have any fucks to give about the situation?

"Have you been drinking?" Victor asked Chelsea as he rubbed a hand over the scruff on his jaw.

"I—just a little. More like a few sips."

"Um."

"The bartender who made the drink was one of the kidnappers!" she rushed to add.

"Was he?" Doubt laced Victor's question.

Victor was not buying what Chelsea was saying. Colt had tried to caution her that going to the local authorities might not be the best plan. She'd responded by saying he was crazy.

Maybe...

But I'm also right.

"There is no van. There is no blood. No body. There is nothing at all to say you were even here earlier." Victor's tone became clipped as his hand fell back to his side. "Please do not waste my time on some sort of hoax."

She scampered toward him. "This isn't a hoax." Chelsea pointed to her throat. "Do you see where he cut me?"

Victor squinted. Squinted some more. "No?"

A hard exhale burst from her as Chelsea stumbled back. She glanced beseechingly at Colt. "Tell him!"

Colt shrugged. "Two men in a van took her. I followed. Got her away from them."

Victor took a few halting steps toward him. "Are you some sort of...security for her?"

Colt opened his mouth.

"No, he's an accountant," Chelsea explained with a wave in Colt's general direction. "He happened to be in the right place at the right time, and I am eternally grateful to him."

Eternally grateful. Colt filed that bit away for later. Good to know. He could work with some eternal gratitude from her.

"But now I need your help, Officer—" Chelsea continued.

"Chief." His chin lifted.

"Chief. I need your help! These men are dangerous! You have to help me find them. What if...what if they have some sort of operation going on the island? An operation where they are abducting single women?"

Victor tilted his head as he seemed to consider that possibility. "I think I would have heard about disappearances on my island."

Her mouth opened. Closed. Opened again. "You—"

"Go back to your hotel, miss. I will investigate more tomorrow. In the morning, after you've rested and the alcohol is out of your system, we can talk again."

"But—but—" She kind of sputtered to a stop as she gaped at the *chief* in disbelief.

Victor turned away. Headed for his little white patrol car.

Chelsea rushed to follow him.

Colt didn't rush. He took his time and did a thorough sweep of the crime scene. This wasn't some amateur cleanup. Fast, efficient, and thorough.

Concerning.

What is going on? And he definitely had a bad feeling about the local law enforcement. He'd never encountered someone who wanted to help a victim *less*. Like that didn't make Chief Victor Sorenz seem suspicious.

"He left!"

Colt looked up. Chelsea stood in the doorway, with the setting sun behind her and still just dressed in that filmy, see-through coverup of hers that left *nothing* to his imagination. When he'd approached her on the beach, she'd been wearing the smallest red bikini in the world. A bikini that had nearly sent him to his knees right then and there. One that *had* sent aching arousal flooding through him. His dick had gotten so hard and eager that he'd had to turn away.

Colt had stared at the churning waves and tried to cool down, but that hadn't helped anything. Then she'd spoken in that husky, sensual voice of hers. A voice that had rolled right over his body, and he'd turned to look at her—

Only to see dawning horror appear on her lovely face when she'd realized exactly who he was. Hardly the reunion he'd optimistically fantasized about.

"Colt?" Her hands went to her hips. Fisted. Her dark hair—thick and lustrous—tumbled over her shoulders. Her bold green gaze met his stare with disbelief plain to see in her eyes. "Can you believe that?" Her full lips tightened in anger. "He just left. Didn't even examine the area! Didn't try to collect any evidence. Didn't dust for prints—didn't do any of the stuff that they do on TV shows!"

He didn't point out that this wasn't a TV show and that he doubted the chief's budget extended to a crime scene analysis team.

"When I followed him out, I tried to tell him that the Jeep had been hit by a stray bullet, and he barely even slowed down to listen to me!"

Even more suspicious. Colt didn't just think the man was inept. He thought the chief might just be involved in whatever madness was happening. "I think you need to leave the island." ASAP.

"What?"

"You heard me." He closed in on her. As he drew nearer, her scent wrapped around him. Seductive. Light. Feminine. Sexy. The faintest trace of lavender and vanilla. "You need to get the hell out of here."

"I..." Her head tipped back as she looked up at him. "My flight doesn't leave for a week. This is day one of my trip. Day *one*."

Easy solution. "Book another flight. You were nearly taken." *So you should get the hell out of here.*

"But...but they aren't going to come after me again. I mean...they *won't*."

He stared back at her. Colt had no idea what might happen next.

"One of the men worked at the hotel," she said. Her voice was uncertain. Scared. He hated for her to be scared. "The jerk with the knife—the one you shot. I have to tell the manager that a criminal is working there." Chelsea sucked in a deep breath. "What if he tries this tactic on other guests?"

"Are you *sure* he worked for the hotel?" His instincts said no.

"He was at the bar. He made my drink. A tropical knockout. That's—that's what Brian called it. Brian was the blond," she admitted miserably.

Brian. His eyes narrowed. "Got to tell you, sweetheart..."

She tensed.

"Your new boyfriend is a real bastard. If I were you, I'd consider dumping his ass." *Or how about I just eliminate the sonofabitch for you?*

Her hands twisted in front of her. "He's not my boyfriend."

"No?" *Keep the eagerness out of your voice.*

Her long lashes swept down to conceal her gaze. "No."

The plot just kept thickening. "Let's get the hell out of here, and I want you to tell me everything." Because being out in the open? That was too dangerous. Until he had a better handle on what was going down, he needed to play things safe—and keep an extra close watch on Chelsea.

Why is someone after her? Chelsea was an interior designer with a bustling business in Atlanta. She worked with high-end clients—hell, Colt had originally made his way into her life because one of her clients had been a target of his.

Chelsea thought he was an accountant. That he had worked in the office one floor below hers in the Atlanta high-rise, but she'd been wrong. Mostly because he'd lied to her. Something she was probably not going to easily forgive but...

They headed back outside. Chelsea gave out a little cry of surprise and bent down. When she straightened, she had a sunscreen bottle gripped in her hand, and she grinned as if she'd just won a major prize. "This proves we were here!"

"Uh, yeah, sweetheart," he urged her toward the Jeep. "I remember being here. You don't have to prove anything to me. And I highly doubt a bottle of old sunscreen would have done anything to get the chief on our side."

He took the sunscreen. Put it in the back of the Jeep. Once she was settled, he did one more quick visual of the area. *Remote. Hidden.* If he hadn't followed that van when it left the hotel, no one would have known that Chelsea had been taken to this spot. It was so far off the beaten path that...

No one would have heard her screams.

His teeth ground together as Colt jumped into the driver's seat.

"What is it?" Chelsea asked him softly. "You look mad."

He cranked the vehicle. "Mad doesn't fucking begin to cover it." He got them the hell out of there. But as they zoomed away from the scene, he made sure to check his rearview and to keep a careful watch on the roads around him. *Is someone out there watching us now?*

"Look, I-I appreciate you rushing to help me. It was incredibly kind—and brave—of you to do that, and I'm really, really sorry that your Jeep was hit. I can pay for damages—"

"Don't be sorry. Not my Jeep."

"If you'll just tell me how much—wait. What?"

"Not my Jeep. Don't worry about the damages." He'd take care of things.

"Uh, who does the Jeep belong to? And how did you get it?"

Probably wasn't the best time to tell her that he'd stolen the Jeep. Colt opted to redirect the conversation. "He wasn't your boyfriend." An excellent point to know.

From the corner of his eye, he saw her hands twist in her lap. "No." Very definite. "In fact, I, um..." She cleared her throat. The wind whipped her hair back. "I hadn't met him until today."

He braked hard at a stop sign. Turned his head toward her. "What. The. Fuck?"

Chelsea winced. "So...confession?"

He didn't take his eyes off her. "I'd like to hear this."

"You made me nervous on the beach. So I just picked a guy at random, I waved to him, ran away from you, and the next thing I knew..." Her hand rose and rubbed over her jaw. Against the faint bruise that lined her skin. "He was shoving me into the back of the van. He said something about me having 'made' him on the beach and...and we were gone."

Sonofa—His grip tightened on the wheel. "New rule." Each word was bitten out. "No random guys. *Ever.*" Or he'd rip them fucking apart.

"Not like I make a habit of running up to strangers," Chelsea muttered as she looked away. "Extenuating circumstances, all right? I wasn't expecting to see my ex on the beach."

You should have expected me. I told you I'd be back for you. He accelerated. Kept scanning around the Jeep.

"He offered to get me a drink. I let him. I mean, what was the harm? The drinks were free. Then I walked away after just taking a sip or two of the drink." Now her words were clipped, and she still hadn't looked back at Colt. "I was heading to my room when I heard someone coming up behind me. I spun around, he was there, and that's when he said that I'd, uh, made him."

Not good. Colt was realizing that she was specifically targeted. From the sound of things, the guy had been watching her. Waiting for the moment to strike.

"He said something about so much for doing things the 'easy way' and he pretty much scared me to death because I knew the hard way had to be coming."

Fuck. "Your drink was probably drugged. Jerk must have thought he could get you away quickly, but when you bailed on him at the bar, he had to reevaluate."

"I screamed." She kept looking out of the window. "He was stronger than I was. He picked me up, I fought him, but he still dumped me in the van."

The silence ticked past as he headed for the hotel. He wished that he'd torn the bastard apart.

"How did you find me?" Chelsea finally asked.

Colt forced his jaw to unclench. "Heard your scream." A scream that would no doubt haunt his dreams. "Got there in time to see him put you in the van." Rage rose, but he choked it down. "I tailed the SOB."

"It was truly incredibly nice of you to help me, but...you could have just called the cops."

Something told him that Victor wouldn't have been a whole lot of help. *I will be getting my buddies to dig into his life, ASAP.* "I'll remember that for next time."

"Good. Because you're not Clark Kent, you know. If you'd been shot, those bullets wouldn't have bounced off you." Her voice went even huskier than normal. "The last thing I would want is for you to get hurt because of me."

And what's the first thing you want, baby? Colt knew exactly what the first thing he wanted was—her.

"But there won't *be* a next time," Chelsea continued doggedly. "One abduction per lifetime is more than enough, thank you. I'll talk to the hotel manager. I'll talk to the chief tomorrow. We'll figure this all out. They'll catch those creeps, and it will be over."

His lips pressed together. In Colt's experience, nothing was ever that easy. But it just didn't seem like the right moment to shatter her illusions. She'd already had one hell of a day.

***

"Can you believe that?" Chelsea fumed as she stood in front of her hotel room door. "The manager said only four people were employed as bartenders at this hotel—and that they were all women!"

Yes, he could believe it. Mostly because he'd heard the manager say those exact words to Chelsea when she'd rushed into the guy's office.

"And what was up with the valet attendant?" Chelsea wanted to know. Her hands fluttered in the air. The see-through cover up stretched wondrously. "All he could do was sputter when you handed him the keys to that Jeep. That was just weird."

"Um." Colt wasn't touching that one. He'd slipped the valet attendant some cash. As for the bullet hole on the back of the vehicle, it was on his to-do list. He'd pay for repairs.

"This has been the worst day ever." Her shoulders sagged as her hands fell to her sides. "I just want to go inside and crawl into bed."

And I just want to come inside and crawl into bed with you. Oh, what a sweet, hot temptation.

But she kept standing in front of her door. And not issuing an invitation so he cleared his throat and told her, "I think it would be best if you let me come inside."

Just like that, her shoulders snapped to attention once more. "Excuse me?"

He was already booked in the room right next to hers. A little bribe at check-in had taken care of the matter and gotten Colt the adjoining room. "You're in danger, Chelsea." Obviously. "I don't think you should be alone."

She stared up at him. Had her eyes become even deeper, even greener in the last two months? It sure looked that way to him. It sure looked—

Her hand lifted. Pressed to his cheek. She had the softest skin. He wanted her hands touching him everywhere. And she was touching him as if—

"Don't let this go to your head," Chelsea told him with a faint smile. "We both got lucky today."

Lucky? Oh, he'd like to get lucky with—

"But you were out of your league with those men."

The hell he'd been. Talk about insulting. He'd kicked their asses. Had she missed that bit of awesomeness? She shouldn't have missed it. Chelsea had been right *there*.

"They could have hurt you, Colt. And, honestly, *you* could have shot *me*."

What. The. Fuck. "Not a possibility."

"Of course, it was. Look, I get that you were bluffing. I get that you wouldn't have actually *fired* when you told that guy holding me that you were going to take the shot, but...face facts, when you're holding a gun, anything can happen.

Sweaty fingers get trigger twitchy." She patted his cheek. "You can't play hero again."

Play hero? He hadn't been playing anything. He'd been saving her gorgeous ass. What had happened to her being eternally grateful?

"You can't come into my room and be some—some bodyguard. That's just not going to work. First, I don't need a bodyguard. Not like those men will come for me again. One of them is probably in a clinic—I'm sure Victor is searching the local area now for him—"

Yeah, Colt doubted that. He'd lay odds that Victor was somewhere sleeping.

"And two..." Her hand fell. "I am *not* inviting you into my room because if I do, things will—well, things will get..." She trailed off. Did an *ahem* before primly continuing, "Things might get mixed up. We're exes. We shouldn't be bunking in the same room. We shouldn't do that because—" Now she just stopped talking entirely.

He waited a minute. Inhaled the utterly intoxicating lavender and vanilla scent that was pure Chelsea.

She stared at him. Blinked her incredible eyes.

So Colt decided to finish for her. "Because we still want each other?"

Her tongue darted out. Tapped her top lip. That full, luscious lip.

"Because when we're close, you can feel the need just below the surface?" Colt pushed.

"Well..."

He wanted her mouth so he eased closer. Leaned toward her. Put one hand on the doorframe to her right. "Because when we kiss, things get hot, very, very fast. And you know that if we go beyond kissing, there will be no stopping—"

Her hand flew to his chest. "It has been a long day."

Hell. It had been. She'd been through a nightmare, and now she had his horny ass messing with her. His chin jerked up. "Right." Adrenaline and fury still coursed through him. *What if I hadn't found her?* But he needed to get his emotions under control. One wrong move, and he could screw up everything with her.

This was his second chance. He couldn't blow it. Wouldn't. "You shouldn't be alone," he growled. "I can sleep on the floor. Be a perfect freaking gentleman." If that was what she wanted him to be.

A little furrow appeared between her brows. "Isn't that what you always were? Other than being late—or not showing up, I mean, that certainly wasn't very gentlemanly. But when it came to the physical side of things..." Her hand motioned between them. "It was just kisses. You never pushed for more. Sometimes, I wasn't even sure you wanted more."

Oh, hell, yes, he'd wanted more. She'd never understand the level of restraint he'd used with her.

"That control of yours was always in perfect place. I was the one to go wild. You were the one to pull back."

Because he hadn't wanted to take her when he was lying to her. It just hadn't felt right. Mostly because she *did* feel right. After a lifetime of wrong, Chelsea was his right. And he'd lied to her over and over again.

"Can I tell you a secret?" she asked him, voice hushed even though no one else was around to overhear them.

"You can tell me anything." Everything.

"I hated your control. Just once, I would have liked to see you without it. Maybe then I wouldn't have felt like you were freezing me. Or always putting me second."

Dammit. "Chelsea—"

"I'm tired and shaky, and I think I have a whole lot of adrenaline coursing through me. I suspect it's making me say things I shouldn't." She pressed her lips together. Retreated a half step. "Yes, let's go with that excuse, okay? Or maybe just forget I said anything."

He would not forget. When it came to Chelsea, he never forgot a damn thing. He couldn't.

She shoved her hand into her bag. She'd been clutching that bag ever since he'd seen her in the garage. Her hand came out with the keycard for her room, and she swiped it over her lock. The light flashed to green, and Chelsea pushed open her door.

"Chelsea..." Colt caught himself reaching for her. His hand fisted.

She looked back.

"Turns out," Colt tried what he hoped was a reassuring smile, "I'm right next door." He inclined his head to the right. "So if you need anything or if you get scared, just knock on the connecting door."

Her amazing eyes narrowed. "You're in the room next door?"

"Um."

"That's quite a coincidence."

Not really. "I didn't expect our reunion to go this way."

She took a step into her room. Stopped. Glanced back at him as if she couldn't help herself. "How did you expect it to wind up?"

Not with you being kidnapped. "In my best fantasies, you threw your arms around me and kissed me like your life depended on it."

Chelsea blinked. "And in your worst fantasies?"

You told me that you didn't want me any longer. That I had to stay out of your life. "My worst fantasy now involves some jerk shoving you in the back of a van."

"That's my worst fantasy, too."

He should move. Walk away. Let her rest.

He kept standing there and drinking her in. "I'm glad you're okay."

"And I'm really glad you were there to help me."

Baby, from here on out, I will always be there for you.

"Maybe we could try being friends," Chelsea continued as she lingered in the open doorway. "We didn't work well as lovers so...maybe that's what we should be. Friends."

Oh, hell, no. She was not about to friend-zone him. "We weren't lovers."

She backed up a little, retreating more into her room. "No...almost, though. That last night—I thought that would be when we crossed the line."

And I left her. Talk about a dumbass move. "I only left because it was urgent. Life or death."

One delicate eyebrow arched. "An accounting emergency. Yes, you said that."

"No, I—" It hadn't been an accounting emergency. He needed to tell her the truth. But this hardly seemed the time to drop a bombshell on her. "I don't want to be your friend." Talk about hell.

She flinched.

Crap. Could he not stop screwing up with her? "I want you," he added roughly. "That hasn't changed. I see you, and I want you. I hear your voice, and I want you. I can't be some platonic friend with you." When it came to her, he was far too savage. Too desperate, hungry, and primal. But she didn't get that. She'd only seen him as the controlled, restrained guy. The jerk in the fancy suits. The fellow behind the glasses who calculated numbers and worked on tax returns.

God save me.

That undercover mission had been killer. "I don't want to be your friend," he said roughly, "but I'll take whatever I can get. If you don't want me anymore, if you don't want to see..." Hell, he was rambling. He needed to end this scene before it got worse. "Good night, Chelsea."

But he didn't walk away. He kept drinking her in.

She looked down at the floor. "I don't want to be your friend, either."

His heart rate surged. *Glance up at me. Let me see your eyes. Let me see...*

She tilted her head up. Stared at him. "I don't know what we are. What we'll be. But you're right. Friendship is off the table." A deep breath. "Thanks for saving me."

Thank me with a kiss. Thank me with—

Nope. That would be an asshole thing to say. He was trying hard not to be an asshole. Mostly. At least with her. Other people would have to take what they got. "I'm not leaving until you lock the door."

"You're trying to be a hero again." A wan smile.

No, he wasn't. "I'm just trying to make sure you're safe."

She took another step back. "Good night, Colt."

"Good night, Chelsea."

She shut the door. A moment later, he heard the lock click into place.

***

"*I don't want to be your friend.*" His words rang in her head as Chelsea turned around and put her back to the door. When she strained, she could hear the pad of his steps as he left and headed to the room right next door.

It was probably wrong, but she'd really liked his answer because...she didn't want to be his friend, either. She didn't typically want to jump her friends, and when it came to Colt—well, she *did* want to jump him. Jump him. Throw her arms around him. Kiss him passionately. Have crazy-hot sex with him all night long.

A long exhale escaped her. The day had been too insane. She needed a hot shower. She needed to sink into bed. She needed to sleep. Tomorrow, she'd deal with Colt. And Brian, if that had even been his real name. And she'd handle Victor and his investigation.

Tomorrow.

She pushed away from the door and began to strip as she made her way to the shower.

And ten minutes later, when she came out of the bathroom with the towel wrapped around her body and her wet hair sliding over her shoulders, Chelsea saw the man in the black ski mask waiting near the foot of her bed—and she screamed as loudly as she could. Still screaming, she ran toward the door that connected her room to Colt's. She knocked as frantically as she could. No, Chelsea didn't *knock*. She pounded hard and—

The man in the ski mask locked his arms around her and yanked her back against him.

CHAPTER THREE

"Yeah, I don't like the situation at all," Colt said into his phone as he talked to his buddy Pierce Jennings. "Some assholes grab her from the hotel, and the local law does nothing? Acts bored by the whole thing?" His jaw locked. "The scene feels wrong."

"Well, abductions, in general," Pierce returned, voice mild, "are, you know, wrong."

"Don't be a smartass. This is *Chelsea*. He practically took her right in front of me and then the other dumbass put a knife to her throat and—" Colt broke off because he thought he'd just heard a thump.

"Tell me how I can help." No hesitation from Pierce. "You want me on the next flight down there? You want—"

"I want us to start with the police chief on the island. Victor Sorenz. I need to know if I can count on him should more danger come Chelsea's way." Though all of his instincts screamed the answer at him, and it was a most resounding *no*. "Dig up everything you can find on the guy." Pierce worked with Colt at Wilde—an elite protection and security firm with a headquarters based in Atlanta. When it came to digging, Wilde was the best. If Victor had secrets, they'd find them.

"You're supposed to be on vacation," Pierce reminded him.

Hard to be on vacation when the woman of your dreams was being targeted—

Thud. Thud. Thud. "What in the hell?"

"What's going on?" Alertness. Worry.

"She's knocking on my door."

"Uh, okay, good, then your plan to win her back is—"

"*She's knocking on my fucking door.*" Not good. "Chelsea needs me."

"Wait!"

There was no waiting. He hung up the call and bounded for the door. He'd put on jeans after he first got into his room. Just an old, worn pair and nothing else. He grabbed for the knife in the nightstand drawer, hid it behind his back with one hand, and unlocked the connecting door with the other.

Or rather, he unlocked *his* side. He quickly realized that Chelsea's door was still locked. "Chelsea!" He pounded his fist on the door. "Open up!"

Silence. The kind of thick, heavy silence that made him nervous. As a rule, Colt didn't feel nervous. Normally, his nerves were rock steady. This was not a normal situation. This was Chelsea.

"Baby, I'm coming in." Maybe he was making a mistake, but he'd deal with that issue later. He'd told her that if she needed him to knock. She'd knocked. Now she wasn't answering, and he wasn't waiting. Colt lifted his foot and slammed it into the door. The second kick had the lock breaking and her door flying inward. He surged inside, and the sight before him caused fury to pour through his whole body.

Chelsea—wearing nothing but a towel that appeared ready to fall at any moment—was being hauled toward an open patio door by some piece of crap in a black ski mask, black pants, and a black shirt.

"The hell you're taking her," Colt snarled as he lifted his knife.

Chelsea took that moment to slam her heel into the jerk's shin. He swore, a vicious curse in a voice that sounded vaguely familiar, and then he shoved Chelsea forward—pushing her toward Colt. She stumbled, seemed about to fall, and Colt dropped his knife as he leapt forward to catch her.

Her attacker turned and flew through the open patio door. His blond hair peeked out from the back of his ski mask.

"He was waiting when I got out of the shower!" Chelsea cried, speaking frantically. "He tried to force me to go with him—"

And he was getting away. Colt righted her, snatched up his knife, and snapped, "Call hotel security. *Stay here.*" Then he rushed out, giving chase.

"What are you doing?" Chelsea yelled after him.

Trying to catch the bad guy. That was the plan, anyway. He ran onto the patio. Her room was located on the first floor—a bad mistake. On the first floor, it was far too easy for someone to just walk straight up to your patio—and patio doors were notoriously easy to force open. The bastard he was after had a head start on Colt, but the guy wasn't as fast as Colt. Colt bounded forward and—

Rat-tat-tat.

He dove to the ground. *Are you fucking kidding me?* Someone had just *shot* at him. And it hadn't been the jerk he'd been chasing. Must have been the guy's partner. Colt craned up and saw his prey escaping. The bastard hauled ass toward a dark van—*oh, yeah, like I haven't seen you before*—that waited about ten feet away. The driver pointed a gun out his window.

The man in the ski mask jumped into the van, and they squealed away.

Colt glared after the perps, then surged upright and rushed back to Chelsea's room. The patio door was still open, and he hurried inside.

The first thing he noticed? The towel was gone. Chelsea had hauled on a pair of cut-off shorts and a t-shirt, and she was frantically talking into her phone. "Yes, yes, a man just broke into my room! I need help immediately!"

"Chelsea."

She spun toward him. Lowered the phone. Her bottom lip trembled. "Colt...what is happening?"

Two abduction attempts in twenty-four hours. "Do you trust me?" he asked her.

"No. Absolutely, I do not. We've been over this. Why would you think that I trusted you?"

Well, shit. "You're gonna need to start." *If you want to stay alive.*

Her gaze darted to the knife. Then back to his face. She swallowed. "You look very comfortable holding that knife."

He was comfortable.

"As comfortable as you looked holding the gun in that garage."

He *had* been comfortable with that weapon, too.

She bit her lower lip. He didn't like the gathering fear in her eyes. Not fear about her attack. Fear that seemed directed at *him*. "Who are you?" Chelsea asked.

Colt opened his mouth.

And heard the fierce knocking at the door. The hotel security staff. The cavalry had arrived. Too late, though, because the bad guys were long gone.

***

He prowled the suite like a caged lion. Chelsea could practically feel the rage pouring from Colt. The hotel staff had searched the grounds, they'd put in a call to the police chief, and they'd taken her statement—though it wasn't like she'd been able to give much of a description.

Tall guy. He'd felt strong, muscled. And he'd been wearing a ski mask. She hadn't seen his face. Didn't remember if there had been holes for his eyes in the mask. She just remembered being terrified.

And then Colt had kicked in the door and come to her rescue. Again.

Had the attacker been the same man, Brian, who'd taken her before? Colt had growled something to the hotel staff about blond hair, and

Brian *had* been a blond. But if it had been him, why bother wearing a ski mask this time?

She sat on the couch with her legs curled under her body and watched Colt pace. Tension rolled from him. As she watched him, he tossed a glare toward the closed balcony doors. She cleared her throat. "This is a safe location. We're on the top floor. There is no way that anyone is going to scale up *four floors* to get in the balcony door."

He whirled toward her. "Why were you on the ground floor in the first place?"

"I...it was a good room. I could walk right out and be on the beach."

Colt advanced on her. "So you requested the first floor?"

"Uh, no, I was assigned it when I checked in but—"

"We need to get the hell out of here."

Chelsea blinked. "Excuse me?"

"I don't like this place."

"It's an award-winning hotel." Though after two attacks, she couldn't exactly say that she loved the place, either. *One star due to repeated safety threats. Do not recommend.*

"You were abducted from here, baby. Some bastard was in your room tonight."

"Do you think it was the same bastard?"

His brow scrunched.

"I mean, the same man as before. I heard you say you saw his blond hair. Do you think it was Brian again?" She held her breath.

"Yeah, he had the same build. Same height. Voice seemed familiar."

A low exhale. "Why did he bother with the mask?" *If* it had been him. "I'd already seen his face."

"Yeah, but only you and I had. He had to come right up to the first floor. Maybe he was afraid someone else would see him trying to break in. Maybe there are cameras out there that the hotel staff neglected to tell us about, and he didn't want to be on them. There is some fucking reason."

"The hotel staff would have told us—"

"If it's an inside job, they wouldn't tell us jackshit. They would do everything they could to make the situation harder for us."

An inside job. Her heart squeezed. "Look, Colt, I appreciate you—"

He stalked toward her. His eyes gleamed. "Don't."

"Excuse me?"

"Don't give me your gratitude or your appreciation. Because I'm about to scare the hell out of you."

She was already plenty scared enough. "There are two bedrooms in this suite." The ever-so-fancy suite she'd been given by the hotel staff as they tried to make up for the events that had occurred. "Would you mind staying in the second bedroom?" She hated to even ask, but she was *terrified*. "It's just...if you stay on the first floor, and I'm all the way up here—"

"You'll be isolated," he finished gruffly. "Yes, I already realized that. I suspect it might even be one of the reasons you were given this floor, and it's yet another reason we need to get the hell out of here." He stopped right in front of her. Towered over her as she remained curled up on the couch. "Who wants you?"

She did not have a ready response for that question. *I thought you did. And then things imploded and—*

"Who is targeting you, Chelsea? What enemies do you have? Who is going to this much effort to take you?"

Wow. "Hold on." She jumped off the couch. He didn't back up, so the result of her jump was that they were practically touching. She could feel the heat of his body against her. "I don't have enemies! I am a nice person. People typically *like* me." At least, she hoped they did. Did she have bitchy days? Absolutely. Who didn't? But, in general, it wasn't as if she went around town making enemies left and right. She didn't egg houses. She didn't key cars. She never poached on another woman's man. "I'm an interior decorator! I don't run in the kind of circles that would be causing this—this—"

"You're being targeted. Hard. They came after you *twice.* I thought I knew everything about you." A muscle flexed along his jaw. "Your report came up making you look practically spotless. Two speeding tickets. No arrests. One broken engagement from years ago. You—"

"Stop." She put her hand on his chest. A move that she'd needed to make because her knees had just gotten a little unsteady. "*Stop.*"

His jaw hardened.

"You..." A deep inhale. "It sounds like you've done some kind of-of digging into my life." Which made no sense. "Why would you have any report on me?" Why on earth would Colt investigate her?

"Chelsea..."

This was crazy. Everything was so out of control.

"Chelsea, I'm not who you think I am."

She was still touching him. He'd jerked on a dark shirt to go with his jeans. When he'd come rushing into her room, he'd kicked in the door. A real badass, and, honestly, *hot* move. And she'd gaped as he stood in the doorway, clad only in a pair of jeans that hung low on his hips, and with a knife gripped in his hand. His expression had been absolutely lethal. For a moment, she truly had thought that she was staring at a stranger.

Then the jerk holding her had shoved Chelsea forward. Colt had dropped the knife to catch her. She'd seen the worry in his dark eyes and realized—*no, it's not a stranger. It's Colt.*

But...

Her hand slid back to her side. Fisted because she sort of missed touching him. "I don't understand."

He backed up a step—finally. One hand raked through his hair. "Yeah. You're not gonna like this."

So far, there had been nothing that she'd liked about her trip from hell. But she forced a laugh just because—because she was nervous. Sometimes, she laughed when she was nervous. A habit Chelsea wished she could break. "Is this the part where you tell me your name isn't Colt Easton?"

His jaw hardened. "No, that's my name."

Relief had her shoulders sagging. Okay, so he was just exaggerating and making her feel—

"That part was true, at least. But everything else..." A wince. "I'm sorry, sweetheart, but everything else was a lie."

***

"What in the hell is going on?" he snarled into the phone. "It's one woman. *One*. You're telling me that she got away from you twice? What in the hell kind of shit show is happening down there? This job should have been a cakewalk for you!"

Brian Lambert knew he was skating on dangerously thin ice. "It's not her, okay? If it was just her, I could handle the situation, no problem." Honestly, this mess was on the boss. "You never told me that she'd have some hulking boyfriend rushing to save her."

"What?"

"You said she'd been involved with some lame pencil-pusher back home. That she'd ditched him and was coming down here to cry alone in the sand." He sucked in a breath. "Well, she's *not* crying, and she's not alone. She's got this guy with some serious bad vibes shadowing her every move. The man knows how to handle himself, and he is not afraid to fight dirty." He could still see the way the bastard had gripped that knife. The dangerous intensity in his eyes had iced Brian's insides. In that instant, he'd been sure the jerk would gut him. Would just slice him from throat to groin if he had half the chance. "This prick is not here to play."

"Neither the fuck am I."

Easy for the boss to say. He wasn't the one doing the dirty work. "It's the same guy from the pics you sent me. The one she dated in Atlanta." Only he looked a whole lot scarier in person. In the pics, he'd looked like any other rich asshole. "He just won't let us get close to her."

"Then get him the hell out of the picture."

Brian almost didn't breathe. "What are you saying?"

"I'm saying you get her. You bring her to me. *That* is what I'm paying you for. If someone is in your way, then take the bastard *out* of the way. Simple enough."

No, it wasn't. Murder was never simple. And it tended to make Brian a bit squeamish. "But—"

"I'll throw in a bonus. Just get the job done. If you can't do it, I'll find someone else who can."

He considered telling the boss to fuck himself. He also considered... "Just how much of a bonus are we talking?"

CHAPTER FOUR

I'm sorry, sweetheart, but everything else was a lie.

She laughed.

He didn't.

Chelsea's laughter kind of caught in her throat, choking her, and then it died away. "That's not funny." *So why did I laugh?* She'd been battling that nervous laugh all her life, and she'd never hated it more than she did in that moment.

"It's not supposed to be funny." He sounded all grim and ominous, and really, she was at her limit on grim and ominous.

Chelsea felt like she was running on fumes—fumes and adrenaline. She could still feel the masked man's hands on her arms. He'd been yanking her toward the open patio door—a door that she *knew* had been locked before she got into the shower, and she'd been so afraid that Colt wouldn't hear her and that he wouldn't come to help her.

But he'd come rushing to the rescue again. Looking like a serious badass. Only now he was saying...

What was he saying? "I don't understand." Her temples throbbed.

"I know, sweetheart, and this is going to piss you off..."

No woman liked to hear that statement. Ever. Especially from an ex.

"But I was undercover when we met before."

She blinked. "Undercover?"

He sawed a hand over the stubble on his jaw. "You ever hear of a protection firm called Wilde?"

"Well, sure." She spoke slowly as she added, "Almost everyone has. They protect the rich and famous. Royalty. Celebrities." They were a big deal not just in Atlanta, but in the whole US.

"They do more than babysit the wealthy. A lot of our jobs are dangerous and definitely way, way off the radar." Again, more grim and ominous, and also...

A lot of our jobs...He'd said "our" in a very definite way. She backed up a step. Hit the edge of the couch, so she shimmied to the right. It suddenly felt very imperative to put some distance between the two of them. "You're saying that you work for them? For Wilde?"

"Yes."

"As an accountant?" Hopeful.

A negative shake of his head. "No, baby. I've never been an accountant a day in my life."

The drumming of her heartbeat seemed extremely loud and fast as it echoed in her ears.

"I'm a fixer. I make problems go away. I lock up the kind of bad guys who would give you nightmares, and I eliminate dangerous threats before they ever have a chance to materialize."

She stared at him. Or gaped. Her temples continued to throb.

"I provide protection to clients in certain high-risk situations. I put myself between them and the threats that come." He moved closer to her. Positioned his body in her path. "I also take on undercover missions when I need to discover secrets—secrets that can be lethal." A pause. "When we met, I was working undercover."

An undercover accountant. *No, he's never been an accountant.* Her skin felt too hot, then too cold.

"You were working for a target," he explained.

"A target?"

"Theodore Beasley."

Another laugh sputtered out of her. This one was more from disbelief than nerves. "Are you seriously telling me that nice Mr. Theo..." An ever-so-dapper retired insurance salesman. "You're honestly trying to say he was dangerous?"

"Your Mr. Theo is a retired jewel thief. Or, he was supposed to be retired. A client at Wilde had reason to suspect Theo might have been involved in a recent theft. I was doing recon work to uncover the truth for that client."

She blinked. Hugged herself tighter. "Your recon work involved using me?" Her hand rubbed against her chest because an ache had lodged in her heart. *He didn't approach me that first day because he liked me. I looked into his eyes and got lost. He looked at me and saw...*

Someone to use?

She blinked again because everything had gotten a little blurry.

"You were the easiest way to gain access."

Her teeth snapped together. "Did you just call me *easy?*"

"Shit." Horror widened his eyes. "That is not what I meant. At all. Because you were doing decorating work for him, you had a key to his house. His alarm code. You had all of his security information. You had layouts of every room, every possible place where he could have a hidden safe—he'd given you that information on a silver platter."

Now her mouth hit the floor. "Are you saying—are you admitting you *stole* that information from me?" Oh, jeez. She'd let him into her office. She'd left him alone there several times. She hadn't even thought to shut down her computer or—

His head tilted a little as he studied her. "Will it help or hurt if I tell you that Theodore *did* steal from my client so I was mostly working to return property?"

Her cheeks burned, displacing some of the lingering cold. "It doesn't help or hurt." Actually, it did hurt. Her chest ached all the more. "You used me."

"I—"

"You acted like you were interested in me, and you were stealing from me! You were pretending all along!" He'd been pretending while she'd been falling for him? "You're an asshole."

His shoulders squared. "Yes."

"A lying bastard."

His chin lifted. His dark and turbulent gaze met hers. "Yes."

"Get the hell out!" This was too painful. Too heartbreaking. *What is he doing? What game is he playing now—*

"No."

"What?"

"You need me. I'm not leaving you."

Anger hummed through every nerve in her body. "Apparently, I don't even *know* you!" Stranger danger, that was what she had. A very dangerous stranger standing right in front of her.

"My job was a lie. How I felt about you wasn't. Those are two very different things."

"How you felt about me?" Her voice was getting too high, and there was no way she could bring it back down. "You didn't feel anything for me! You barely showed up for our dates, and when you did, you were distracted." Now she got it. He'd just been using her. She'd been falling for him, spinning fantasies about them together, while he'd just been busy stealing intel on some sort of jewel thief client of hers. And sweet Mr. Theo had been a jewel thief? In what world was that even possible? *Oh, wait, how do I know Colt isn't lying to me right now?*

He reached out with his hands as if he'd touch her, then seemed to catch himself. "*You* were the distraction."

What was that even supposed to mean? She didn't know, but it felt insulting.

"I had a job to do. The goal was easy. The mission was simple. Then you sashayed into my path—"

"First of all, I don't sashay anywhere—"

"Wearing your red heels with your hair tumbling over your shoulders and that blood-red lipstick you favor and all I could think about was getting close to you."

Like she was supposed to believe that. He was a confessed *liar*. "Are you on a mission now?"

"What?"

"Are you trying to get close to me again? Do I have another client on your list? You think you can romance me and—"

"What I told you on the beach was the truth. I'm here because I want a second chance with you. The case ended, but I kept hanging around you. Kept pretending to be a damn accountant because I didn't want to tell you the truth and have you look at me..." His gaze searched hers as the faint lines around his mouth deepened. "The way you are right now."

What way was that? Like he was a lying jerk who'd used her and manipulated her? How did he expect her to look at him? Like he was her prince charming and they were going to live happily ever after together?

"I wanted to tell you who I really was. I had hoped to do it the last night we were together, but then I got called away on another case. I had to leave immediately, and there just wasn't time for an explanation." He moved ever closer. So close that his rich, masculine scent wrapped around her. "Then, at first, I told myself you might be better without me. You had broken up with me. You made it clear you didn't want me close to you."

She didn't speak.

"But I couldn't get you out of my head. Every time that I closed my eyes, you were there. I have never wanted anyone as badly as I want you."

She stared straight into his eyes and whispered, "*Liar.*" Because it was just too much. She was having the worst day of her life. And he had the gall to still keep spinning stories to her. Chelsea's hand lifted, and her index finger pointed toward the door. "Get out."

"You're in danger. You might be pissed at me—"

"*Might* be?" she bit out. "Let me clarify for you. There is no *might* about it."

"Fair enough. You *are* pissed at me, but you still need me."

"I don't see how—"

"You're in danger. My job is to protect people when danger comes. I know how to keep you safe. If you don't believe anything else I'm saying, believe that. I can handle dangerous situations. I'm the man you need right now." His gaze hardened. "Even though you clearly want to tell me to go to hell."

"Go to hell." Yes, she did want to say that. So she did. Then decided to say it again because it had felt so good the first time. "Go to hell and take your lies with you."

Instead of *going* anywhere, he held his ground. His gaze glittered. "Been in hell ever since I left you. I can't get you out of my head. When I close my eyes, you slip into my dreams."

The lies just would not stop. She stopped pointing at the door and jabbed her index finger into his chest. "No more."

"No more?"

"I was the one who wanted you. I was the one who pushed for more and more. You were the one with the iron-clad control. The one who was always restrained even when I was about to come just from kissing you." Oh, great. That had been said out loud. One excruciatingly embarrassing admission. When she got angry—and she was really, really angry—she stopped being able to monitor herself.

Screw monitoring. "You were manipulating me from the first moment. I was going crazy for you. I wanted you, but you never—"

"*Don't think I never wanted you.*"

Her lips clamped together.

"Every time I looked at you, my dick got hard."

Well, give the man a cookie.

"You starred in more of my fantasies than you can imagine."

Oh, really? Yet he'd been able to walk away time and time again.

"You sent me into more cold showers than I can count."

Like *she* hadn't been dipping under the cold water after their dates? "You played me." Worse, he'd played with her. Made her believe he was someone else.

No wonder he's not wearing his glasses. Something that had been nagging at her. Those adorable Clark Kent glasses were gone. She'd thought maybe he'd started wearing contacts, but, hell, maybe the man didn't even *need* glasses and that idea just enraged her all the more. She'd liked those damn glasses.

"I had to use every bit of willpower I had because I was trying to not scare you away. You wanted me because I was *safe,*" he gritted out.

Her eyelashes flickered. "I have no idea what you mean."

He leaned closer to her. Gave her that truly killer smile of his. "Now who is lying?"

Damn him. "You didn't want me. You didn't—"

She saw the expression change in his eyes. A flare of heat that should have warned her, but Chelsea was way past the point of heeding any warning. She was riding a righteous fury and a simmering surge of adrenaline.

His hands flew out. Wrapped around her arms and hauled her close. "I've never wanted anyone more." A growl. A rumble of dark desire. And then...

His mouth was on hers. Or maybe her mouth was on his. Because she was on her tiptoes and her hands had grabbed tightly to his shoulders. Had she pulled him toward her? Or had he pulled her toward him? Did it matter?

No.

What mattered was how the kiss felt. How she felt. The desire careening through her blood and obliterating the terrible chill that had filled her ever since some bastard had thrown her into the back of a van. In that instant, she wasn't afraid. She was suddenly burning up on the inside. Her mouth was open. His was open. She tasted him and moaned as her whole body tightened with a need that she couldn't deny. A need that she always experienced when they touched or kissed.

A powerful attraction that went far, far beyond the norm. Far beyond her experience with any other man.

It should have made her wary. It never had. It had just made her feel alive.

But he always held back.

Only...not this time. This time, she could feel a difference in him. A savagery that was barely below his surface. A primal need that seemed to fill the very air around them. He kissed her roughly. Deeply. Possession and lust all twisted together and her nails sank into his shoulders because she wanted more. To hell with everything else, she wanted—

Liar, liar. He'd been lying to her. Was he still lying to her? And when she wanted him so badly, how could she trust herself, much less him?

Even as a moan wanted to slip from her, she pushed against him. Put some needed space between them as Chelsea tore her mouth from his. Her ragged breathing sounded far too loud. When she looked into his eyes, they burned with dark need. The same need had to be reflected in her own gaze, and she wanted to look away. To hide how she felt.

"My desire for you was never a lie. I held back because you mattered. You will always matter." His hands were curled around her waist. She didn't even remember them dropping down there, but now she was acutely aware of the warm weight of his touch against her. "You know we'd be fantastic together in bed."

Yes, she'd always rather hoped they would be.

"I want to touch and kiss every inch of you," he continued in a voice gone all growly and rough and bedroom fantastic. "I want to see you come for me over and over. In my dreams, you have, and you are beautiful when you come."

Her nipples were tight. Her hips were arching against him. She hadn't put quite enough space between her lower body and his, and her lower body was just moving with a mind of its own. A mind that was tempted...

No.

She took a few steps back, breaking from his hold. "Sex doesn't solve problems."

"Nope. It just feels good."

Her eyes narrowed. "I am not having sex with you."

"Fine, but I am still going to protect you."

Chelsea opened her mouth. Stopped. She wasn't sure what to say.

"My protection and what happens between us personally are two separate things." He exhaled. Clenched his hands into powerful fists. "Maybe I should apologize for the kiss."

She still wasn't sure if he'd kissed her or if she'd kissed him.

"But I wanted you to know that I have always wanted you. My attraction to you was never a lie. It will never be a lie. I'm pretty sure when I take my last breath on this earth, I'll die wanting you."

She licked her lips. Still tasted him.

"Holding back with you each time was torture. Know that. But I'm not pretending any longer. The nice guy—the buttoned-down guy who said the polite things all the time—he's gone."

No more Clark Kent? "I did notice you weren't wearing your glasses."

"The lenses had no prescription. They were just—"

"So you'd look less threatening. Just like the clothes you wore." Clothes that had hidden the true extent of his strength from her. Until she'd seen him on the beach and thought...

Wow.

"I was playing a role. I needed to blend. There is no more playing. There is—" He broke off because his pocket was ringing.

A frown pulled at her brows as he pulled the phone out. *Hello! Like that call can't wait?*

He peered at the screen. "I need to take this."

"Oh, by all means," she groused. "Not like we're in the middle of some big, important discussion." Not like they were in the middle of their—whatever it was—Fight? Drama? Breakup? Only they had already broken up and—

He put the phone to his ear. "Talk to me, Pierce."

Who was Pierce?

As he listened to whatever the mysterious Pierce said, she noticed that Colt's square jaw hardened even more. His eyes narrowed, and his nostrils flared. Then... "Sonofabitch."

Okay, Pierce was obviously delivering very bad news. She took another step back.

Colt shot forward and wrapped a hand around her wrist. "No, you don't leave my sight."

Excuse me?

His gaze blazed at her, but he spoke into the phone saying, "I'm talking to her. Yes, I think she's trying to ditch me, and that shit isn't happening. I'll stay with her. I'll get her somewhere safe for the night, and at first light, we are getting off this island."

Pierce's voice was an indistinct rumble.

Colt's hold seemed to brand her skin.

"On it. Don't worry. She's the only one I trust here." Then he hung up. Shoved the phone back into his pocket with his left hand while his right held her captive. "Sweetheart, you're in serious trouble."

Like she hadn't already figured that out.

"The police chief is on the take."

She blinked.

"Pierce just found a wire transfer to the guy's account. Victor got paid twenty grand the day before you arrived on the island."

"I—" That looked bad. Super suspicious but... "How did your friend find that out?"

"Because we have associates who know how to look at financials that other people think are private. A little more digging showed Pierce that the guy has a history of looking the other way. I already knew he was doing a jackshit investigation—seriously, when a kidnapping victim comes to you, you never say you will follow up *the next day*. He did zero crime scene analysis. The man just wanted to get us away from there as fast as possible." A hard exhale. His grip tightened on her. "He's in on what's happening. He's the only law on this island, and I'm getting you out of here."

Leaving was a great goal. Not like this was the dream vacation she'd had in mind, either. "We'll just bunk down here tonight and then tomorrow, we can—"

He shook his head.

"What's wrong with sleeping here tonight?"

"My gut says the hotel staff is involved, too. They put you in that first-floor room. The person working at the bar was part of the abduction. You know that screams shady."

She swallowed. "But the owner said that guy wasn't employed here."

"And you believe him?"

Chelsea certainly had her share of doubts. Voice low, she said, "It was rated as a five-star hotel online. It had lots and lots of great reviews." She'd checked the place out before booking, and there had been no red flags.

"Fuck the reviews. We are getting the hell out of here—right now—because I don't trust that another attempt won't come during the night. I need us as far away from this place as possible."

He wanted her to run off into the night with him. He'd just admitted to lying to her. But he had saved her—twice now—so... "Yes." A quick, decisive nod. "I don't know why this is happening." She was *nobody*. Not a famous celebrity. Not some rich heiress. She shouldn't be on anyone's radar. "But I would like to go home now, please." Home where she was safe.

He tugged her close. Pressed a soft kiss to her forehead. "I'll get you home, I promise." He inhaled and let her go. "But first, get your bag and let's get the hell out of here."

***

They were running away. Brian peered into the hotel's parking garage and saw Chelsea and her asshole ex-boyfriend rushing toward a small convertible. The lights from the lot shone down on the vehicle, and he could make out the rental sticker on the back. Chelsea didn't have a rental yet, so he knew it had to be the ex's car.

Where do you think you're taking her?

Chelsea wasn't just going to slip away. If she slipped away...*the boss will crucify me.* He lifted his weapon. Took aim. He'd just nick the bastard. Put him out of commission and then get Chelsea. Easy. The prick deserved it, anyway, because of the wound he'd given Micah. He and Micah always worked jobs together. He trusted his buddy. Now Micah was out of the picture because of the stupid bullet wound he'd gotten, and Brian had been teamed up with a young SOB he didn't know.

That prick's fault. No one had warned Brian the accountant would prove to be such a pain in his ass. The boss had promised to do more digging on the guy. But in the meantime...*I'm supposed to make sure he doesn't screw anything else up for me.* And this was the perfect opportunity to take care of the jerk.

Brian just had to wait to make sure that Chelsea wasn't in the way.

The ex took her bag. Tossed it into the trunk with his duffel. Looked around.

Before the man could spot him, Brian jerked back behind a cement column as his heart thudded in his ears.

"Where are we going?" Chelsea's voice seemed to echo around him.

"We'll figure that part out once we are the hell away from here." The ex's answer. Grim.

Brian peeked around the column. The ex had opened the passenger side door for Chelsea. She slid inside, and he turned away. Began heading for the driver's side—

Got you now. A perfect target.

Brian stepped forward a little more because he wanted to make sure the shot was good. He lifted the weapon higher...

CHAPTER FIVE

Her phone was in her bag. Dammit. Chelsea shoved open the passenger door and hopped out. "Hold on," she called to Colt. "I need to get—"

Gun.

She saw the gun pointing from behind the nearby column. A gun that was aimed right at Colt. And she lost it.

Screaming as loudly as she could, Chelsea barreled her body into Colt's. They hit hard and tumbled onto the cement. She expected to hear a gun blasting. She'd even braced herself to feel a bullet thudding into her body. Chelsea was ready for the pain. She feared it, but she was ready for it, and—

"Sweetheart," Colt's voice vibrated from beneath her because she was on top of him. Her body had flattened along the length of his when she took him down in a mighty tackle. "What in the hell are you doing?"

She cracked open her eyes. She'd shut them, anticipating the bullet. A bullet that had not come rushing at her. "Gun," she whispered.

His eyes widened. "What?"

"A gun was pointing out from behind the column. It was aimed at you and I—" *Saved you. Jumped in front of a bullet.*

OhmyGod. She'd jumped in front of a bullet—well, she'd been *willing* to jump in front of a bullet, but no bullet had actually fired and—

"The fuck you say," he rumbled.

The fuck, yes, she had said.

He rolled, twisted, and basically shoved her beneath the car. "Do not *move*."

Obviously, he planned to profusely thank her later. In the meantime, she opted not to move and to remain hidden beneath the car. She saw his feet rush away as he raced toward the cement column. Her heart pounded hard, and she pressed her belly down on the cement. Her head lifted, just a little as she fought to see what was happening.

There was no explosion of gunfire. An excellent sign.

No thuds of fists hitting or other telltale fighting sounds. Another wonderful sign.

Then she saw Colt's tennis shoes running back toward her. She crawled forward, and he hauled her out from beneath the vehicle.

"No one was there."

"Someone *was* there." Her instant response. Or, at least, someone *had* been here. "Whoever it was had a gun aimed at you!" But the person hadn't fired.

Because I got in the way?

A muscle jerked along Colt's clenched jaw. "We are going to have a serious fucking discussion," he gritted out as he practically dragged her back to the passenger side. Pushed her in. Slammed the door. "*Do not get out*."

She still needed her phone. But...

He had already bolted around the car. Jumped in the driver's seat. The engine growled, he shifted hard into reverse, and the next thing she knew, they were flying away from that garage like they were in a race. Her hand braced against the dash even as she looked back. Someone *had* been there. They could be followed as they fled into the night.

She didn't even know *where* they were going. Did Colt? Or were they just driving blind? "The, um, airport won't be open." The teeny, tiny airport. "Neither will the main dock." She knew that boats dropped off visitors and picked them up both in the morning and an hour before sunset.

"Pierce will text me the location of a safe house."

A safe house? She looked back again. Saw only darkness behind them. That was good, though, wasn't it? Meant they weren't being tailed. "How is your friend going to find a safe house on this island so fast?"

"Because Wilde has connections."

Oh. Yes. He worked for what basically amounted to some secret millionaire security corporation. She guessed the people at Wilde just snapped their fingers and all sorts of luxury places opened for them. Perhaps the safe house on the island might even be a home that belonged to a former client or something.

Because he's not a pencil pusher. He's some kind of commando. "I don't think we're being followed."

She heard the beep of a text.

He pulled the phone from his pocket. Handed it to her. "Give me the directions."

His buddy had already come through with the safe house? Talk about fast.

"I'm not going to forget what you did," he growled before she could start with the directions.

Her hold tightened on his phone. "You mean me, saving your life? I should certainly hope not. It was a pretty unforgettable act on my part."

The top of the convertible was up, and the tension inside the ride thickened. "I mean *you*," he emphasized, "putting yourself at risk. That's not how this relationship works."

"Oh, sure..." She glanced down at the directions. "Turn right up ahead." Chelsea cleared her throat. "I guess you think I should have just let the guy shoot you. Because having you all bloody on the pavement would have been the best plan. After he shot you, then he could have turned the gun on me—now go left—and then we both could have been dead together. Fabulous idea there. I can see where you'd obviously make a top-notch Wilde agent."

He rumbled. Or growled. Did some sort of deep vibrating thing in his throat that told her she'd pissed him off. So what? She was feeling more than a little *on the edge* herself. This sort of thing did not happen to her. She did not get involved in life-or-death drama situations. She did not want to be involved in these situations.

Chelsea looked back yet again. "The road is still dark."

"I'm keeping my eye out for tails."

Of course, he was. All while driving like he was some sort of Nascar contender. "I guess he could be following us, just with his lights off." She squinted as she peered back. "But you are going helluva fast..."

"Your seatbelt is on."

Yes, but he was still going helluva fast *so*...

"Don't ever fucking get between me and a bullet again."

"Technically, he didn't fire. Take a left. Then we stay on this road until..." She squinted at the phone. "Until we hit the water?" That was certainly what it looked like on the screen.

He took the left. Stayed on the road. His fingers gripped the wheel way too tightly, and his muscles were thick with tension. The road curved and dipped. Twisted like a snake cutting through the grass. There weren't any houses nearby. In fact, this part of the island appeared pretty uninhabited. If she was looking to take someone away, to keep them prisoner from civilization, she'd pick this place. Perfect hideaway spot. "Uh, you're sure this is safe? A good location? Because if this was a horror movie, it looks like you'd be taking me to the perfect place to..." But she stopped.

He didn't. "To kill you?"

"Yes."

"You really don't trust me."

She'd told him that before. Why did he seem surprised? And maybe even...hurt? "Colt..."

"You're willing to take a bullet for me, willing to put yourself between me and danger, but you don't trust me. I really fucked up with you, didn't I?"

Her fingers fiddled with the seatbelt strap.

"Just so you know, sweetheart, killing you would never, ever be an option for me. I would never physically hurt you in any way. But I would kick the asses of anyone who did. The people after you? I am going to make them regret they ever even learned your name."

***

It wasn't a luxury mansion. Not some enchanted place on the sea. It was more of an old fisherman's hut—house?—that seemed to have been forgotten. Palm trees swayed overhead, and the pounding of the ocean surf filled her ears as Chelsea stood in what passed for a den. A den and kitchen and bedroom all in one.

The bathroom was to the right. It was the only other room in the place.

There was no bed, but a big, oversized couch waited in the middle of the room. A kitchen table and a small stove perched to the left.

Colt had left to hide the car. She shifted from foot to foot as she surveyed the scene. Overhead, she could have sworn that the thatched roof swayed with her movements. The place did not feel secure to her. Not at all. And she was thinking maybe they should have just camped out in the tiny airport—

The door opened. Colt strode inside. He was looking at his phone. "Got the security feed up and running. I'll get a notification if anyone appears within five miles of this place." He glanced up at her. "We have the ocean to our backs and the lone road in front of the house. There are cameras and alarm sensors set up all along the road, so if we get any unwelcome guests, we'll know."

She hadn't seen cameras or sensors, but the moon and stars had been covered by clouds, so maybe she just hadn't been able to see things clearly. Or maybe they'd been cleverly hidden. "Why is this place so well armed?"

"Because a former client needed to go off-grid for a while, and this was the location where Wilde stashed him. Wilde safe houses are scattered all over the globe."

Something interesting to know.

He pointed toward the fridge. "It's stocked. The safe houses are always kept stocked. So if you're hungry or thirsty—"

"I'm just tired." More like on the verge of collapsing. "I want to sleep. It's been an incredibly long day." Horrifically long. Never-ending.

He walked toward the couch. Toward her. She backed up because she thought maybe he was coming to—

He tossed aside the couch cushions. Grabbed a handle and yanked out a mattress. "It converts," he explained, his voice a little gruff. "Might be somewhat lumpy, but it's clean. There are some pillows and covers in the closet." He unfolded the mattress. Made quick work of grabbing the promised covers and pillows, and he had a bed set up for her in moments.

She darted a glance at the converted bed. Then at him. This was one of those awkward one-bed situations that appeared in rom-com movies. In those movies, these moments were fun. Sexy.

In real life...she felt tense. Nervous. Edgy. She should say—

"Don't worry," Colt assured her with a quirk of his lips. A smile that never reached his eyes. "I'm planning to bunk on the floor. The bed is all yours."

And that was just annoying. The man didn't even seem mildly tempted to share a bed with her. He didn't seem to feel even a drop of the tension that rocked her. Fuming, Chelsea kicked off her sandals. Just left on her cut-off shorts and her top. She had zero idea why, but she suddenly felt incensed. "And there it is. That control of yours flashing again. I get it. The single bed makes you have zero desire to—"

"Fuck you all night long?"

She sort of plopped on the mattress. Grabbed the covers. Pulled them up. And ignored the tremble that slid over her body at his low, deep words.

"I don't need a bed to want to do that, baby. I can fuck you up against a door. A wall. On the floor. On the beach. Anywhere that tickles your fancy. But you just told me you were exhausted, so this hardly seemed like the moment to make my move."

Her lips pressed together. "Could you turn off the light?" So he couldn't see her crimson cheeks. They had to be on fire because they burned like crazy.

He flipped off the light. Plunged them into darkness. He'd kept one pillow and a blanket.

When her eyes adjusted to the darkness, she realized that he'd settled onto the floor with that pillow and blanket. He'd stretched out just a little bit away from her.

If she'd reached out her hand, she could have touched him.

Instead, her hand balled in a fist, and she curled it under her chin.

"I need to know why they're after you."

Chelsea yawned. "I have no idea. If I knew, I would have told you before now." She hadn't been the one keeping secrets. "Maybe I just have bad luck."

"No. They are targeting you. Coming after you again and again. And they want you alive."

She inched a little closer to the side of the mattress. Toward him. "You're sure about that?"

"If they'd wanted you dead, they never would have put you in the van in the first place. They would have killed you immediately."

A lump rose in her throat.

"And tonight, if the guy was aiming at me—"

"He *was*." She knew what she'd seen. There had been no "if" about the situation.

"Then the only reason he didn't fire is because you were in danger of getting hit." Anger pulsed in Colt's words. "Let me say again...don't ever get between me and a bullet."

"Well, if you could not have bullets aimed at you, then I wouldn't have to get involved."

"Chelsea..."

"It's my fault." She shifted more on the bed. "Like you said, they're targeting me. You're the one who played hero and saved me. If it wasn't for me, you wouldn't be in this mess at all." And if it wasn't for him...Chelsea rolled and stared up at the darkness above her. This was the first time she'd actually just had a moment to get off the roller coaster of adrenaline and *think*. "I don't know what would have happened to me if you hadn't been there." She had to blink away tears, and she was so very grateful for the darkness. All bravado and mockery completely gone, she told him, "Thank you for saving me. I will always be grateful to you."

"Screw that. I don't want your gratitude."

"I-I don't know the going rate for Wilde protection." Though she suspected it must be stupid high. Rich-people-with-money-to-burn high. The kind of clients that she loved to have at her interior decorating business because they would go for the most expensive pieces she could find. "But I can pay you." Maybe on an installment plan?

"Don't want your money, either."

Dammit. "Then what *do* you want?"

"Aw, Chelsea, why ask a question when you know the answer?"

If she'd known the answer, she wouldn't have asked. She floundered and squeaked, "Me?" Only to realize, no, he couldn't be serious. But... "You just want sex with me?"

"I want you." Flat. "And I will do whatever it takes to protect you. Consider me your personal bodyguard from here on out. I don't plan to leave your side until we have you safe and sound in that condo you love so much. The one that gives you those amazing sunrise views. I know how much you love a good sunrise."

She did. Tried to catch them as often as she could. "The day is fresh at sunrise," Chelsea heard herself whisper. "Anything can happen. The bad things are gone. The light is coming out." Something her mother had told her a lifetime ago. When they'd made it through a very, very bad night. A night so bad that Chelsea didn't talk about it to anyone. Ever.

"I'll keep the bad things away from you. You have my word on that." A pause. "But you'll have to trust me."

He'd saved her at least twice so far. She did trust him to keep her safe. But trusting him with her heart was an entirely different matter. "The first time I saw you, I thought you had the most incredible eyes I'd ever seen. So deep and dark and warm. When I looked into them, I thought..." But she trailed away. Maybe there had already been enough confessions for one night.

"What did you think?"

I'm safe with him. She still had the same thought. "Good night, Colt."

"Want to know what I thought the first time I saw you?"

"No." Yes. Absolutely. But she squeezed her eyes closed. "Maybe we shouldn't focus on the past. Easier to just go forward."

"You're offering me a fresh start?"

Was she? Her stomach did a little quiver. "Are you holding other secrets?"

"I have a lot of secrets."

She'd suspected as much.

"But none that can hurt you."

Her breath released on a little sigh of relief.

"What about you, sweetheart? What secrets are you holding from me? Because I can't help you—I can't get a handle on who is after you and what they want—if you aren't being truthful with me."

She didn't know what to tell him. "I have no idea why anyone is after me. I'm nobody."

"Bullshit." Low. Rough. Almost angry. "You're always someone important to me."

That was sweet. Made her stomach quiver more. "I don't run in dangerous circles." Another yawn. Sleep pulled at her. "Don't know any state secrets. Haven't made any shady deals with bad guys. I don't...don't break laws. I try to be good. I try..." The last ended in a sigh as she slipped into sleep.

***

You are good. The best thing to ever happen to me. No, she wasn't a damn *thing*. She was Chelsea. The woman who'd walked away. The woman who haunted him.

The woman who was being hunted, and she seemed to have no idea why.

Her breathing had deepened. Colt knew she was asleep.

When he'd imagined the first night he'd spend with Chelsea, he had *never* pictured this scenario. His fantasies had not involved him sleeping on the floor and her bunking on a lumpy pullout bed. But he was close to her. She was safe.

And in order to get to her, any SOB who came calling would have to go through Colt first.

He eased out of his shoes. Made sure his knife was within reaching distance. The knife and the gun that he'd taken from that prick at the garage.

His phone vibrated, and he picked it up. Scanned the screen and saw the message from Pierce. *Are you in a secure location?*

Hardly the Ritz, but, yeah, they were safe. He texted back, *Inside the safe house. Good security, but you could have warned me it was a hole in the wall.*

Three dots. Then, *With five minutes' worth of notice, you're lucky it was even a hole.*

A grim smile curled Colt's lips. Pierce had a point.

Another text appeared. *You getting off the island at first light?*

His smile slid away. *That's the plan.* But he was already worried about a slew of potential problems with that plan. His gaze darted to Chelsea. Still sleeping.

Still perfect.

Fuck. He had it bad.

Once more, his phone vibrated. *Did she tell you why they were after her?*

This was the part that got tricky. And the part that was going to make him feel like a heel. But in order to keep her safe, there were just certain things that had to be done. He texted, *She claims she doesn't know.* He believed that claim. She hadn't shown any tells that would indicate she was lying, and her confusion had been clear. When she'd told him that she was a nobody...

Hell, no, sweetheart. Stop the thought right there. She was definitely someone important to him. The most important person. Though she didn't believe that because he'd screwed up things so thoroughly before.

Jaw clenching, he fired out one more text. One that, if Chelsea had seen it, the words would have infuriated her. *I missed something before when I looked at her background.* His fault. She hadn't seemed like any threat. What you saw—a beautiful, intelligent, fun woman—was what he'd gotten.

Except...

He hesitated, just a moment, then typed out, *Dig into her background again. See if anything raises red flags for you.*

Three dots. Pierce was sure firing back fast on his texts. *Does she know you're doing this?*

Easy answer. *No.*

Another fast reply. *You sure digging into her life is going to get you what you want?*

What he wanted—her. A shot at a second chance. To see if they could make it work. To see if the insane chemistry he had with her—chemistry he'd never experienced with anyone else—would survive the hype. What he *needed*, though...he needed her safe. So if he had to do things she wouldn't like, then he'd do them. He'd lose her all over again if it meant he could ensure she remained safe. So his final text was short and sweet. *Do it.*

CHAPTER SIX

She jerked awake, her lips clamping shut to hold back a scream. Something had woken her. *Someone*. And she thought that maybe one of her attackers had come—

"Just the wind, Chelsea. The house is so close to the shore that it takes a pounding. You're safe. Nothing to worry about."

She'd already bolted upright, and now she turned to peer at him. Or, rather, to peer down at his shadowy form. Her eyes narrowed as Chelsea strained to see him in the darkness. She was pretty sure his hands were folded behind his head. The covers seemed bunched near his waist. "You're awake." Obviously. Not the most brilliant observation to make, but she was always groggy after waking. It seemed to take a few minutes for her mind to start processing.

I'm in the house—hut—with Colt. The waves are crashing outside, and the wind is blowing. Everything is fine. No bad guys.

"I'm awake." Flat.

She leaned over and peered at him a little more. "It's hot in here."

"No air conditioning. Sorry."

Like she needed an apology when she was simply happy to have a safe place for crashing. But there was just—something felt off. An odd tension filled the room, and she'd sort of been rambling and looking for something to say. Chelsea had no idea how much time had passed, she only knew that the little hut felt even smaller than before. Or maybe Colt felt even bigger.

His rumbling voice asked, "Do you want something?"

Her lips clamped together. The middle of the night—or whatever time it was—when she was half asleep and a wee bit confused—that was definitely not the prime time to blurt out...*You.*

"Chelsea?"

She loved the way he said her name. All deep and dark and with the faintest hint of a rough caress seeming to underscore the word. No one had ever said her name quite like he did.

He said he wants you. He came all this way for a chance to be with you again. "What if it's not as good as we think?" She slapped her hand over her mouth. Oh, damn. She'd done it. She could *not* have conversations with people when she first woke up. She needed five minutes of waking time, then she needed caffeine, *then* she could talk. This in-the-dark-conversation bit wasn't for her.

"What did you say?" He sat up. She saw his shadowy form move jerkily.

So Chelsea jumped from the bed. Took a few hurried steps away. "I need some fresh air. I just, ah, it's okay if I go outside, isn't it? Your cameras and alarms would have said if someone was approaching the house."

"No one is approaching."

"Great." She inched toward the sliding glass door. "I'll just cool down real fast and be right back."

The sudden light from his phone illuminated the hard angles of his face. Made him look extra intense. Dangerous. Without the glasses, it was quite the dramatic change. Those glasses had softened him.

Okay, I will never make fun of Lois Lane again. Because she used to wonder, how the heck had the woman not realized who she was truly dealing with? But...

Maybe Lois had seen what she wanted to see.

Maybe I did, too. Without the glasses, he looks about twenty times fiercer. Or maybe he looked extra fierce because Chelsea had now seen him in action. All up close and dangerous.

He tapped a little on his phone's screen. Maybe he was deactivating some sensors so they wouldn't start screaming when she went outside. Or—

He stood up. Came closer. His body brushed against hers. All warm and hard and strong, and she jumped back as if she'd been burned.

Way to overreact and not play things cool.

"Easy," he murmured. "If you're going outside, then I'm coming with you. I'm supposed to be keeping watch on you, remember?"

And she'd been trying to put some necessary space between them, but this hardly seemed the right moment to explain that. She bobbed her head, thinking he'd see the movement, then he led the way to the sliding glass door. After unlocking it, he pulled it open, and the wind and the scent of the ocean immediately swept over her.

Her hair lifted lightly and blew in the breeze. Chelsea sucked in a deep breath as she followed Colt outside. Her feet were bare, and her toes immediately curled into the sand. The clouds had passed. When she tilted her head back, she could see what looked like a million stars glittering over her head. The moon was a thick sliver in the distance—the stars were what shone the brightest.

The stars shone and the waves crashed, and instead of getting space from Colt, being out there with him...on the beach, with palm trees swaying nearby...

It felt incredibly romantic.

Incredibly sexual.

Or perhaps she just felt sexual being near him.

"Better?" he asked as he leaned under one of the palm trees.

"Um." No. Worse in so many ways. She licked her lips. Forced herself to look out at the waves. They crashed hard against the shore only to withdraw, to sweep back. To crash again.

"I have to tell you something I've wondered about for over two months..."

She kept staring at the waves.

"Was amazing sex really on your agenda for that last night?"

Now she had to gulp. *Play it cool.* "I had thought it was time for things to go to the next level." What she'd really wanted was to break his control. To get through that shield that seemed to surround him. Her toes dug a little deeper into the sand. "But it might not have been amazing."

He shoved away from the palm tree. "Excuse me?"

"I overshare in the middle of the night. You should know that about me. I'm oversharing now." She caught a flying lock of her hair and tucked it behind her ear.

"You don't think sex with me would be amazing." He stalked toward her.

She refused to retreat. "That's not what I said."

"Uh, yes, sweetheart, it sure seemed like it was." He stopped right beside her. "I can guarantee you, sex would be phenomenal for us."

He didn't get what she was saying. "All the potential is there." She turned to fully face him. Motioned between them. "We have this nice attraction thing going on. Very strong. Very basic."

"So glad you noticed it."

He'd better not be mocking her. Her mind scrambled as she tried to figure out a way to explain the situation. "It's like when you're baking a cake..."

"Sex with me is like baking?" A hard rumble.

The waves crashed. "You have all these ingredients...*We* have ingredients. We have attraction. We have the fact that, quite frankly, you are a stellar kisser. The best I've ever known."

"Thanks. Appreciate that." Dry. Still rumbly.

"But when you put the cake in the oven, things still might not bake properly." She should stop talking. Yet she couldn't. "Maybe the oven timer goes too long. Maybe the oven is too hot for the cake mix. Maybe...Maybe it just doesn't work."

He took her hand in his. His fingers rubbed gently along her palm. Pressed. Stroked. "We'd work just fine."

"Things have been fine before." That was the problem. "You kind of want more than fine." Because otherwise, all of that crazy attraction they had...it just—

"I can give you more than fine."

Promises, promises. This time, she managed to clamp her lips together and hold back that response. Barely.

He laughed softly. A chuckle that seemed to dance along her nerve endings even as he kept stroking her palm. Since when was a palm so sensitive? And what was he doing to the pad beneath her thumb? That was just all kinds of sensual.

"Want me to prove it?" Colt asked.

This was probably not the proving time. "If we fizzle, then you came all this way for nothing." Truth.

"No. Told you already, I came for you." His left hand rose. Slid under her jaw. Tilted her head back. "When you want me to stop, say the word..."

"I..." *What's the opposite of stop?* "Go."

"Chelsea?"

She arched toward him. Lifted onto her toes. This time, she was sure, her mouth pressed to his. She kissed him first. She kissed him with a reckless abandon because she had been wanting him for a long time. Too long. And maybe it wouldn't be as good as she'd hoped between them.

Maybe she'd built things up in her mind too much. But there was only one way to find out for sure.

He's not pretending to be someone else any longer. He'd damn well better not hold back on me. Because she wanted the real man. She wanted his passion and need and power. She wanted him.

His mouth opened. His tongue thrust against hers. A savage growl spilled from him, and Colt hauled her closer. He took over the kiss. Desire pounded through her body even as those waves kept pounding and pounding against the shore.

In the light of the day, she would have thought of a million reasons why what they were doing was wrong. But, it wasn't day. It was night, and it was always easier to hide in the darkness. So her hands clamped around his shoulders. She pushed her body tightly against his. Her toes weren't digging into the sand any longer. Chelsea pushed up off the sand so she could get higher, get closer. His kiss had electricity charging through her veins. Her whole body was alive and tight and aching. And maybe things between them would be like she'd imagined. Not *fine*. More like the amazing explosions on the Fourth of July.

His hands slid down to her waist, and he lifted her up. Held her easily against him, and it seemed like the most natural thing in the world to wrap her legs around his hips. When she did, the hard length of his arousal shoved against her core. The *extremely* hard and long length of his arousal. The undeniable length.

The—

Colt lifted his mouth from hers. "I couldn't sleep because I wanted you so much," Colt confessed.

The ragged sounds of her breaths were drowned out by the pounding waves.

"You are so fucking beautiful." His mouth took hers again. He kissed her deep and hard and passionately even as he took a few steps forward.

She felt something rough and hard against her back and realized it was one of the palm trees. The tree was behind her. He was in front of her. Her hips rocked against him even as his right hand slid down to curl under her thigh. She felt his fingers brush over the juncture of her thighs just for a moment as he shifted position.

Her whole body tightened. She yearned. Wanted.

Her hand rose to press to his cheek, and she kissed him again. Bit his lower lip in a sensual caress and was rewarded by that savage growl of his. She loved the primitive sound. Loved the way he felt. The fierce strength of his body and...

She was riding his erection. Lifting and rolling her hips over the thick length of his dick. She hadn't even realized what she was doing, not at first. She just ached. Her sex ached, and she'd been rocking instinctively. Chelsea wanted him inside of her.

She wanted *him*.

He eased away, but only so he could slide that wicked hand of his right against her core. He still held her with his other hand. Braced her body easily against the tree. But his fingers slid under the edge of her cut-offs. Worked up a little higher. Brushed over her sensitive sex.

Her body jerked. "Colt?"

"Fine, my ass. Baby, we are going to burn each other alive."

That sounded, uh, painful, but—

But he was stroking her clit. His fingers were inside of her shorts, but still outside of her underwear. The thin underwear that separated her from his touch. He stroked, then squeezed, and his mouth was on her neck. Licking. Sucking. Biting lightly. Her breath came faster. Her heart pounded so hard it seemed to shake her chest.

He kept stroking.

The damn panties needed to *go*. She wanted his hand on her. Wanted his fingers *in* her. She opened her mouth to tell him...

His fingers slid under the panties.

She moaned. The surf took the sound. Drowned it.

The tree swayed behind her. His fingers were *on* her clit. His thumb pressing. His index finger joining it to squeeze. Then he moved to push one finger into her.

"Fucking tight..."

Well, yes, it had been a while. A long while. At least a year, but this hardly seemed the moment to tell him—

"You are going to feel fantastic."

He already did feel pretty fantastic to her. So fantastic that her whole body was shivery, and she could feel the promise of release beckoning to her. Close. Almost there. Her hips rocked harder.

He gave a rough, deep laugh. "You are *hot*."

She was about to go right up in flames if his fingers could just—

He worked her clit. Fast. Hard. A little rough in an ever-so-amazing way. And she came. Pleasure seemed to splinter her nerve endings apart as her hips jerked against him. Her eyes squeezed closed, and her mouth opened—

He kissed her. Took her moans and gasps and caressed her carefully even as the orgasm kept rolling and rolling within her. When it was done, when little after-shocks hummed through her...

"I sincerely hope," Colt growled, "that was better than fine. If not, do allow me to try again."

Her head tipped back. Through the fronds at the top of the tree, she could see the stars. "That was—"

A beep. Quick. Followed by two more.

He stiffened against her. Stiffened. Then carefully lowered her until her feet touched the sand.

"Colt?" Uncertainty pushed away the lovely post-climax haze.

"Company." He had his phone out and was staring at the screen. He'd yanked it from his back pocket. "Sonofabitch is heading toward the front of the house."

Wait. They had company while they had just been—been—

"You stay here."

"Stay here? Don't we need to run?" She thought running sounded way better than staying.

"I want to interrogate him."

Interrogate. Her heart still pounded. Her body still shook. And he was in his interrogation mode. Switching gears that fast—how did he do it?

Maybe he wasn't as involved as I was. Maybe it didn't matter—

"No. Whatever you're thinking, no. I want you like hell burning right now, baby, but I have to take care of this threat. Stay here. Don't get some crazy idea to run and put yourself between me and a bullet again."

She hadn't been thinking that. She'd been thinking they should run together.

"Hide behind the tree," Colt directed her. "Keep out of sight. He'll think you're inside. He doesn't realize I'm aware he's coming. That gives me the benefit of surprise. I can take him."

Colt sounded awfully certain, and she didn't want to rain on his certainty parade but… "How do you know it's just one person?"

"I can see him. The feeds show on my phone. An asshole in black, wearing a hoodie and closing in."

The man who'd come to her hotel room had also been wearing black.

"Just because he's the only one in view doesn't mean he won't have backup planning to rush in soon," Colt added grimly. "All the more reason for you to stay *here*." He kissed her. A fast, hard kiss. "If I'm not back in five minutes, then I want you to run like hell away from the scene."

He expected her to just leave him?

"But I'll be back. I'll always come back for you."

With those words, he left her.

Chelsea backed toward the tree and realized she very much needed to find a weapon.

***

He waited just beyond the front door. Colt kept his body pressed to the wood. He'd made sure the alarms wouldn't sound. When that door opened, he wanted the SOB to think that he'd eased inside and was the one in control.

For a very, very fleeting moment, he wanted the guy to think that.

Colt barely breathed as the door began to inch open. The perp had picked the lock. He wasn't making a sound as he crept inside. The door opened a little more.

Colt had kept all the lights off inside so the figure advanced in the dark. Big, shadowy. And with a gun clutched in his right hand.

No, asshole, you don't get to bring a gun when you come after her.

Just as soundlessly, Colt moved forward. He advanced until...Colt pushed his own gun into the base of the intruder's back. "You're gonna want to drop that weapon of yours. Right now."

The figure tensed. But, wisely, the guy didn't pull some dumbass move like trying to whirl and attack Colt. A move like that just would have resulted in the SOB getting shot.

The intruder did drop his gun. Then he lifted his hands into the air.

Colt began to pat him down as he looked for another weapon—

"I get that it's been a long time since you've seen me, Colt," the man announced. "But really, there's no need to get so handsy. Especially since you haven't even bought me dinner or simply a glass of wine—"

What the fuck? Colt knew that voice. He knew—

He grabbed the guy's shoulder and spun him around. But there wasn't enough light for him to see the man's features clearly. Hell. Colt slammed his fist into the nearby light switch. Illumination flooded into the room. He blinked. Then glared.

"Hi, friend," the intruder sang out with a taunting grin. "Long time no see, am I right?"

Fucking hell. He was looking at a *criminal.* A man wanted across the globe. A man who'd just come after Chelsea with a gun. *Friend, my ass.*

Colt shoved his gun into the waistband of his jeans.

"I get that you're probably surprised to see me," the man continued. "And, know what? Frankly, I'm surprised to see you. Thought you'd be stateside taking care of *Wilde* business. But, nope, you just had to pop up here and get right in the middle of my—"

Colt drew back his fist and decked him.

CHAPTER SEVEN

The sliding glass door opened. A big form emerged. Wide shoulders. Powerful chest. Angry walk.

Colt.

She'd recognize his angry walk anywhere. And when he drew closer, as she peered from behind her precious tree, she could see his face. Partially, anyway. As much as the stars allowed her to see.

He stopped. Put his hands on his hips. "Is that a coconut you're holding?"

She stood up. Kept clutching her coconut. "I thought I could either hurl it at an attacker." She had a good throwing arm. Shortstop, baby. Or at least, she had been shortstop, back in high school. While the coconut was certainly bigger than a softball, she'd known she could still manage a powerful toss with it. "Or I could just slam it into his head if he got too close."

Colt looked behind him. "I like the slamming-it-into-his-head idea. Holds definite merit."

She maintained her position behind the tree. "Is it safe now?"

"Safe is a very relative term." One hand rose to shove through his hair. "I've incapacitated him, and I thought you might want to be there for the interrogation."

Absolutely, she did. Chelsea scampered forward, with her precious coconut. He would have no idea how excited she'd been to find that damn thing. Colt led the way inside. Lights were blazing in there so it was easy for her to see...

The man tied to the chair, with a giant cloth shoved into his mouth.

Chelsea staggered to a stop. Vaguely, she wondered where Colt had gotten the rope. Had it just been stashed in the hut?

The man's gaze immediately jumped to her. He started angrily mumbling something behind the cloth.

"His cheek looks red," Chelsea noted.

The cloth flew from the man's mouth and hit the floor. "That's because the asshole next to you *hit* me!"

Colt crossed his arms over his chest.

"Well..." Chelsea cleared her throat. Was she supposed to be playing some sort of good cop role? Maybe bad cop? Colt must have brought her in to the interrogation to help out so... "You're lucky that's all he did." She gripped her coconut harder. "We don't enjoy having people stalk us, and if you don't tell us everything right now—"

"Us?" The bound man squinted at her. Then his gaze jumped to Colt. "What the hell is she talking about, Colt? Since when do you have an 'us' with her?"

He knows Colt's name. But, okay, maybe Colt had introduced himself...*to the man he'd tied up?* And there was just such a familiarity to the stranger's tone as he spoke to Colt...

She got a very, very bad feeling.

"Is this a Wilde job?" the man wanted to know in the next instant. "Or are you freelance?"

She inched closer to Colt. "How does he know you?"

"How does he know *you*?" the guy fired back as his brows furrowed. "And why is he willing to hit and tie up his friend for you?"

His friend? Those two words set off every red flag imaginable, and Chelsea retreated back—

But she didn't get far. Colt's hand flew out and curled around her wrist. His head jerked toward her. "It's not what you think," he said in his deep, probably-meant-to-be-reassuring voice. "First, he's not my friend."

"Hurts," the stranger grunted. "In my heart of hearts, it hurts."

"Fuck you." An instant retort, but Colt kept focusing on Chelsea. "I previously worked a case that involved Remy."

She flickered a glance toward "Remy" as he continued to sit in the chair and struggle a bit against his ropes.

Remy flashed her a broad smile. Perfect features. Charming grin. Thick hair and gleaming eyes. That charming grin promised he wasn't a threat, and maybe she would have believed it...

If he hadn't just tracked her across the island.

"His real name is Rembrandt," Colt explained.

A wince from the other man. "I truly prefer Remy. So much easier to say."

Colt grunted. "On a good day, he's an art forger and an art thief."

And Colt *knew* this man? The guy considered Colt to be his *friend?* She wet her lips. "On a bad day? What is he then?" She risked another glance his way.

Remy lost his grin. His gleaming gaze hardened. "You don't want to know."

Oh, damn. *Damn.* Her attention lingered on him. "Why are you after me?"

"How about you answer my questions, then I'll answer yours? Sound good?"

"No." She shook her head. "It sounds terrible. *You're* the one tied up in a chair. You have to answer our questions or—or—" Or she really didn't know what would happen. Something bad, though.

Remy sighed. "Colt, are you truly going to become physical with me—again? I let you get the one punch in because...okay, my bad, sneaking in with the gun probably wasn't the *nicest* move I could make. In my defense, though, you know I don't tend to be nice. Neither do you, though. So, why be judgy?" Then his gaze dropped to Colt's hand—the hand that still circled Chelsea's wrist. "Hell. Tell me this isn't personal."

Colt let her go. He turned his gaze on Remy. "I don't have to tell you anything."

"Uh, yes, you do." Even though he was tied to a chair, Remy managed to appear completely relaxed. "You don't realize it yet—or, maybe you do, considering the way you rushed from the hotel—but you have found yourself in the middle of one serious clusterfuck of a situation." A pause. "I sincerely hope that some of your Wilde brethren are waiting in the shadows nearby to give you much needed backup."

Colt tilted his head to the right. "Where is *your* backup? In particular, I mean that friend of yours that likes to get into trouble with you? Constantine, wasn't it?"

A roll of one shoulder. Or as much of a roll as Remy could probably manage with the ropes. "This time, I have a new partner. You've actually met him already."

Chelsea's breath froze in her lungs because if he was about to say that his partner was that Brian asshole and Remy was there to help abduct her—

"I believe you stole his sporty blue Jeep recently. Left a lovely bullet hole in the back. That was not very considerate of you." A quick laugh. "Though, honestly, from what I hear, the dumbass just gave you the keys to the ride. A super amateur move, especially for a CIA operative."

CIA operative. "You're CIA?" she whispered. What in the world would a CIA agent want with her?

"Um."

"That's not a yes," Chelsea informed him and she was impressed with how crisp she sounded. As if she wasn't shaking apart on the inside.

Another semi-shrug from Remy. "It's not a no, either, though, is it?"

He *still* wasn't answering. But he was looking straight at her. "It was supposed to be such an easy mission. Get you to the island. Get close to you. But..." He cleared his throat. "I suppose Colt beat me to the punch, eh?"

The drumming of her heartbeat suddenly seemed very, very loud. Her skin also felt very, very cold and clammy despite the heat of the tropical night.

"You supposed to seduce—ahem, I mean, *charm* the location out of her, Colt?" Remy asked. "Is that your current mission? I have got to give props to Wilde. I had no idea the company was even involved in this game. But here you are, two steps ahead of me. Bravo. I would clap, but you tied me up."

"I do not understand what is happening." Though she definitely got the disgusting inference that this Remy character was making. He'd planned to charm her? Try to seduce her? She could feel rage pouring through her body and darkening her cheeks. She lifted the coconut that she still held. "First, let me begin by saying that you are *not* my type. Not at all. So your charm routine would not have gotten far."

His gaze darted from her face to the coconut. What could have been real alarm flashed for the briefest of moments in his eyes. "Uh, Colt..."

"Second, Colt is my *ex*."

Now Remy's eyes widened. "Ex?" A wince. "Colt, friend, that sucks for you. She's gorgeous, and she's taking this whole situation with a lot of pretty good control—"

"*Third...*" Okay, that was like a shout and obviously a sign that she had zero control. But she rushed to the bound man. "Third—the location of what? What are you talking about? Why are strangers after me? Why was I kidnapped? Why is this happening?" Each word seemed to get louder and louder.

"Ahem. Colt?" A faint line of sweat dotted Remy's noble-looking brow. "I think she is about to slam that thing into my head, and if I'm unconscious, I can't talk."

Colt took his time advancing. Then he held out his hand to her. "There's a chance he is working as a CIA operative. Remy has been freelance with them before. If you assault him, he could try to get you arrested and that's just drama that we don't need right now."

She peered at his outstretched hand. Then back up at him. *Fine.* She slammed the coconut into his palm. "You are not charming me!" Chelsea snapped.

"Tell me something I don't already know." Colt tossed aside the coconut. Glared at Remy. "You are really screwing up my plans."

"What *are* your plans? And who are you working for?" Remy pounced.

"Her."

Remy waited, as if expecting more. When nothing else was forthcoming, he exhaled on a loud sigh. "Your social skills have not improved since we last crossed paths. You need to elaborate a bit more. If I see that we're on the same team, I might be able to help you out—"

She could feel her knees trembling. Everything was so horribly out of control.

"We're not on the same team." Colt's cold reply. "I'm on *her* team. My plans involve her. I'm working for *her*. The person who gets my loyalty on this island? *Her*."

Remy pursed his lips. “So, if it came down to a choice between me and—”

“Her,” he snapped. “I will choose *her*. That’s why your ass is tied to the chair and she’s at my side.”

“Even though she’s a criminal?” Remy asked, voice all silky smooth.

Chelsea sucked in a deep breath. She was no criminal. *How dare—*

“Even though she’s more of a thief than I am?” the jerk added ever so casually.

“I am *not,*” Chelsea fired hotly. What an ass!

He flickered his gaze over her. “Even though she’s hidden a pearl necklace worth well over a million dollars?”

Chelsea laughed. The two men didn’t. They did frown at her.

“Did I say something amusing?” Remy wanted to know. His tone was different. Stiffer. His gaze more alert.

Her nervous laughter had struck again. “I haven’t hidden some pearl necklace. This isn’t a pirate movie. This is my *life*. Men are chasing me. I was kidnapped—”

“Because you are in possession of something that a few very dangerous individuals want badly.” His thick eyebrows rose even as Remy tilted his head toward Colt. “You wanted me to talk, so I’m talking. You know I tend to, ah, excel in the area of forgeries and thefts. When it came to the attention of some powerful people that a certain missing, three-strand natural pearl necklace—one valued at approximately 1.4 million American dollars—was suddenly in play again, I was pulled into the investigation. The investigation led me to your lovely ex. Me...and others."

This was absurd.

"The chain of the necklace is made of 180 pearls. They vary in size, and as I said, they are all natural. They were painstakingly matched by a master, and the diamond clasp of the necklace—well, it is certainly a thing of beauty itself." A low whistle, as if the image in his mind impressed Remy.

"I do not own any pearl necklace. Not even a single one, okay?" She rarely bothered wearing any jewelry. "Your intel is wrong. Or you're just lying." Her money was on option two. Maybe this was some weird divide and conquer strategy he was trying on her and Colt.

Remy seemed to assess her. "If you give me the necklace now, we can end this. I can take you into custody and—"

"I am not a jewel thief! I don't have your pearl necklace!" Frantic, her gaze jumped to Colt. And she realized he had been watching her. "You believe me, don't you?"

He stared back at her.

"Colt?" Her stomach squeezed. Ten minutes ago, she'd nearly been making love with him beneath a palm tree. His hands had been all over her. She could still feel his touch. And now...

Now he stared at her as if she was a stranger.

"You trust me, don't you?" Chelsea asked. As soon as those words were out of her mouth, she wished that she could take them back. She bit her lower lip because she knew what his answer would be.

No. He didn't trust her.

Because he'd asked for *her* trust, and she hadn't given it to him. She hadn't—

"Yes, baby, I trust you. If you say you don't have the necklace, I believe you."

Tears stung her eyes. She ignored the bound man and leapt for Colt. She wrapped her arms tightly around him and squeezed him as hard as she could. "Thank you."

There was a rustle behind her and—

The sound of ropes dropping? Hitting the floor?

Colt spun her behind him and faced off against the man who had somehow escaped the ropes that bound him. A man who now stood—completely free—in front of the chair. Remy's expression was twisted in disgust. "It is *personal* between you. Jeez. Do you know how bad that is? She is in the middle of a powder keg, she blinks those big, sexy eyes of hers at you...and you go to mush. That's just fucking wrong. I expected more."

Colt shoved a knife against Remy's throat. "Tell me again how I'm mush."

Remy's lashes flickered. "I may have...been mistaken."

"You've been *mistaken* all night. Let me be clear, we are not friends. Never have been. I don't trust you, not for a second. I get that you and Pierce might have some sort of truce going on, but Pierce happens to be in love with your sister. You remember her, don't you? The woman you *abandoned* for years."

Because Chelsea was watching Remy so closely, she saw the stiffening of his square jaw. "Sometimes, protection looks a lot like abandonment," he gritted.

"And sometimes, an asshole thief just looks like an asshole thief," Colt snarled right back. "You came in here with a gun, and you say you're after some million-dollar necklace. Your history doesn't exactly lead me to think you're on the up and up. So either start explaining—fast but in great detail—or maybe I'll be calling the cops on you."

Remy smiled at him. "If you call the local cops, the chief will just arrest you. He'll lock you away." His stare drifted to Chelsea. "And he'll deliver her to whoever put ten grand in his bank account two hours ago. That, of course, was just the most recent transaction." A pause. He didn't seem to care about the knife that was still pressed to his throat. "Though I suspect you realize you can't trust dear Victor. That would be why you rushed to this hole-in-the-wall in the dead of the night, yes? You ran here instead of seeking comfort and protection from the local law."

Chelsea inched forward. "Were you the one in the garage? The one who was aiming a gun at Colt?"

"I'd shake my head no, but then your *ex* here might just cut my skin with his shiny knife."

Colt continued to press said shiny knife to Remy's throat. "How did you know where we were?"

"Because I accessed video footage of you leaving the parking area. I saw the rental sticker on your convertible. Got those friendly folks at the CIA to do a bit of hacking work for me. Turns out, the rentals on the island all have GPS tracking devices on them. You know, in case some crazy tourist gets lost and needs help."

Her breath shuddered out. "If you weren't the one with the gun in the parking garage, then—"

"Then I suspect it was probably one of the men who tried kidnapping you before. I also think that individual will be able to trace your car just as I did. I got here first, which is an advantage for us, but we should expect his arrival soon enough." His gaze returned to Colt. "Instead of slicing my delicate skin, how about we reach a truce? Because from where I'm standing, you could use some help."

Colt didn't lower the knife. The tension was so tight that it seemed to thicken the air and push against Chelsea's skin.

"You don't have backup," Remy stated bluntly. "You came to this island alone. You came for her. And now you are trying to figure out how the hell to get her away from here. To get her out of here *alive*."

She had to swallow—twice—to clear the lump in her throat. "Being dead isn't an option that I want to consider."

"It's not on the table. Ever." A flat announcement from Colt.

Remy kept his body stiff. "You give me the necklace, and I can help you."

"I can't give you something I don't have!" She inched closer to Colt.

A sigh from Remy as his eyelashes flickered. "Dammit, I think I'm starting to believe you."

How lovely.

He and Colt continued their stare-off.

"You won't be able to fly her off the island," Remy finally said. "Victor will ground all the planes. I'm sure the ten grand he received was payment to shut down the flights. Probably to close the main dock, too."

Did Victor have the authority to do all that? Chelsea wasn't quite sure how that—

Remy arched one eyebrow. "I can get a boat to you. If she's off the island, that's step one toward her survival. Once we're clear of this tropical hell, we can take her to a secure facility."

Such a bad feeling. When he said "secure facility" why did Chelsea immediately think...prison?

"Victor will have the airport and dock covered with local people who are loyal to him. They won't let you just board a ferry or hitch a ride on someone else's boat. You'll need me to bring a boat to an out-of-the-way location for you." His smile stretched and made his gaze gleam. "I guess when it comes down to it, you'll just have to suck it up and trust me. *If* you want your lady friend—oh, so sorry, your *ex*—to get out of this mess unharmed."

"I really don't fucking like you," Colt muttered.

Chelsea shared that feeling.

Remy's smile widened even more. "I don't care. You don't have to like me. In this instance, you *do* need me, though."

Chelsea held her breath as Colt lowered the knife.

"Excellent. We have an agreement." Remy glanced at his watch. "Give me two hours, then meet me at the beach on the north shore, approximately three miles from this location. Stay out of sight. I'll be the one coming on the boat to save the day." He lifted his head. Met Colt's stare once again. "First, though, I have to check back in with a nervous partner. Convince him that all is well. And assure him that we are close to achieving our mission objective."

"The mission objective," Chelsea repeated. "Me."

"You're a means to an end."

Harsh.

"The end is the necklace. Its recovery is the goal. Whatever has to be done to achieve that goal, I'll do." He straightened his shoulders. "I would recommend getting away from this location immediately. As I said, I suspect others will trail you. Hide in the uninhabited portion of the island. I'm sure the two of you can find a way to pass the time until our rendezvous." He strode for the door.

Colt moved into his path. "How do I know you aren't setting a trap?"

"Because I love my sister." Low. So low that Chelsea almost couldn't make out his words. "And you helped her, so now I will help you. Debt paid."

Colt assessed him, then stepped back. "I'll see you in two hours."

Remy held out his hand. "I'd like my gun back."

"I'm sure you have another somewhere." A shark's smile. "See you soon."

Cursing, Remy slipped from the hut. Colt shut the door behind him. Locked it. Stood for just a moment with his back to Chelsea.

She struggled for something to say and finally landed on, "Interesting friend you have there."

"Remy isn't a friend. He's a dangerous criminal, a shady CIA operative, and a man you don't want to cross." He turned his head, looking over his shoulder at her. "But he's also a brother who does love his sister. She might be the only thing he cares about in this world, and since he thinks he owes me for helping her, he just might be our best ticket off this island."

"Who is Pierce? I get that he's the guy you've been texting, he's your friend, but—" But she wanted to know more about him because his name just kept popping up in conversations.

"He's my partner at Wilde."

She hadn't met him before. "Was he also undercover somewhere when you met me?"

"No. He was in the background. I was running lead. Usually, your Wilde partner is always close but the partner stays hidden unless it's necessary to be seen."

So that was why Remy had wanted to know where Colt's backup was. But this wasn't a case. And there was no backup. "I don't know anything about the necklace."

He turned toward her. Stared. Then closed in. *Stalked* toward her. Her shoulders couldn't help but tense. Her whole body tensed. There was just something about the hooded stare he was giving her. As if he couldn't quite decide if she was lying or telling the truth. "I don't," Chelsea insisted. "If I had some million-dollar necklace, don't you think I would have been living in a much bigger place? Or that I would have expanded my business sooner? Or, I don't know, given up the business entirely and run away to some tropical—"

She stopped because...

Ahem. She was on a tropical island. And running to the island hadn't worked so well. "There's a mistake. I don't have the necklace."

His hand lifted. Pressed to her cheek. She found herself wanting to turn into his touch. "You have me," Colt told her softly. "I will get you to safety."

She smiled at him. Relief bloomed inside of her.

He bent his head. His mouth brushed over hers. It was a tender kiss. So careful.

It made her want more.

"Get your bag ready, but take *only* what you need because we'll be on foot. If Remy found us, then, yes, others can, too. They *will.* We'll hide out until the boat comes for us."

Okay. Good plan.

"While you get ready, I'm going to do a quick check outside to make sure the area is clear for our departure. Don't want any other surprise visitors waiting out there for us." His hand slid from her cheek. "Everything will be all right."

Wonderful words. Fabulous words. And once she was off this island, she'd actually believe them.

***

Colt slipped into the night. Made sure to stay in the shadows. He'd already done a perimeter check and also peered at the security footage via his phone. No one else was around. He was secure, for the moment.

He contacted his partner and put the phone to his ear. Part of him was damn glad he still had cell service, but he knew that was a double-edged sword. Since he could call out, others could track him, too. Which meant...

I'll need to go dark soon.

Pierce answered on the second ring. "What's happening?" No protest about the time. Just worry.

"Got a surprise visit a bit ago—from Remy."

"*What the fuck?*"

"My reaction, too." Low. "Says that he's working with the CIA and that Chelsea is the target. Jerk was claiming she had some necklace—"

"Uh, Colt..."

Shit. He knew what that particular tone meant. "You found something."

"Yeah, I found something. Something you are not going to like."

There was nothing about this mess he did like.

"Your Chelsea was a peripheral player in the situation with Theodore Beasley, so we didn't go back far enough in her background."

Chelsea isn't a criminal. She hasn't done anything wrong. He knew this truth in his gut.

"I did a little more digging, and it's all tentative, but...her mother is raising red flags."

"What?"

"Her mom's life seems to have started the day Chelsea was born. Before that, she didn't exist."

Sonofabitch. "New identity."

"Yep. I'm thinking she traded something in order to get a new name for herself and her daughter. And a new name usually means you're running from someone who happens to be very scary."

"Her mother died a year ago," Colt said softly. The death still hurt Chelsea. When they'd been together before, whenever she mentioned her mom, pain had slid into Chelsea's voice.

"Chelsea doesn't have any other family that I can find." Pierce's voice was flat. "Her father wasn't listed on the birth certificate. So it's possible she doesn't know anything about him."

He understood what his partner was saying. And what he wasn't. "You think it's possible Chelsea is hiding details about her past."

Pierce's silence was affirmation. Dammit.

Time to cut to the chase. "The necklace Remy is after? He said it was worth over a million dollars. He's supposed to retrieve it, but Chelsea claims to have zero idea what he's talking about."

What Remy was talking about—and what others were hunting her to possess.

Pierce whistled.

"He's going to get us off the island," Colt said. The waves pounded in the distance. "I'm going dark because my location is already compromised. When I'm clear, I'll contact you again."

"I do *not* like this plan."

Join the club. "Not like there are a ton of options. Remy says the boat is coming in two hours. If you don't hear from me in three..."

"I will send in the freaking cavalry."

They might be too late. "Just make sure that Chelsea gets away." His one request.

"I'll make sure I know every damn thing there is to know about your mystery lady," Pierce promised. "And I will always have my partner's back."

Colt hung up the phone. Stared out into the night. So much for the vacation time he'd anticipated. The secrets kept coming, and he wasn't sure what—or who—would be after them next.

One thing he *did* know...

His gaze swung back to the hut.

I will fucking destroy anyone who tries to hurt Chelsea.

CHAPTER EIGHT

They left the vehicle. Most of Chelsea's belongings. She ran with him toward the waiting darkness, and the very fact that she was so quiet told him that Chelsea had to be terrified.

The woman had never been the type to be at a loss for words.

He kept one hand locked with hers as they navigated over the terrain. He could hear the fast and hard chirping of insects. The pounding of the water. He stayed as close to the shore as he could, and the treetops swayed overhead. The trees were thicker here, their tops denser, but there was still enough starlight trickling down for him to see where they were headed. If he'd turned on his phone and used the light from it, the illumination could have given away their location to anyone hunting them.

And as far as hunters...

The first cry came about forty-five minutes after they'd left the little cabin.

"*Chelsea!*" A man's booming voice cut through the night. At first, the bugs screamed louder in reaction to the cry, then everything seemed to go dead silent.

Colt immediately stopped and crouched, pulling Chelsea down with him. He knew the bastard had found the hut. Found the hut, the abandoned convertible, and realized that the only place they could go—well, it was either into the water or trek across the island on foot.

The guy had opted to follow them on foot.

"Chelsea, I am here to help you!" the man shouted.

Her knees pressed into the ground beside Colt.

He shook his head.

"The man with you—you don't really know him!"

Ah, tricky bastard. Had he been digging into Colt's life?

"You think you do, but he's been lying to you since day one."

Fair enough, he had lied. But what he hadn't done? Fucking kidnapped her. *So good luck getting her to buy your story, asshole.* It was rather hard to go back from a kidnapping attempt. *If* it was the bastard who'd tried to take her—twice—and Colt's gut said it was. The fellow just didn't have the sense to give up. Maybe a bullet could help with that problem.

"He's not who you believe he is!" Another shout. This one...closer. Colt listened intently. Only one man was talking, but he doubted the guy had come alone.

"He's working for a company called Wilde! They hired him to retrieve a very important piece of property—property he thinks you have."

Well, well. Someone was singing a new tune. Twisting truths and lies together. An effective tactic that Colt had actually employed in the past.

"He'll do anything to retrieve that property!" Definitely closer. "I'm afraid that you are in danger as long as you are close to him."

She inched even closer to Colt. His fingers squeezed hers.

"I'm with the CIA!"

Now that gave Colt pause. Surely this wasn't Remy's so-called partner? If so...

"If you can get away from him, come to me!" A desperate plea. "I will protect you. I will get you off this island and back to American soil. You cannot trust him! He wants to take you away. Take you to the people he works for—he will turn you over to them, and I fear you will never be seen again!"

None of that was on Colt's agenda. He stared at the shadowy planes of Chelsea's face. There was so much he wanted to say to her. He needed her to keep believing in him. He needed her to understand that he would never sell her out. Turning her over to some enemy was never going to be in the cards.

But he couldn't say a word.

So he did what he could—he leaned forward, and he kissed her. A soft, careful brush of his lips over hers, and in that kiss, he told her...

Count on me.

He felt a slight tremble work over her body.

She nodded against him.

"Chelsea!" Not so pleading. More angry. Rage cracking through the fake surface. "We don't have fucking time to waste! Come out! Let me help you!"

Colt's lips stayed against hers. *Don't make a sound, baby.*

The man was close. So close that Colt knew he might need to—

"Fucking bitch." A snarl. Then the rush of footsteps as the man swung away and headed in the opposite direction. The rush of *two* sets of footsteps because he had not been alone.

Colt also didn't think the guy had been CIA.

His mouth lifted from hers. They were still crouched low, and he let go of her hand. Let go just so he could move his fingers and press a fingertip to her lips so she'd know they couldn't make a sound.

He felt her nod against him.

He had two guns. The gun he'd originally taken from the bastard who'd kidnapped Chelsea. And Remy's gun. He gave Remy's gun to her. Pressed it into her hands. If necessary, she had to be ready to fight.

For a time, he remained still. Listening. Waiting. The footsteps faded away. Eventually, the insects started chirping again. He tugged Chelsea to her feet, and they took off once more. Moving slowly, silently. The night wrapped around him and Chelsea as they ditched the men who hunted them.

***

Fucking lost. That was what he was. Brian spun around, glaring at the stupid trees and vegetation all around him. His hand lifted, and he slapped at a damn mosquito that buzzed near his neck.

While he'd waited to get access to the rental car's GPS, his boss had come through with intel on Colt Easton. A freaking security agent. Not some accountant, but a dick who'd been working undercover.

He's after the same prize. You can't let him win. The boss's order. So Brian had thought he'd try his hand at playing hero. Try to spin the story so that Chelsea would doubt her lover. A woman had to be pissed when she found out that she'd been tricked. But...

She hadn't called back to him.

He was stomping through the freaking wilds of the island, shouting to her wherever he went, and she wouldn't respond to him.

He needed more men. More eyes. And not just the barely legal kid the boss had sent with him tonight.

"It's not like they can get away," the kid said in a voice that cracked a little. "I mean, what are they gonna do, swim for it?"

He could hear the crash of the water. Not too far away. He hadn't even gone toward the beach because...no, they couldn't swim away. And they didn't have a boat. Victor had eyes at the marinas but...

How else do you get off the island?

***

"I don't see anything." She bobbed a little next to Colt as she peered out at the darkness. "Isn't it time? Shouldn't the boat be here?"

Provided they could trust Remy, yes, the boat should be arriving. Colt's eyes narrowed as he stared out at the waves. They were in the right location, but he didn't see any lights to indicate a boat was coming toward them.

But Remy would come in with lights off. In case anyone else was watching. "We're going into the water."

"Excuse me?"

"We'll put the guns in your bag." Though they'd still get soaked, and with the way his luck was going, they wouldn't fire after being drenched. "We'll swim out."

"Out to what?"

Out to the boat that had damn well better be coming.

In that instant, he saw the brief flash of a green light.

Hell, yes. "Out to the boat that's waiting."

"He's not, um, coming to shore?"

"That would attract too much attention." He took the guns, put them in her bag, and slung the strap over his shoulder. "We swim to him. We get on the boat. We get the hell away from this tropical nightmare. Piece of cake." He started to rise.

She grabbed his arm and pulled him back down. "I should tell you something that is semi-important about myself."

Baby, please don't tell me that you're some jewel thief who—

"I am not the best swimmer in the world."

"What?" The last thing he'd expected to hear in that instance.

"I'm okay. Like, you know, I can handle myself just fine in a pool. And in shallows. But I am not exactly what you'd call a super deep, open waters kind of woman."

He absorbed this info. Shook his head. "You came to a tropical island...and you can't swim." Fuck.

"I *can* swim. I'm just not Michael Phelps." A rushed whisper. "So I just wanted to warn you, in case I become some kind of dead weight—"

She wasn't going to be a dead anything. "I will drag you onto the boat. Don't worry, sweetheart, you're not sinking on my watch. Because I happen to be one hell of a swimmer. When you're a SEAL, you have to be." Once more, he rose.

She clamped tighter to his arm. "You were a SEAL? Since when?"

Since, yeah...that was something else they'd discuss...later. When they weren't on a dark beach with bad guys searching for them and waves crashing before them. "You won't be drowning with me. Count on it." The water was a second home to him. "Ready?"

"No, but let's do it anyway."

Damn straight. They raced toward the beach. The green light didn't flash again, but he suspected that Remy would be waiting a certain amount of time before he gave them another signal. Colt remembered exactly where that light had been, and as they waded into the surf, he angled his body in the direction—

"Chelsea!" A booming shout from behind them. Back on the beach.

She looked back. Colt didn't. He grabbed her and practically tossed her into the deeper water. In the next instant, he dove after her. He heard the thunder of gunfire, saw the water erupt near him, but he didn't stop. He stayed deep and he grabbed her wrist and he kicked forward with all of his power. He wasn't about to go up to the surface, not yet. They had to get farther from the shore. So he swam and swam, and hell, yes, he kept her with him. Colt could hold his breath for three minutes, no problem, but he doubted that Chelsea could do the same.

Her hand twisted in his grip. She jerked against him.

He immediately catapulted them to the surface. Their heads broke the water. She sucked in a gasping breath. His gaze swung toward the beach. *Not far enough away yet.* So he hauled her back down with him. They kicked and surged forward. He let her hand go so she could maneuver better, but he kept his body right beside hers. They pushed and swam and when she faltered...

His arm wrapped around her stomach and, once more, they broke the surface. He treaded water to keep them above the water's edge. They'd traveled a good distance from the beach. The waves lifted them, rocked them, and Chelsea sucked in more frantic breaths.

"Where...where is the boat?" she croaked.

He scanned the water. Waited. Looked for that green light.

If I can see the light, the people on the beach might see it, too. Unfortunate. But...

The light flashed. The briefest of glimpses, and he hauled ass. At first, he kept his grip on Chelsea, but she pushed against him. "I...I can do it."

So he let her.

Until she began to slow. And falter. Then he just locked tight to her and got them through the waves. Waves that were getting rougher and harder and that pushed against them as they tried to reach the boat that waited.

That had better be Remy's bastard self on that boat. Because if it was someone else, if this was a trap...

Then Colt and Chelsea were screwed to hell and back.

He could see the boat now. The V-shaped hull rocked as the vessel—maybe a thirty or thirty-five-footer—waited. A man stood behind the steering wheel. Shadowy. And—

"Hurry the hell up," Remy blasted. "You think I got all damn night to sit in the ocean waiting for you?"

There was a small ladder at the stern. He grabbed it with one hand and guided Chelsea to it with the other. She struggled to haul herself up, he gave her a push, and water coursed down her body as she flopped onto the boat. He followed her quickly, and as soon as he was out of the water—

Remy punched it. The boat's engine growled to life, and the vessel shot forward. Chelsea had just gotten to her feet and she stumbled, but Colt caught her before she could fall. He pulled her close against him. Held her tight.

"We're safe now?" she whispered.

He looked over her shoulder and stared at Remy's back. Safe, provided they could truly trust an art thief who enjoyed playing deadly games with the CIA.

He and Chelsea maneuvered to the middle of the boat. Spray shot from the water around them as Remy drove like a true bat out of hell. "Can you try not to kill us?" Colt groused.

Chelsea sagged onto the boat seat. Tilted back her head.

He dropped the bag he'd kept slung across his shoulder. "Where are we going?" he asked Remy. He *had* noticed the guy hadn't answered his first question.

"I'm taking you to a place that is a little more friendly—and with a law enforcement team that's not so blatantly on the take." Remy didn't look back. His grip remained steady on the wheel. "So many strings had to be pulled for your ungrateful ass, by the way. So many. When we get there, you follow my lead, got it? And then we'll work out payback."

"You never said anything about payback." He should have expected this development. "I thought you were doing this because Wilde helped your sister." He sat beside Chelsea. A lock of wet hair slid over her cheek. Gently, he brushed it back.

Her head turned toward him. "I didn't drown."

He smiled. "No, I think you might have an Olympic swim career in your future, after all."

A soft laugh slipped from her. "Liar."

Yes, he was.

Remy's voice rose as he told him, "If you want the CIA's help, there's always a payment needed."

Fuck. "I thought *you* were helping us."

"Well, I'm currently in bed with the CIA so..." The boat bumped into the waves. Seemed to jump into the air, then hit back down. "The payment will be simple. Just one thing. Don't act like it's such a big deal."

Everything with Remy was a big deal. "Where is your partner?" A pause. "Not, by any chance, running around on the island, shouting for Chelsea, and telling her that she can't trust me?"

"What?" Remy swiveled to look at him. "Why would Ty be doing that?"

He felt water dripping down his face. "Where is he?"

"Getting things in motion." He turned to the front again. "His job was to keep Victor busy while I spirited you away. Ty is only a semi-dick. He understands that getting Chelsea to a more controlled environment is important."

"You never said he'd be helping you."

"I never said he wouldn't, now did I? What the hell did you expect? Me to work miracles all by my little old self?" The boat bumped again. "Dammit. How about you sit back, put your arm around the lovely lady who is shivering and shaking..."

She *was* shivering and shaking. Hell. Colt immediately hauled her closer.

"And do try to get in a loving mood—or at least, look loving—because we really need the people at the hotel to buy that you're some hot and heavy honeymooners, okay?"

Chelsea stiffened.

Colt's jaw dropped. "What?"

"You're welcome." Remy revved the engine even more. "By the way, that payback I mentioned? I prefer it in the form of a 1.4 million-dollar pearl necklace. Let's try to make that happen, shall we?"

The guy was such a dick.

CHAPTER NINE

"You're checked in under assumed names." Remy threw open the doors to the honeymoon suite. "You can't keep your hands off each other. You're totally devoted. Sexually obsessed. And that's why you will *not* be leaving this room."

Chelsea crept inside. She felt like a drowned rat. The boat ride had seemed to last forever, and there had been more than a few times when she feared she might be sick. The combination of swallowing some salt water during that frantic swim and the hard bobbing of the boat as it hit the waves had not led to the most amazing experience ever.

However, she'd been alive. She'd been on her way to safety, so she'd just kept her issues to herself and tried to breathe her way through the nausea.

At the moment, she was so happy to be on solid ground that she could have fallen to the floor and kissed the gleaming tiles.

Remy had rushed them through the dark lobby of what looked like an uber-expensive hotel. Chelsea couldn't recall the name of the place. She should have paid more attention, but he'd directed her to keep her head down. Colt had pulled her close, nuzzled her against him, and the skeleton crew of staff members who'd been up at that hellacious hour had probably just seen a loving—but exhausted—couple.

Her hair had dried on the trip. Remy had given her fresh clothes before she'd gone inside. The clothes hadn't made her feel any less like a drowned rat, but they had made her look better. Not like Remy wanted the staff to know she and her "husband" had needed to take a frantic survival swim that night.

Remy shut the doors as she and Colt lingered in the entranceway. "The hotel has top-notch security. *Real* security, and even a few agents who are working undercover." He wiggled his brows. "They'll be watching the room, so don't think you two can duck and run without us knowing. You're working with us now, and a partnership *is* a partnership."

"I don't have the necklace," she said wearily. When would he get that? She couldn't wave her hands in the air and magically produce something that she just didn't possess.

"I believe you."

Her head snapped toward him.

"But I think you may just be the only person who can help to find it. Thus, the partnership."

"How am I supposed to find a necklace that I've never even seen?" It was an impossible task.

"I've got faith in you. After you've rested a bit and you have a chance to think, who knows what you'll remember?"

"Remember?" What an odd word choice. "I think I would remember a million-dollar necklace."

Remy slanted a glance toward Colt. "Not if the last time you saw it, you were a child. We assumed she'd given it to you, but something else must have happened."

"She?" What on earth was he talking about now? And could he just have this talk later, please? Fumes were keeping her going, and Chelsea feared she'd be collapsing any moment. A bed would be heaven.

Remy's attention lingered on Colt. "Why haven't you told her yet?"

"It's time for you to go." Colt grabbed Remy and ushered him—or shoved him—toward the door. "Come back after she's had at least five hours of sleep."

She stumbled after them. The new tennis shoes Remy had given her were a little tight. "Told me what?"

Remy looked back. "Being in the dark fucking sucks." Grim. "I know. I had to stay in the dark far too long. I'm still there." He jerked away from Colt. "Your mother kept secrets from you. Now your boyfriend is doing it, too. Sorry, correction, *ex*-boyfriend," he said when she opened her mouth.

But she hadn't been about to correct him on the ex issue. She'd been about to tell him that he was wrong. Her mother had been an elementary school teacher. One of the nicest, most caring people in the world. Her life had been an open book.

Except for that one night.

"It's believed that your mother stole the necklace from a very powerful man. She took it when she left him. Took it and—" But Remy stopped. Cleared his throat. "You know what? I'll be back in five hours. If you get hungry, order room service, but tell them to leave the tray outside. Don't let anyone in this room but me." He wrenched open the door.

"Thank you," Chelsea called after him.

Remy paused.

"I will do everything I can to pay you back for this, but I truly don't remember any pearl necklace. My mom and I lived in a two-bedroom house in the middle of nowhere." A little speck town in the heart of Georgia. "If she'd been sitting on a million dollars, don't you think she would have used that money?"

The faint lines near his mouth bracketed. His head tilted toward Colt. "I'm assuming I don't need to tell you to stay close to her?"

"Try to get me away."

"Good answer. By the way, me and Wilde? Even now. So don't think you can call me in for any favors." He pulled the door shut behind him. The faint click seemed very, very loud.

But when Colt flipped the extra locks on the door—those clicks were even louder.

She stood there, with her arms wrapped around her stomach, and her hair still smelling like the ocean. All of her wanted to go and collapse in the bed that waited, but first... "Shower," she murmured. Bone tired, Chelsea turned away.

"Aren't you going to ask me what secrets he meant?"

Honestly, she was just too tired to ask. "I don't think I can handle another surprise right now." She could barely handle putting one foot in front of the other. When she'd been swimming in that water, when those people had been on the beach behind them and shooting...Chelsea had truly thought they might die. He'd had to pull her, had to tuck her against his body, and practically carry her through the waves to safety. Without him...

She swallowed. "You saved my life. Thank you."

"Told you before, I don't want your thanks. That's not what this is about."

Right. Before, he'd said he didn't want thanks. He'd told her...

I want you.

She crept through the suite. It was massive, consisting of a sitting area with a plush couch and a giant TV. A door to the right led to the bedroom. The king-size bed's covers had been turned down. And rose petals had been sprinkled on the sheets.

Soft music played in the bedroom. Faint lighting illuminated the scene. Red roses waited on the nightstand, right next to a chilled bottle of champagne.

Chelsea swallowed. "I guess Remy told them that we were coming?"

"He's setting the scene. Probably put in the order to have everything like this so it would look more legitimate."

Right. Legitimate. Colt had followed her into the bedroom, and when she glanced back, he appeared big, fierce, and sexy. How was that fair? She probably looked like she'd been through a hurricane, and he looked hot.

She shouldn't be thinking he looked good enough to eat. She should be thinking about climbing into bed and sleeping. Not hotness. Not sexiness. Quickly, she pushed open the bathroom door.

A heart-shaped hot tub waited for her. The water jetted softly, sending the rose petals on top dancing around. "I suppose he told them to get that ready, too?"

She felt Colt closing in behind her.

"Yeah." His voice deepened even more. "I'm sure he did. You go in first. I'll shower when you're done."

A shower had been her original plan, but the hot tub tempted her tired muscles. She should have reached her limit when it came to water but...

But when he walked out and shut the door behind him, leaving her alone in the bathroom, Chelsea stripped. She stepped into the tub, lowered her body in the warm water, tipped back her head and closed her eyes...

And promptly fell asleep.

***

He didn't hear a sound from the bathroom. Colt checked the clock on the wall. Chelsea had looked utterly exhausted—beautiful still, always beautiful—but so weary as she made her way into the bathroom. He knew she wanted to crash.

But she hadn't come back out yet.

He made his way toward the bathroom. His knuckles rapped on the door. "Uh, Chelsea?"

Nothing. No response.

He tried again. Louder. "Chelsea?"

Again, nothing. Alarm flared through him, and he threw open the door. He rushed inside to see—

Chelsea. With her arms spread over the back of the tub, her head tilted back, her gorgeous body naked beneath the water and...

Her eyes closed.

Fuck me. He hurried toward her. Turned off the hot tub. The scent of the flowers teased his nose as he reached for her. "Baby..." He slid his arms under her. "You can't fall asleep in here."

Her eyes opened, she blinked a little blearily, then her eyelids immediately closed again.

He lifted her out of the tub. Her warm, wet body curled against him as she wrapped one arm around his neck. He thought that her mouth brushed against him.

Sweet hell.

She was naked, and in his arms, and he'd had this fantasy about a thousand times. Well, no, correction, she hadn't been *sleeping* in his fantasy. She'd been a super active participant in his dreams.

"Baby, I need to dry you off." He carried her away from the tub. "Can you stand?"

He was pretty sure she murmured yes, so he lowered her carefully until her feet touched the thick rug. But Colt kept a hand on her waist, just in case.

She wavered only a little bit.

And he tried to ignore just how fucking perfect her body was as he grabbed for a towel with his free hand. There had to be some kind of reward for this. For being tortured by everything he wanted so much and by—

"Dry," he growled. Dry enough, anyway. He'd basically swiped the towel over her and was just gonna call it done. Because her tight, pert nipples were pushing toward him. She was fucking *bare* between her legs—shaved or waxed, just fucking mind-blowingly hot and he could barely think. *Could barely breathe.* He could see her. All of her. He wanted to part her thighs. He wanted to put his hands on here *there* and not get her dry, but get her wet. Get her so wet that she was moaning and twisting and coming for him.

The way she'd been beneath that palm tree. The way he wanted her again and again.

Not now. Not now because she's dead on her feet.

He scooped her into his arms. Double-timed it to the bed. Lowered her onto the mattress and immediately yanked the covers up over her. Rose petals went flying. His breath sawed in and out. In and out. "Safer place to sleep," he assured her. "Way safer. No risk of drowning or—"

"I thought I was going to drown." Her words were all slurred together. Sleep slurred. "I was sure I'd sink beneath the water, and I didn't want to tell you because you were..."

He leaned toward her. "What, baby?"

"Working so hard to get us to the boat." At least, that was what he thought she said. The words had come out all together in a tangle.

He brushed back her hair. "Told you, you're not gonna drown on my watch. If you'd sunk, I would have just shot down and pulled you back up."

Her eyes had closed.

He turned away.

Her hand flew out. Caught his wrist. "Where are you going?"

His translation of the rumble that had come from her. What she'd sleepily said...*Whereugo?*

"Quick shower." He knew it would be a very icy one.

"Come back to me."

Comebackme.

"I will."

***

His skin was covered with chill bumps when he left the bathroom. The cold shower hadn't helped much to ease his giant erection, but he was clean, at least. He began to creep past the bed.

"Colt?"

Sleepy. Confused.

He exhaled. "It's okay. You're safe. I'm just going to bunk on the couch."

"Stay."

"I am. I'm staying on the couch," he assured her. No way would he leave her alone.

"Stay." Fitful.

He moved closer to the bed. It was huge. But so was he. And if he crawled in that bed with her, there would be no bullshit about him staying on one side and her on the other. He'd be in her space. If he touched her... "Bad idea."

"Scared," she muttered.

Fuck, if she was scared, then he'd stay. "Scoot over."

She didn't. He slid beneath the covers beside her and started to scoot her so she would—

She rolled toward him. Took up all the space on his side as she proceeded to climb on top of him. She snuggled close. Her breath teased his skin. "Better." A sigh.

She went boneless on top of him.

Colt swallowed. Stared up at the ceiling. Better? It was hell. It was a nightmare. It was also...

His arms closed around her. *Better than anything I've had in a long time.* Some of the tension eased from his heart. His head tilted, and he brushed a kiss over her temple. "You're right. It is better." Another soft kiss. "Good night, sweetheart."

***

Her eyes opened. The usual grogginess she felt upon first waking had Chelsea ever-so-slowly stretching...

Until she realized that her stretches were hampered by the arms around her. By the body beneath her. The strong, hard, male body.

She sucked in a breath, and her head shot up.

"Oh, fuck!" A startled explanation from the man beneath her—because she'd just clipped his chin. She'd just clipped *Colt's* chin.

They were in bed. Both naked. She was on top of him. Her legs straddled his hips and slid down his body, and his dick—a very long, very thick, very erect dick nudged toward—

"*How* did this happen?" Chelsea cried as she scampered off him. As she scampered, her knee slipped between them and her eyes widened as she came dangerously close to kneeing him right in the—

He spun, quickly, and pinned her beneath him. "Nothing happened," he rushed to say. "Absolutely nothing. You were scared and you asked me to stay with you, so I did. Then you climbed on top of me, went to sleep, and so did I. That's it. Sleep. Not sex. Sleep. And I woke up hard because—well, that happens. It happens even more if I wake up and *you* are near me because I happen to want you more than I want anything else in this world." His hands had curled under the pillow beneath her. "Nothing happened," he repeated.

She couldn't look away from his deep, intense stare. Sunlight drifted through the curtains, providing her with enough illumination to see him. "How did I get in bed?" The last thing she could clearly remember was climbing into the hot tub.

His mouth hitched into a half-smile. "Found you sleeping in the tub." The smile vanished. "Not safe, baby. So I got you out, I dried you off, and I tucked you in."

He'd tucked her in? That was...

"Hell. Just so you know. Seeing you was hell, but the damn thing is, I can't remember the last time I slept so well."

"We were..." Chelsea cleared her throat. "Dead tired."

"Been dead tired plenty of times before. I slept well because I was with you." His jaw locked. He pushed away. Climbed off her. Started to slide from beneath the sheets. Then he stilled. "Yeah, I'm butt naked so you might want to look away."

She didn't look away.

He rose from the bed. Had his back turned to her. Her gaze lingered on his back. Those broad shoulders. Those strong muscles. Chelsea pulled the covers closer even as her gaze dipped slowly down to the butt in question.

The best ass she'd ever seen.

"You're not looking away, are you?"

Nope. Her tongue swiped over her lower lip. "You saw me naked last night." She was still naked. "My turn."

A nod of his head. "Fair enough."

Then he spun toward her.

Her gaze was still focused on his lower body, so when he turned...

Oh, hello. She'd felt his erection against her. The hard, wide width. The long length. The heat. But seeing him was just—

"I'll be taking another cold shower," he mumbled. "Be back and—"

Her hand flew out. Caught his wrist. "Stay."

He peered down at her hand as if her fingers were the most fascinating things he'd ever seen in his life. "You said that last night."

She had? "I'm not sure what I meant last night but what I mean right now..."

His gaze lifted. Locked on her face.

She wanted to be very, very clear about this. There was no going back. “I want to make love with you, Colt. I want you.” There. Done. Chelsea held her breath—

And he pounced.

CHAPTER TEN

When a man held too tightly to his control, for too long...eventually, he knew that control would shatter. It was, after all, only a matter of time.

His time had come.

I want to make love with you, Colt. I want you.

Soft, hesitant words had just pounded into his control with the strength of a sledgehammer. The restraint he'd had? The restraint he'd clung to desperately for so long?

Gone.

Colt tumbled Chelsea back into the bed. The covers tangled between them, and he growled as he shoved them out of the way. He wanted to touch her. To put his hands and his mouth all over every single inch of her.

And he would.

Her breasts thrust toward him. Curving and perfect with their tight nipples. His mouth closed around one nipple, and she bucked off the bed.

"Colt!"

His hand snaked between their bodies. Wedged down between her legs. Her legs had parted for him, and his fingers went straight to her core. She wasn't wet yet, but she fucking would be.

He laved her nipple, sucked, and strummed her clit. Her whole body jolted, and he did it again. Again.

Then he began to kiss a path down her body. Because for what he wanted to do, the way he wanted to fuck her, she had to be completely ready. She had to take all of him and scream with pleasure. She had to be warm and wet, and she had to be raking her nails down his back as she urged him to just go faster and harder in her.

Faster and harder.

He shoved more of the damn covers out of his way. They hit the floor with a rustle. His hands closed over her thighs, and he pushed them even farther apart. For a moment, he just stopped to stare at her. His dick was so hard he ached, and he was gazing at a freaking masterpiece.

"Uh, Colt?"

"I am going to eat you alive."

"Colt—"

"No, I'm just going to eat you until you come. Scream for me, baby." He put his mouth on her. Licked her clit. Sucked. Then thrust his tongue into her.

Her hips jerked in reaction so he grabbed them with his hands, and he brought her closer. Held her there so he could taste and taste and taste. His tongue greedily lapped at her as she cried out his name.

Not enough. Not yet.

He wanted to feel her come against his mouth. She was close, but not there. *Not yet.* So he licked faster. Harder. He tasted and feasted and she—

Came. Her sex shoved against his mouth, and she cried out. A muffled sound as her body shuddered. He could feel the trembles in her thighs. Could taste her pleasure. And he just lapped it up.

He made sure she rode out every second of that climax, and his head slowly lifted. When it did, he realized that she'd covered her mouth with one hand. That was why her cry of release had been muffled.

As he stared at her, her eyes widened. Her hand slowly lowered. "I..." Her tongue swept out to lick her lips. "Was afraid the walls were thin..."

"We're in the honeymoon suite." His voice was savage. Too rough. He felt too rough. Too rough. Too hungry. Too primal. *Want in. Want to slam deep and never let go.* "If they haven't put thick walls in this part of the suite, then they're idiots. There's one loud activity people like to do in the bedroom of the honeymoon suite."

Fuck.

Only one thing he wanted to do in that instance—*fuck my bride.*

But she wasn't his bride.

She is mine.

He positioned his cock at the entrance to her body and—

Dammit!

Protection. His gaze shot around the room. Latched onto the nightstand. He bolted from the bed.

"Colt?"

He wrenched open the top drawer. Sure the hell enough, a box of condoms waited inside. And when he reached for that box, a slip of paper fell from the top.

Courtesy of your awesome friend Remy. A careful, handwritten note penned on a bit of the hotel's stationery.

The sonofabitch. But, hell, yes, Colt was grateful. He grabbed a condom from the box, ripped open the packet, and rolled that baby on. Maybe his fingers shook a little bit. He was barely holding on.

He spun back for the bed. Chelsea's eyes met his. Her dark hair spread on the pillow behind her. Her hand lifted toward him.

He was a goner.

He lunged back for the bed. Jumped on top. Put his cock at her core. His breath sawed in and out, in and out. He should probably be going slower, but when you had wanted something for so long, needed something so much...

Fuck slow.

He drove into her. Sank into her and absolutely lost what was left of his mind. There was no more holding back. There was no thought of restraint. There was only need. Pounding, driving, consuming need. He sank as far into her as he could go. He grabbed her legs and wrapped them around his waist. She ground against him, and her moans urged him on. Faster. Deeper. Harder.

He gave her everything. Took everything. Her sex squeezed around him as she cried out in pleasure, and he just pounded into her even faster. He could feel his orgasm drawing close, but he didn't want this moment to end. Colt didn't want to stop. He never wanted—

Pleasure. Enough to gut him. Blind him. Cause him to roar out his release as he held her tighter than he had ever held anyone or anything else in his life. Pleasure so strong that he knew that nothing else would ever be this good.

Pleasure so good...that he knew he would fight the devil himself if it meant he could have Chelsea again.

His heartbeat thundered in his ears as his lashes slowly lifted, and he looked at her.

Stared at her face.

Memorized every single thing about her.

And knew...

Mine.

***

"It's not my fault she left the island." Victor leaned back in his office chair and crossed his arms over his chest. "I had men at the dock and main marina. The airport was shut down. I did my job."

The man who'd introduced himself as Brian Lambert slowly shook his blond head. "If you'd done your job, Chelsea Ember would be here right now. She's not. She's in the wind, and my boss—the man who paid you a considerable amount of money to keep her here—well, he's not very happy."

Victor snorted. "Twenty grand isn't considerable."

"You were given more than twenty. You were paid before she arrived. Then you were paid after—"

"Yeah, well, no one said anything about a kidnapping attempt! That shit was out of control. I deserved the twenty grand just for covering that crap up." And kidnapping a woman? That made him uncomfortable. It was all fine to look the other way for a few drug drops. Maybe the occasional gun deal. But kidnapping? No. "This was more than I bargained for."

Brian glanced around the small office. "You were given a golden ticket, and you fucked up."

Truth be told, Victor was actually kind of glad the woman was gone. He didn't exactly want her blood on his hands. He had a daughter who wasn't much younger than Chelsea Ember had been and—

"We want to know where she is," Brian continued flatly.

He laughed. "What the hell do you want me to do? Look into some crystal ball for you?"

"You will call the authorities on the nearby islands. The places someone could access by boat. You will tell them that Chelsea is a wanted criminal. You'll send them her description. If they see her, you tell them to apprehend her on sight and—"

"*You* don't tell me what to do." Now he stood. The old chair—the chair he'd intended to replace at least a dozen times—squeaked behind him. "I'm not some flunky. I'm the chief here." His chest thrust out. Did this punk know who he was dealing with?

Brian smiled at him. "You're exactly what I say you are."

Okay, this little piece of shit was about to learn some manners. You treated your elders with respect. "I'm done. And unless *you* want to be hauled into the cell in the back..." He jerked his thumb to the right. "Then you will get your ass out of here, you'll get off *my* island, and you won't ever come back."

"You're not going to make those calls?"

Hell, no, he wasn't. "I don't have any evidence that the woman committed a crime! If I go calling them, they'll ask questions. They might look at *me*. They might—"

"Realize you aren't some honorable cop with a heart of gold? Please. Most people already know. You've been on the take for too long." Disgust curled Brian's lips. "Certainly too long to be growing a conscience now."

Was that what he was doing? Victor rubbed his chest. Maybe. "You never said anything about hurting her."

Brian rolled his eyes. "If she'd cooperated, she wouldn't have been hurt. It could have been a painless transaction for everyone."

"She's got a bodyguard. You know that, right? I did some checking on the guy, and he's—"

Brian's face tightened. "You're not the only one who checked. I know exactly who Colt Easton is."

"He's dangerous." He made Victor nervous. The guy had made him nervous from the very first glance, even before Victor had dug into his life. It had been something about Colt's gaze. So cold. Deadly. "He's—"

"He's the one who took her away. He will be handled, I assure you."

Handled. The hair on his nape rose. "Handled how?"

Brian stared back at him, and Victor could feel his heart rate kicking up. Now the man was just casually talking murder? Right to his face? "I'm the chief of—"

"I don't like violence, honestly, I don't. Maybe I gave you the wrong impression. It's not something I enjoy. Unfortunately, my boss isn't a man you can refuse."

Victor felt a trickle of sweat slide down his face. He knew a threat when he heard one. "Son, you need to just settle down." Casually, carefully, he began to slide his hand toward the holster on his hip.

But Brian whipped out his gun. Pointed it at him. "The boss pays well, and the job has to get done. You screwed up." The gun trembled just a little. "He always makes you pay when you screw up."

No, this wasn't happening. Why the hell wasn't anyone else in that office—

Brian fired.

Victor felt the bullet sink into his chest. He'd never been shot before. There just...wasn't much trouble on the island. He made sure of it. He controlled things. He took care of things and...

The bullet was hot when it first went into him. Burned and then slowly seemed to settle deeper and deeper into him. Everything felt slow, even his movements as he looked down and stared at the hole in his chest.

"I'm sorry," Brian told him. "I am. I didn't want this, and I can promise, it was nothing personal. I really don't like violence. But my boss doesn't take no for an answer, not from anyone."

Victor's chest wasn't hot any longer. It was cold. Icy.

He fumbled for his holster.

Brian fired again.

***

The pounding of her heart echoed in Chelsea's ears. Her lashes lifted, and she found Colt staring down at her. His expression was savage. So intent. Her chest seemed to tighten as she peered up at him.

He leaned forward and brushed a soft kiss over her lips. "Worth the wait."

Yes, well, he'd certainly been, ah, worth it, too. Her sex was still doing a happy tremble around him, and aftershocks of bliss coursed through her.

"I can't believe I ever kept my hands off you in Atlanta."

He was still inside of her. And having a conversation while he was in her? *Hard*. "Uh, you didn't seem to have much trouble."

"Trust me, I did." He withdrew.

She gasped because the friction caused by his withdrawal just made those little aftershocks feel ever so much stronger.

"Be right back."

He headed for the bathroom. She did some quick breathing exercises. Fanned herself. Tried to school her features and get some nonchalant vibes going on. She'd survived a kidnapping attempt—two attempts. She'd jumped into the ocean and swum away from bad guys even though she'd been terrified sharks were lurking beneath that dark surface. Chelsea hadn't even mentioned her shark fear to Colt at the time because, what would have been the point? There hadn't been an option. She'd needed to get in the water and—

"I want you again."

Her head turned toward him. Automatically dipped down. Sure enough, the man spoke the truth. He was more than ready to go a second round.

"Correction," Colt told her as his voice roughened, "I always want you. Back in Atlanta, I wanted to put my hands on you all the time. From the first moment I saw you, I wanted you."

She cleared her throat. "I think it's pretty obvious how I felt about you."

He leaned over the bed. Caged her with his hands. "No, nothing with you has been obvious."

Not even her recent body-shaking orgasm? She'd thought it was pretty obvious—

"Because I had to pretend the whole time. I never knew how you'd feel about the real me. Not that tight-assed dick I had to pretend to be."

She almost smiled at that particular description. "I don't know if I would use those exact words."

"You couldn't see the real me. I couldn't ask for more from you—though I wanted *everything*—while I was pretending to be someone else." He sat on the edge of the bed. Kept caging her with his hands. "You liked who I pretended to be. You liked the safe guy with the glasses who left you with a kiss at the door of your place."

She started to deny his words. Then stopped. Because... "I did like him. He was always polite. Always held the door for me. Didn't push. But it really pissed me off when he was late for our dates. Or when he didn't show at all." *When he left me. When he didn't try to fight for me.* Yet...

He had. He'd come back to fight.

"I might have also thought the glasses were rather sexy," she added in a weak attempt to lighten the mood. Only...truth. She had found the glasses sexy. She missed them.

"I'm not some sweet guy, baby. I don't toe any lines. I don't follow rules. I didn't get an MBA, and I didn't attend some Ivy League school." A muscle flexed along his jaw. "Before I get balls deep in you again, I think you need to know more about the real me."

She already knew quite a bit. He'd risked his life to save her. When she'd needed help, he'd been there. His skills might be a little scary, but when she was with him, she still felt safe.

I like the safe guy...

She liked him.

"I was a SEAL. Hell, once a SEAL, always a SEAL. I don't talk about that time much because that's just not something we do. We take the missions. We get the jobs done. I loved the work.

Hell, maybe I even liked the adrenaline too much."

She was naked. He was naked. And this conversation felt way too intense to have while naked but—

"Didn't find anything to match that adrenaline rush, until I happened to look up one day, and I got lost in a pair of deep green eyes. I knew I'd met you at the wrong time. In the wrong place. But nothing was going to stop me from getting close to you."

He was very, very close right then.

She wanted him closer. She wanted him in her again. She wanted the pleasure. The link. *Him.*

"I told myself I'd hold back until you could know the real me. But then another case came up, and you walked." His jaw hardened. "At first, I thought maybe I should let you go. You'd broken up with me. Left my heart shattered beneath the sexiest red heels I'd ever seen in my life."

She jerked. And her hand automatically flew up. Her fingers pressed to his lips. "*Don't.*"

He stilled.

Don't say things you don't mean. Don't say your heart was involved it if wasn't. Don't make me hope. Don't make me go back to that place. Because her heart had been involved. Still was. "I liked him." Correction, "I like *you.*" Soft. Husky.

His lips parted. She felt the light press of his tongue against her fingertips. Desire trembled through her.

"I want you," she told him. "I don't want you holding back *anything.*" The only bright spot in the last twenty-four hours? Or, hell, had it been thirty-six? Forty-eight? She didn't know. Time was a blur. *He* wasn't. "I want you again. I want you right now." Before the CIA came pounding at the door. Before more bad guys showed up. Before Remy put her in custody or her world became even crazier.

"I will give you whatever you want. Always." So deep and dark and sexy.

She pushed against his shoulders. Got him to be the one to move back. To slide onto the mattress beside her. Then Chelsea straddled his hips. Eased down a bit. Her hands pressed to his chest as she peered at him. "I won't lie to you."

His eyes locked with hers.

"And you don't lie to me. Deal?"

"Deal." His hands closed around her hips. He lifted her up, brought her back down, and when he did, she was right over his dick. Her folds were still slick and sensitive, and the length of his cock brushed against her. Not coming inside, just sliding over her. Sending little pulses of pleasure shooting through her. She could probably come just by rocking against him. Just by having his cock slide against her clit again and again.

"First truth," Cole rumbled. "Fucking you is like sinking into paradise. Just as amazing as you said it would be at the restaurant. And all I want to do is fuck you over and over again."

She rode him faster. Rocked against him. Wanted the broad head of his cock to push into her. "Ah, it was pretty spectacular for me, too." More than spectacular. Enough to take her breath away and leave her in hazed-out bliss. Her eyes closed as she began to pant.

"Get the condom."

Her eyes flew right back open. Her sex pushed harder against him.

"Get the condom from the drawer," he gritted. "Because I need *in*."

She wanted him in. Deep and fast. She stretched over him, fumbling for the drawer, and when she moved, his lips curled around her nipple. He licked and sucked and a moan broke from her. Her hips shoved down eagerly against him, and the nightstand suddenly seemed *way* far away.

His tongue rasped over her nipple. "Condom."

"Stop distracting me!" But she loved the way he distracted her. Chelsea had never responded this way to a lover. So completely. Totally. No inhibitions. She just wanted him.

Her fingers managed to grab for the drawer. She hauled it open. Snagged a condom, and on her third attempt, she actually tore the packet open. Then it was time to roll the condom on him, but she hadn't exactly gotten to explore his cock yet. So her fingers lingered. Stroked. *Big*. He was definitely bigger and wider than her other lovers.

"Baby?"

She wanted to put her mouth on him.

"I will not last. I need you too much. Get the condom on. Get me inside."

Biting her lip, she rolled the condom on him. When it was in place, she positioned herself again, moving to press her knees into the mattress as she spread over him and put his cock right at the entrance to her body. She took him inside. One slow inch at a time. She was swollen from her release, and he had to *push* to get in. And that push felt so good that she shivered.

"Can't. Last."

She took a little more. A little more. Her legs eased down onto his thighs, and they felt taut—no, rock hard beneath her. His muscles were so powerful and tough. Everything about him was strong, and she—

Was on her back. He'd tumbled her back. Grabbed her legs and hitched them over his shoulders, and there was no restraint. She stared into his eyes and saw the wildness. The lust. No control. *Gone*. This was what she'd wanted. She'd needed to see him like this, and he was...savage. Primitive. He pounded into her over and over again, and there was no holding back. Not for him. Not for her, either. His fingers pushed between them. Caught her clit. Plucked and rubbed. Fast. His strokes into her body were faster. Faster.

She screamed. A high-pitched, quick cry because the orgasm just exploded through her.

He drove even deeper. Lifted her higher. Powerful surges of his hips against hers that held nothing back. That were frenzied and desperate and consuming. When he came, he choked out her name. His mouth pressed to her throat. He kissed her. Bit lightly.

And she knew he'd done more than just marked her skin. He'd marked *her*. Deep inside. Her whole body felt taken. Possessed.

There was no going back from this.

From him.

***

"Problem."

Remy glanced up as his new partner stomped his way toward his breakfast table. Typical for Ty, a frown already tightened the other man's features. His shirt appeared rumpled, and his hair shot out at multiple angles. His shoes also didn't match which was...well, Ty. "I see multiple problems with this picture," Remy stated as he lowered the newspaper he'd been pretending to read.

Ty dropped himself into the seat across from Remy. "Got word this morning." He looked around. Made sure no one was watching.

No one else was there. Even the waiter was back in the kitchen.

Ty whispered, "Victor Sorenz was shot to death."

Damn. "Someone is not happy that Victor didn't keep Chelsea on the island."

A quick nod. "That's what I was thinking. The major player knows that she's left, so he's hunting her. It won't be long before he tracks her here."

Remy glanced at his watch. "No worries. She won't be here long enough for him to find her."

"We need to get her moving *now*."

And someone needs to switch to decaf. "Five hours haven't passed."

A line appeared between Ty's brows. "What?"

"We will get moving on this case, but Chelsea needs some time to rest." Though, ten to one odds said Chelsea and Colt were not *just* resting in that honeymoon suite. He'd even been a helpful friend and gotten the staff to leave a little present in the nightstand drawer—along with a polite note—so that Colt could enjoy the atmosphere more. *You are welcome.*

"She can rest on the plane," Ty grumbled. "Look, I get that you know that bodyguard bozo..."

He didn't think Colt would enjoy that particular moniker.

"But I don't trust him. There were no leads on the necklace for years. Everyone thought it was long gone, then we got the tip from our boss about Chelsea. Our job is to get the necklace, and in order to do that, we need her. We need—"

He sipped his latte. Delicious. Just what he needed after getting, oh, maybe two hours' worth of sleep. But the annoying CIA operative who was on his very first field mission? Remy could do without him. *Babysitting. That's what they have me doing. Their latest method of torture for me.* How long would it take before the people in charge decided that he'd paid for his crimes?

You break a few dozen laws, and certain individuals got so pissy.

"Are you listening to me?" Ty demanded. Tyler Lawrence Crenshaw, the second. Couldn't forget the *second* part of the equation. Because Tyler Lawrence Crenshaw the *first?* He was still kicking around and pulling way too many strings at the agency. He *was* the boss Ty had referenced.

"I hear you." Another sip. "But I think you need to hear *me*." Ah, what he wouldn't give to be sitting on the French Riviera right now. A paint brush in his hand and a sunrise greeting him. "Colt Easton is not going to let us take Chelsea."

Ty sputtered. Really, sputtered. Then he managed, “He doesn’t have a say in the matter! We are the CIA!”

“Oh, yes, shout it in public. Because that’s the way to keep a low profile.”

“No one is here.” Once more, Ty peered around the area.

“Doesn’t mean the place isn’t bugged.” Remy highly doubted it, but he just wanted to see Ty sweat.

Ty immediately started sweating. But he rallied to say, “Colt Easton is a low-rent bodyguard. He can’t stop us.”

There is no us. He was on Team Colt, but this didn’t seem like the best time to mention that fact so… “You ever hear that you can catch more flies with honey?”

“I have no desire to catch flies.”

He needed to be saved from dumbasses. “You try to take her from him, and Colt will just kick your ass. Do you *want* an ass kicking first thing this morning?” It truly wasn’t the best way to start the day.

Ty lifted his slightly pointed chin. “I’d like to see him try.”

“No, you would not. He’s a former SEAL. And you’re…” *A guy who had his father use his influence to get you this job.* “You’re a nice enough man.” Ty was, surprisingly. He wasn’t a complete douche. With the right training—*oh, yeah, that’s supposed to be my job*—he might be all right. Might. “I’d hate to have to explain why you completely failed on your first big mission.”

"Chief Victor Sorenz is *dead*. That is a failure. That is—"

"He was in on everything. I told you this already. The guy was on the take, and he just looked the other way when Chelsea was abducted. If it weren't for Colt's timely arrival, the mission would have been fucked sideways because the bad guys would have spirited Chelsea away before we ever had the chance to make contact with her. So, while the chief's death is regrettable, we have to stay focused."

"That's...cold."

Yes, it was. He was. He'd had to be in order to survive. "Chelsea is the key, but she has a very fierce guard dog at her side. We try to take her and that dog will rip out our throats without a single hesitation." He'd accessed Colt's classified records. Seen some stuff to make him nervous. And to make him respect Colt even more. "We let her keep the guard dog close...and maybe they will lead us to the treasure we seek."

Ty blinked. "You think she knows where it is?"

"I think Colt won't allow danger to continue stalking her. As long as the necklace is out there, he'll believe she is at risk." The waiter marched out of the kitchen. Remy waved him over and lowered his voice to tell Ty, "Colt will decide that eliminating the risk is his best plan. We'll help with that plan. And we'll get what we both want."

The waiter paused by their table. "What can I get you?"

"Actually, I need to have an order sent up to a friend." He smiled. "He's here on his honeymoon, and I think he and his blushing bride would love some strawberries and champagne for breakfast." He tapped his chin. "You know what? Bet they'll have a killer appetite. Let's send up some French toast, eggs, and whatever amazing pastries you have." He rattled off a few more items, gave instructions for the delivery—for the tray to be left *outside* the suite—and when the waiter disappeared again, Remy looked over to find Ty frowning at him.

"Is this the honey?" Ty asked, seeming genuinely curious. "You're being all nice to get Colt to help us?"

"I'm being all nice because I prefer to have dangerous, scary individuals on my side instead of working against me." He motioned toward Ty. "Consider that my first life lesson to you. Maybe you should write it down somewhere. Got a notebook on you?"

Ty glared at him. "I've had some training. I'm not some amateur—"

"Yes, you are. Because professionals don't get their Jeeps stolen on day one of the mission." Remy crossed his arms over his chest. "Lesson one. The scarier the individual, the more you need that person on your team." He paused. "Colt Easton may present himself in many different forms." Remy knew that Colt could and had. Since Remy enjoyed being more than a bit of a chameleon himself, it was a talent he appreciated. "But at his core, he's a predator. An enemy that you do not want."

Ty tugged at his collar.

"You try taking Chelsea from him, you try making that woman do anything she doesn't like, and that predator will come for your throat."

Ty's eyes had gone wide.

Remy smiled. "So, what do you want for breakfast?"

CHAPTER ELEVEN

A knock tapped on the door. “Breakfast!” A cheery announcement.

Colt glanced toward the door. He’d just been walking into the sitting area, intent on grabbing his phone and seeing if it had survived the dip into the ocean, when he’d heard the knock.

“I’m starving,” Chelsea said from behind him.

He looked back at her. Fresh clothes had been stocked in the bedroom. Remy, striking again. The man seemed to plan for everything. She wore a pair of white capris, a silky blue, sleeveless top, and dainty sandals on her feet. *Gorgeous*. Good enough to eat—

Oh, yeah, I did. And I want to again and again—

Another tap on the door. “Leaving the tray outside. The champagne is chilled. Have a wonderful morning!”

Chelsea’s stomach chose that moment to give the cutest, lowest damn growl.

Her eyes widened in something like horror as she put her hand to her stomach. Then she laughed. Her nervous laugh that made him want to cross to her. Haul her into his arms. And never fucking let go.

"So, yes, I'm pretty much starving." She hurried toward the door, moving to pass him. "I can't remember the last time I ate."

He snagged her wrist. "Let me make sure it's safe. Because, baby, I didn't order anything." His finger slid along her pulse point. Felt the jump. He liked that he could make her pulse race. She sure made his thunder.

Colt let her go and moved to look through the peephole. He opened the door a few cautious inches. A man in the white coat and pants waited near the elevator. "I didn't order anything," Colt called to him.

The guy spun. Looked to be about eighteen. He flashed a nervous grin. "Ah. Sorry. It's courtesy of your friend..." He looked down at the small pad in his hand. "Remy. Said to knock and *loudly* call out that the food was there." His cheeks flushed. "He thought you might be busy."

Remy strikes again.

"And congrats on your marriage!" he added quickly. The elevator doors opened with a ding. A fast wave from the guy. "Enjoy your day!"

He waited until the fellow had disappeared, then Colt wheeled the cart into the suite.

"We are going to owe Remy so much," Chelsea announced as she hurried toward the rolling cart. "Talk about being a hero."

Colt stopped searching the cart—searching it was second nature to him—and he looked up at her. "Did you just call Remy a hero?" Had she missed the part where he told her the jerk was an art thief?

She'd scooped up a strawberry. Held it right before her lips. Stopped before taking a bite. "Is this...wait, you're searching the tray." Alarm flashed on her face. "Do you think it's not from Remy? Is it poison?" Her gaze darted longingly to the strawberry. "Please don't be poison," she murmured to it.

The phone on the hotel's desk rang. "Don't eat yet." But he had a feeling he knew exactly who was calling. Colt sauntered to the phone. Not his phone—the hotel's. He snatched it up on the second ring. "Yes?"

"Who is your best friend?" Remy wanted to know. Colt instantly recognized his voice.

He also instantly replied, "Pierce. Pierce Jennings. I believe you know him. He's the man your sister—"

"You could at least pretend that it was me. What would it hurt?" A sigh. "I sent the food. Figured your suspicious ass wouldn't let your lovely lady eat without verifying it came from me. I've noticed you tend to be a bit overprotective where she's concerned."

Overprotective. Sure, fine. That was one way to describe him.

"Thought you might both be hungry. Also thought you were probably distracted by—oh, who knows what—and you had forgotten to order food. So I helped you out." A pause. "You have twenty minutes—because my partner is ever so impatient—and then I'm afraid we'll be up there for our meeting. You *do* remember the meeting, yes?"

Like he could forget.

"I'll bring new cell phones for you both. Safe ones. Even if your old devices work after your swim, we don't want anyone tracking you."

"You just think of everything, don't you?"

"I do try." Modest.

Colt grunted. "Goodbye, Remy."

"Wait!"

Had that been real alarm? Maybe. He kept the phone at his ear.

"I'm helping you. Giving you the things you want. Remember that. And give me what I want."

Click.

"Colt?" Chelsea took a halting step toward him. She still carefully held her precious strawberry. "Everything okay?"

"The food is safe. It came from Remy. And he'll be here in twenty minutes so we'd better eat as fast as we can." A pause. He looked at the phone. "The sonofabitch hung up on me."

"Did you tell him thank you for the food?"

"Didn't get a chance." *Because I'm pretty sure he threatened me right before he hung up.* A friendly threat, but a threat nonetheless.

Twenty minutes. Not a lot of time to come up with a life-changing plan to catch the bad guys after Chelsea, but he'd always been fast on his feet.

First, though...

Time for some truths.

He helped Chelsea arrange the food at the intimate table for two that waited in the suite. She didn't want the champagne but instead opted for the orange juice, and since he damn well didn't plan on confronting Remy and his CIA buddy while he was drunk, Colt skipped it, too. He did tackle the pastries because they were fucking perfection, and he had never been one to resist a chocolate chip croissant. Oh, hell, no.

At first, he and Chelsea were just busy eating. The fast, desperate eating that happened when you were starving. He couldn't even take the time to admire the beauty of her lush lips closing around the strawberry. Okay, lie, he did admire the scene. He admired everything about her and—

"Why are you looking at me like that?" Her head tilted.

"Like what?" In that instant, he had no idea what he might have revealed to her and that development could certainly prove problematic.

"Like you're surprised." She smiled. "It's me. What about me could possibly surprise you now? You literally know me inside and out."

Oh, baby, I will be getting inside again soon. ASAP. First available opportunity. The two times he'd had her—they'd only whet his appetite. If he'd had his way, he'd still be in her. He'd *stay* in her until they couldn't move.

"You know me." Her lashes flickered. "But there is still so much about you I don't know."

She still had her share of mysteries, too. Those mysteries were the reason she was being hunted. The sooner he learned the full truth, the sooner she'd be safe. As far as his mysteries were concerned... "Let's play a game."

Her delicate brows lifted. "Now?"

Better now than never. "Truth or dare."

"You...you said the CIA guys were coming."

"Yeah, they are." *Fuck them.* "The game won't take long. You want to know my secrets, don't you?"

A nod.

"And I want to know yours."

"But you already do."

No, we're just getting started.

A quick laugh from her. The nervous tremble that sounded a bit breathless. "I haven't played truth or dare since I was thirteen years old," Chelsea admitted.

"Then I'll go easy on you," he said lightly as he snagged another croissant. "Promise."

She took a long swallow of her orange juice.

"In fact, why don't you ask first?"

Interest lit her eyes, replacing the flare of nerves. "You'll answer anything I ask?"

Okay, this could be more dangerous than he'd initially realized. But...*too late*. "Absolutely."

A nod. "Truth or dare?" She snagged another strawberry.

He dragged his gaze from her mouth. Focused on her eyes. "Truth." Because he knew this was what she wanted.

Oh, but the things he could do with her and a dare...

"Why did you stop being a SEAL?"

She went right to the good stuff. "My dad was in the Navy. Served for thirty years before retiring. I'm the youngest of seven sons, and I—"

Chelsea almost dropped the cinnamon roll she'd just picked up. "Did you say 'seven sons' just then? As in...you have six brothers running around out there?"

"Indeed, I do. And they're all in the military. Except for Carter. He has a ranch outside of Dallas where he trains racehorses."

"There are seven of you." She seemed a bit horrified.

"They are going to love you," he assured her. How could they not?

"Seven?"

"Um." The number seemed to bother her. "Probably seems overwhelming, since you were an only child. Just you and your mom, right?"

"Right." She took a small bite of the cinnamon roll. "Seven?"

"Think of it this way..." He winked at her. "I'm lucky number seven. At least, that's what my mom always calls me. Mom and Dad are both still alive. They retired and got a place not too far from Carter. He's the one who settled down. The rest of us scattered, so it was easier for them to pick a home base near him."

Her lashes flickered. "My dad died before I was born."

Tread carefully. "Your mom told you that?"

"Yes. He was a pilot, and he died in a crash while she was pregnant with me."

Colt filed away that info. "I'm sorry, baby." Growing up, he'd always had his loud, boisterous family. They'd moved more times than he could count, going from base to base to base. But the moves hadn't mattered. They'd always been together. He'd always had someone close.

But Chelsea's only family had been her mother, and with her mother's death...

You aren't alone. He didn't want her thinking that. If he had his way, she'd never be alone again. She could have six brothers-in-law to watch out for her, too.

Too fast. She's not ready for that.

"You didn't—we got distracted." Chelsea cleared her throat. "Why did you stop being a SEAL? And you have to tell me the truth."

"I don't plan to tell you any lies." Even if the truth hurt. "I loved the work. I wanted to be a SEAL as long as I could remember. The training was brutal, don't get me wrong, but I knew what I was getting into from the beginning."

She ate and watched him and he remembered. "I met Eric Wilde years ago. A good man. Someone you can count on. Guy's got more money than God, and he should probably be a prick but...I like him. I had friends who liked him, too. Friends that he helped when their own team turned against them." A bloody, violent, devastating betrayal. "Eric saved the lives of people I knew. People I cared about. And when I realized that I wanted more...hell, the longer you're in with the SEALs, the more likely you are to wind up at a desk. They promote you and you train the others and you don't get to see your family and there is always another mission and I..." He stared into her eyes. "I wanted more. The time came when I just wanted more. Eric told me that I could have a job with him, so I took what he offered. Made new friends." *Met you.* "Sometimes, what you want in life changes. So you have to change, too."

"And do you like working at Wilde?"

"That's another question." He gave her a smile. "It's my turn now."

Faint red peeked in her cheeks. "Right. You don't even have to ask—I want truth."

"Do I have any fucking chance with you?"

The red deepened. "I—" She stumbled to a stop. Not a good sign.

"I want a chance. If you get to know the real me and you think I'm an asshole and you walk away, fine. But maybe you won't think that." He angled closer to her. "Maybe you'll think something totally different."

"Like what?"

"You tell me." *Truth or dare, baby.*

Her lashes lowered, shielding her eyes. "You have a chance with a me."

Fuck, yes.

"You saved my life. Giving you a second chance seems like the least I can do."

Screw that. "No." He reached over. Carefully, his fingers curled under her chin. He tipped back her head so he could stare—get lost—in her eyes. "I'm not looking for gratitude. Not looking for some adrenaline-fueled fuck, either." He hoped like hell that hadn't been what she felt when they were together in that bed.

"Can't say that I've actually had a lot of adrenaline-fueled fucks," she whispered.

"They're good. Sure they'd be phenomenal with you." He didn't look away. "I want more. But not because you're *grateful*. Because you want to see what the hell will happen next with us." And, dammit, he realized he was holding his breath.

He had it so bad where she was concerned. She—

"I'm down for adrenaline-fueled fucks with you. I'm also down to see what will happen next." A soft exhale from her. "Truth. Full truth—when I walked out of that restaurant in Atlanta, I wanted you to follow me. I wanted you to say that I mattered more than your case." She hesitated. "What was that case?"

The case. Hell. He couldn't tell her everything, but there was some truth he could offer. "A ten-year-old girl had been kidnapped."

Her eyes widened. "OhmyGod."

"Her father is a man of power and influence, a man with a whole lot of enemies. She was taken as a way of controlling him. He wanted her back. He didn't trust the Feds to do the job, so he called his friend Eric."

"And Eric called you." Tears swam in her eyes. "A kid. I'm so sorry. I had no idea. She needed you, and I was throwing a fit in a restaurant and—"

"No." He cut her off. His fingers caressed her silken skin. "You didn't know. I was lying to you, and *I* am sorry. The case was confidential." Still was and that was why he couldn't tell any names. "I had to go. But I did not want to leave you."

"She's okay?"

"Safe and sound."

"And...the people who took her?"

"Not so safe and sound." He let her go. "Truth or dare."

"I didn't expect this game to be so intense."

It's not a game. "You asked a question." About his case. "So I get to go again."

"Truth," she chose before he could say anything else.

He took a breath and asked the question that haunted him. "What will it take for you to trust me again?"

CHAPTER TWELVE

Chelsea could not look away from the darkness of his eyes.

"Because I'm gonna need you to trust me. Completely. This mess with you isn't over. We're safe for the moment, but we both know those CIA guys are gonna be at the door soon. They want the necklace."

"I don't have it!"

"I know. But I need you to trust me. Trust me to help you get out of this nightmare. Trust me even if things look bad. Even if you think you shouldn't...baby, I need you to trust me with your whole heart."

"Blind trust."

"That's what you gave me before. Didn't realize how much I'd miss it until it was gone."

She put her hands in her lap. They twisted. Fisted. "Do you trust me?"

"Ah...not your turn." Soft. Chiding. "But, I'll give you a free one." He smiled at her. "I would trust you with my life. You could be pointing a gun straight at me, and I wouldn't hesitate."

"What? Colt, in that situation, you should very much hesitate." Any sane person would. "Though, first, why would I be aiming a gun at you?"

"Why indeed?" A shrug. "I'd still trust you. I'd know that I could count on you. You wouldn't hurt me. You aren't the type to hurt anyone."

He was wrong. She'd discovered some rather disturbing truths about herself since coming on her tropical vacation. The first truth? "When I saw that gun pointing at you in the hotel parking garage, I was absolutely terrified."

The faint lines near his eyes tightened. "And yet you ran to put yourself between me and the shooter."

"Because I didn't want you hurt." What she'd realized in that moment that had shocked her? "If I'd had a weapon, if I'd been closer to him, I would have attacked him. I would have done whatever was necessary to keep you safe." Until her trip, she'd never so much as been in a fight. Never been around violence at all except...

Except for that night. But we don't talk about that night. It's a bad dream. Let it go away. See the sunrise. Everything is better when the sun rises. The day is safe and good and...

Her mother's image flashed before Chelsea's eyes.

"Sweetheart?"

She blinked.

"What just made your eyes go dark with pain?"

"It's not your turn," she said. Or maybe it was. She had no idea.

His jaw set. "I can't make it better if I don't know what's hurting you."

"A bad dream. Bad memory. It doesn't matter."

"I think it does. Tell me."

"I don't like small spaces," Chelsea blurted. Oh, damn.

"Can't say I particularly prefer them, either."

No, he didn't understand. "I once had to hide in a closet for a very, very long time."

He got out of his chair. Moved closer to her. "Baby?"

"All night long. I couldn't make a sound. She said not to make a *sound*. And it was so dark in there. And I could hear fireworks and screams. And I thought I'd be trapped in there forever." The food felt too heavy. Her stomach seemed to have knotted. "I cried all night, but I didn't make a sound. When the door opened, she took my hand and we went outside and the sun was coming up." The memory was so strong it hurt. "'The day is fresh at sunrise,'" Chelsea quoted. "She told me, 'Anything can happen. The bad things are gone. The light is coming out.'"

Silence.

Why had she just told him all that? She'd never told anyone else. It had just been her secret. Her and her mother's.

"Sometimes, I would think it was just a bad dream." And why was she still talking? "But...it wasn't?" A question, when she'd meant it to be a statement.

He pressed a kiss to her forehead. "No, I don't think it was."

"I told you...because I do trust you. You'll help me."

A nod.

"You'll keep me safe?"

"Always."

Her shoulders sagged a bit. "I'm scared."

He bent before her. Because he was so big, when he was on his knees, he was still eye-level with her. "They'll have to go through me to get you, and it's not fucking easy to get through me. And I'm gonna call in all my Wilde friends. We will be a wall between you and any threat."

"I don't want you hurt." Never that.

"I'll do the hurting."

Her lips parted.

A rap sounded at the door. Fast. Hard. Not the light, almost happy knock that had come from the delivery guy. Automatically, her stare whipped toward the door.

"Your mother didn't exist until she had you."

Just that fast, her gaze snapped back to him.

"Truth," he told her flatly. "A truth that my friend Pierce discovered when I asked him to dig because I was afraid of what was happening to you. I need more intel so that I can stop the bastards after you. He dug hard and deep and your mother—the day you were born, that was the day that Marilyn Ember first came into existence."

She shook her head because he had to be wrong. There had to be some mistake.

"In order for that to happen, she must have made a deal with someone. She could have been in witness protection, she could have been working with Feds, or hell, maybe it had something to do with the CIA and that's why they are breathing down your neck now. This necklace—my instincts say it's tied to your mother's hidden past."

"A past that has decided to come back for me?" *Now?* What had caused this sudden hunt?

The pounding came again. Harder than before.

"Yes." He didn't look away. "It's going to get worse before it gets better." A warning.

Worse? Worse than a kidnapping? Worse than a desperate swim in the ocean when she thought she might die at any moment?

"Teachers usually have to pass FBI background checks to get their jobs." He watched her so carefully. "In order to get her position, someone powerful helped her. This wasn't some two-bit cover."

Her breath shuddered out.

"Trust me?" He offered his hand to her.

She stared at his palm. The lines. The strength. And she put her hand in his. "Yes." They could do this. They *would* do it.

He rose. So did she. He kept her hand in his. Looked down at her fingers. His hand was so much bigger than hers. His hand practically swallowed hers. Faint calluses lined his fingertips. He brought her hand to his lips. Kissed her knuckles. "Think you can handle one more truth?"

"I'm not sure it's my turn." Were they even keeping track any longer?

"I will never choose anyone over you. I don't care how things look, you're it. That's why I came to the island. That's why I came after you. You don't give up something that's so important without a fight." Another soft kiss. "I will always fight for you." He let her go. Stalked to the door. He stopped and looked through the peephole. "Just your friendly CIA operatives coming by for a visit..." He glanced over at her. "You ready for them?"

Nope, but she nodded.

He swung open the door, and a moment later, Remy strolled in. He flashed her a wide smile. "Did you love breakfast? Weren't those the best croissants you've ever had? I swear, they're even better than the ones I usually have at this tiny little café near the Eiffel Tower."

Another man followed him in. His shoulders were hunched, his frame thinner. While Remy was dressed elegantly, his clothes seemingly tailored for him, the newcomer looked as if he'd borrowed over-sized clothes. And his shoes were mismatched.

"I know." Remy sighed. "I told him you have to look the part, but it's a work in progress."

The other agent flushed. He shoved back his slightly too-long, brown hair. "There was a baggage mix-up."

"There is a store in the hotel." Remy settled on the couch. "Would have taken all of five minutes to fix things." He motioned toward Colt and Chelsea. "Seriously, I got them a whole new wardrobe just like that." He snapped his fingers.

"You got it because you flirted with the salesclerk on the phone. And she had their sizes in stock. Not mine." He strode for Chelsea. Stuck out his hand. "Agent Ty Crenshaw."

She took his hand. Discovered that he had the same faint line of calluses that Colt possessed.

"Chelsea." But, of course, he already knew that. She let him go and motioned toward Colt. "And that's—"

"We've met." Ty's voice became clipped. "You *will* be paying for the damage to the Jeep."

What?

Colt had already shut and locked the door. "Don't we have more important matters to discuss? Matters other than a little bullet hole in a shitty ride?"

Ty huffed. "Yes, we do. We have—"

"You're not gonna like this part," Remy declared from his seat.

"—the matter of murder," Ty finished.

"Here we go." Remy shook his head. "I warned you to build up to this gracefully, but did you listen to my advice? No. The whole reason we are together is so you can benefit from my *years* of expertise. Perhaps even get a little of my amazing social polish so that you can learn to *blend* better."

Ty's mouth tightened.

"What murder?" Colt's voice cut through the room like a knife. Instantly, he'd put himself at Chelsea's side once more.

"I regret to inform you," Ty said, voice stiff, "that Chief Victor Sorenz was murdered shortly after you left the island. He was shot twice, once in the chest and once in the head."

Chelsea jerked back. Her knees did a quick dip, and she quite possibly would have slammed onto her ass if Colt hadn't caught her arm and supported her.

"Got you," he murmured. "Always."

Her breath panted out, and all she could think about—it wasn't Victor, though she *hated* that anyone had been killed. She remembered the parking garage. The gun pointing at Colt from behind the cement column.

What if the shooter had fired? What if Colt had been the one to die?

"You can see why you need police protection." Ty's shoulders straightened. "We will make sure—"

"So, the chief of police just died," Colt interrupted to say. "That doesn't exactly scream safety to me."

A sigh escaped Remy. He kept his position on the couch. "This is why you should have let me do most of the talking, Ty. We went over this." He waved one hand vaguely in the air as he fired a grimace toward Colt and Chelsea. "He's overzealous, but we're working on that tendency."

Her heartbeat seemed to echo in her ears. Faster. Harder. "Do you know who killed the chief?"

"Actually, yes." Remy seemed pleased to share this news. "Turns out that Victor had a very tiny security camera installed near his station's entrance. Good for him. Good for us because we saw that a tall, blond male—probably in his late twenties, maybe early thirties—strolled right in and was the only person to go in that office during our kill time."

She flinched.

"Sorry. But, hey, I could tell by your expression that the blond might be familiar, yes?" He waited, all expectant-like.

"Yes." A hiss of breath. "The first day—the man who took me. H-he said his name was Brian. He was blond. About an inch or two shorter than Colt. Similar builds."

"Give us more." Remy's expression hardened. "The video was too grainy for good details. I need eyes, nose, jaw, tattoos, any distinguishing features..."

His image flashed in her mind. "Blue eyes. Hawkish nose. Hard jaw. Not as square as Colt's. And, ah, no tattoos. None that I saw, anyway. I don't remember much else about him—"

"Six-foot-one, approximately one hundred and eighty pounds. Mole to the right of his upper lip. A small scar slid through his left eyebrow." Colt seemed to be ticking off details at a rapid rate. "Spoke with a faint midwestern accent. I figure he was right at thirty. No tats. But he should be sporting one hell of a bruise on his jaw."

"You saw him, too," Ty noted.

Remy rolled his eyes. "Of course, Colt saw him. Who do you think gave the dick the bruise? The blond hit Chelsea—can't you see the darkness near her jaw? So Colt decked him back. Though, honestly..." His eyebrows sunk low. "I'm surprised you didn't do more than just hit him."

Colt rolled one powerful shoulder in a shrug. "I shot his partner."

Both Remy and Ty straightened at that bit of news.

"Sorry." Colt didn't sound the least bit apologetic. "Things moved fast, so I didn't get to share that with you earlier. There were two men who originally took Chelsea. One was working as a bartender at her hotel. The other was scoping out the beach for her—that one was the blond, Brian. They took her to an abandoned garage. I followed. When I rushed in, I drove my fist into the jaw of the bastard who'd hit her, and then the other prick..." His voice roughened with the memory. "He put a knife to her throat. So it seemed only fair that I put a bullet in him."

Ty's eyes had gone very, very wide. "Fair?"

"Ahem." Remy cleared his throat.

Ty whipped his head toward him.

"You see what I mean now? This is what I was talking about. Obviously, Colt gets pissy and protective where Chelsea is concerned. And in response, we tread lightly around him. We don't just try dragging her away."

Colt surged in front of Chelsea, shielding her with his body. "I'd like to see you fucking *try*."

She put her hands on his back. Peeked around his shoulder. "I'm not going anywhere without Colt."

"Damn straight." His back was hard with tension beneath her touch.

"That's what I told my partner," Remy returned without missing a beat. "Said it would be utterly pointless to try separating you. That Colt would just pull some super-fierce special forces moves on us and someone would wind up hurt. That someone would most likely be Ty."

None of the tension had left Colt yet. "I go where she goes," he growled.

"Again, I told him that would be your response." Remy rose from the couch. Stalked toward the leftover breakfast. "But it would certainly help matters along if we had a lead to follow. Know what I mean? A direction to take. It would make Ty feel better and stop all of this silly talk about dragging Chelsea away from you."

"You sonofabitch," Colt breathed.

"Do you kiss your mother with that mouth?" Remy didn't wait for a response, but picked up a croissant. Nibbled. "So good." He motioned with the croissant and angled it toward Chelsea. "You kiss her with that mouth?"

"Don't worry about what I do with her." A flat retort from Colt.

"But I do worry. Because I'm a helper. Didn't you notice that already? Without me and my help, you'd still be trapped on that island. Without me—well, without me and my intervention, the CIA might just think that Chelsea would be better off in custody. Or they might think that she is some sort of international jewel thief who should be interrogated."

He was threatening her. She got that. She just didn't understand. Was Remy the bad guy? On their side? A manipulative ass?

"We just need a lead." Remy wiped away the crumbs from his fingertips. "Something that can help us to figure out who put this line of dominos into motion. Truly, the pearl necklace had fallen from memory for most people, then suddenly, the hunt is on again. A hunt focused on Chelsea."

If she knew anything, she would have told him by now.

"If someone could just point us in the right direction so we're not simply sitting here and waiting for that Brian bastard to close in and start taking shots at all of us..." Another despondent sigh. "If only."

"Bastard." But Colt seemed almost admiring. "You know I have a lead, don't you?"

Her surprise had to flash on her face. Chelsea hurriedly snapped her open mouth closed so she didn't say...*You do, since when?*

Ty took two, hurried steps forward, then seemed to catch himself.

Remy smiled a rather Cheshire-cat type of grin. "Why did I think that might be the case? Oh, right. Because you work for Wilde, and I've started to think that organization has better resources than even the CIA." He flickered a glance toward Ty. "No offense to you and your esteemed family."

"Tell us about the lead." Ty's hands fisted and clenched. "People are dying. We need to get moving."

She wanted to know about the lead. Why hadn't Colt mentioned it to her before? Granted, they'd been a bit busy swimming for their lives and then having hot, frantic sex but...

Maybe over breakfast? Would it have killed him to mention a lead to her then?

"We want a private flight that will take us back to Atlanta." Colt's demand came out as cool-as-could-be. "One that is arranged by Wilde because I want a pilot on the flight that I can trust. I can make a phone call to Pierce, and the plane will be ready within the hour."

"Within the hour?" Ty repeated. "You think Wilde is that good?"

"They are," Remy assured him. He also nodded. "Fine. Wilde gets the flight. But Ty and I are on board with you. *And* you tell us everything you know about the lead you have."

"I tell you *after* the plane is in the air. And when we're stateside, then I will go in to interrogate him." Colt was adamant. "This shit is personal, so I'm handling it. Not something that is up for debate."

Remy seemed to weigh him. Then he reached into his back pocket and tossed a phone toward Colt. "Fine." His shoulders straightened. "Give my regards to Pierce, and I will see you—within the hour—for that promised flight." Remy inclined his head toward Chelsea before he gave her a phone, too. "Already been setup with the password and contacts you had on your old phone. You're welcome."

How had he known her password? *CIA.* She hurriedly put the phone on a nearby table.

Remy sauntered for the door. He grabbed Ty's shoulder. "We're leaving."

"But they didn't tell us anything—"

"We're going to see what we can dig up on that Brian bastard, and then we're telling our boss we are going to Atlanta for a lead." He paused near the door. Looked back at Colt. "You know the danger is just going to follow us to Atlanta?"

"That's my home turf. I have the advantage there."

Colt seemed so confident. Ty looked as if he wanted to argue, but Remy shoved him out the door. A moment later, Colt flipped the locks, and he glanced down at the phone in his hand. "They're probably monitoring the calls."

"Excuse me?" She felt rooted to the spot.

"They're going to listen to my conversation with Pierce. The CIA loves to do shit like that. Always getting into other people's business." He put the phone to his ear. Waited.

She still didn't move. "Uh, Colt...?"

"Pierce," he said. And nodded. He'd already gotten his friend on the line?

Then Colt mouthed to her, *One second.*

Seriously?

"Remy got us off the island." He spoke quickly into the phone. "He and his CIA buddy have housed us in a high-end hotel." He rattled off the location. "I need a secure flight off this island, and I need it yesterday. Four passengers. Me, Chelsea, and the two agents." He listened to something Pierce said, and his eyes narrowed. Then his gaze swept over her, and he asked, "Baby, was your ID in that bag we brought with us?"

The soaking wet bag? Yes. "My passport was in there."

His left hand shoved back a lock of hair that had fallen over his forehead. "Make sure IDs won't be an issue, just in case," he told Pierce. "And return to yesterday, when I met Chelsea. Lock it down."

What? What on earth was he talking about? But suspicion began to churn inside of her.

"Thanks, man. Knew I could count on you. And, yes, yes, your good friend Remy gave me the phone." A pause. "Right. He sends his regards. Uh, huh. Sure. I can tell him that. No problem."

He hung up. Focused on her. "The plane will be ready soon. We're going the hell home."

She sucked in a breath. Let it out. Sucked it in again. Nope. Not helping. She was not calming down. The police chief had been murdered. The CIA operatives were probably right outside and... "What lead?" she rasped.

He closed the distance between them. Leaned toward her. Brushed his lips over her cheek.

She shivered. "You just talked in code to your partner, didn't you?" Whispered.

"Yes." His breath blew lightly over the shell of her ear.

Another shiver swept over her. "Don't leave me in the dark. Tell me."

"You aren't going to like it." Soft. Right at her ear.

What about this mess had she liked? Other than about ten blissful moments that she'd had on the beach before everything had detonated on her? And she'd liked the incredible sex with Colt. More than *liked* it.

But Chelsea thought about what she'd heard him tell Pierce. *Return to yesterday, when I met Chelsea.* She realized he must have meant back to the case that Colt had been working when he first met her, but that had been—

"Mr. Theo?" she gasped.

His mouth remained at her ear, and, voice barely a breath, he said, "It's no damn coincidence that the man was once a master jewel thief, and now you're being hunted by people who think you have a million-dollar necklace."

But...

But Theodore Beasley was so nice. And he was in his eighties. And he was—

Lock it down. Those had been Colt's other words to Pierce. She realized he'd ordered guards to be put on Theodore until she and Colt could get back to Atlanta.

"He's our starting point," Colt explained. "And we will be *ending* this threat. You'll be safe. You won't be hunted. I swear it."

***

Thirty minutes later, the CIA operatives were at the door again. Chelsea and Colt left the honeymoon suite without a backward glance. All Chelsea wanted to do was get home. Colt's arm curled around her shoulders as they made their way through the hotel.

His lips brushed against her temple.

They probably looked like a honeymooning couple. He held her so tightly against him, as if he couldn't let her go.

Remy talked inanely. Laughed easily. Seemed to not have a care in the world.

Ty carried the bags.

Soon they were in front of a black SUV that waited right next to the valet stand.

"Obvious," Colt groused. But he opened the back door for Chelsea. Gave her a reassuring nod. "Almost over."

Was it?

She scooted inside.

Remy slapped him on the shoulder. "Guessing that phone call went well." A whistle.

"Pierce is certainly a man of action, isn't he? Good to know."

Colt turned his head. Met Remy's eyes. "I gave him your message."

"Oh?" Remy's eyebrows climbed. "And what did he say?"

"If you fucking screw me over, you're a dead man. And even your sister won't be able to stop him."

Remy swallowed. "Pierce. Such a...pleasant fellow."

Chelsea fumbled with her seatbelt as she watched them.

"Of course, you don't have to worry about Pierce," Colt sounded as easy and carefree as Remy had been moments before.

An act. A lie.

Colt was very, very good at pretending.

Probably even better than Remy.

"You don't have to worry," Colt repeated as he slid into the vehicle and sat next to Chelsea, but kept his gaze on Remy. "Because if you do anything to hurt her in any way..." He caught Chelsea's hand in his. Twined his fingers with her. "I'll kill you long before Pierce ever has the chance to get close."

CHAPTER THIRTEEN

They'd reached cruising altitude. Next stop, Atlanta. Home sweet home.

Colt gazed out the window. Calculated. Planned. His first order of business would be an interrogation with Theodore Beasley. No fucking way was it a coincidence that a master jewel thief had been involved in the case that brought Colt into Chelsea's life—and now someone thought she possessed a million-dollar necklace.

"I don't think you're supposed to threaten CIA personnel."

It was the first time Chelsea had spoken since they'd left the hotel. His head turned toward her. She sat across from him with her spine ramrod straight. Beautiful. Delicate. So fucking perfect that he wanted to haul her into his arms and never let go—

"Do you often threaten to kill people?" she asked carefully.

"Truth?"

Her lashes flickered. "Hardly the time for a dare, is it?"

"It depends on the dare. Personally, I'd be up for joining the mile high club with you."

Her cheeks immediately flushed crimson. "We are not alone."

Nope. They weren't. Ty was in the cockpit with the pilot—a female agent from Wilde that Colt knew and trusted—and Remy was heading their way right that very moment.

"Pity," Colt said. It was. "Next time." His fingers tapped against the armrest as he considered her question. "And probably more often than you'd like."

"Excuse me?"

"The threats. They come more often than you'd like, but I promise, usually the people deserve the threats. Not like they are some sweet folks baking brownies and trying to make the world a better place. The people I face are more like the type who want to burn the world down around their enemies, and they don't care who they hurt in the process."

Remy lowered himself into the seat next to Chelsea.

"Speak of the devil," Colt drawled.

"You're wrong about me." Mild. "I don't want to burn down the world. What would be the point in that? Too much beauty would be destroyed." Remy's head tilted in consideration. "Though I do confess to liking to watch the flames dance every now and then." He looked at Chelsea. Colt didn't like the hooded gaze that Remy sent her. "What about you? Do you ever want to just watch the fire and see what it can do?"

She shook her head. "No. I'm not the type who likes to get burned."

"And not the type to be pouring the gasoline, either?"

"No."

"Excellent to know." He settled more comfortably in the seat. "And your mother? What type was she?"

"*Don't,*" Colt snapped.

"Look, I get that you have a soft spot for Chelsea. She's a beautiful woman and quite charming." He patted her hand. "You are," he assured Chelsea.

Colt looked at their hands, then back at Remy. "Do you think I am fucking around with you?"

"I think you believe that you can leave me out of the action, and that is just not something I can allow. You have your end game. I have mine. You don't get to hold back on me. Not after I've already done so much for you." His hand lifted away from Chelsea. "I know her mother didn't exist until Chelsea was born. I'm digging now, and it's only a matter of time until I find out who she really was." A shrug. "It would speed things along if Chelsea just told me—"

"I can't tell you what I don't know." Anger hummed in her voice. "My mother was Marilyn Ember. She taught the third grade at Cranerock Elementary School. She baked cupcakes for the kids in her class, and at Halloween, she gave out special candy apples that she spent hours making to the children in the neighborhood. Everyone who met her—they loved her. She didn't want to burn down *anything*."

"Then maybe it was your father." Remy's voice hardened. "Not the first time that the old man is the one who likes the fire. I certainly know about that shit."

Colt knew Remy's father was in a class by himself. A very dangerous one.

"My father died before I was born," Chelsea said. "He was killed in a plane crash."

"I'm sorry." Remy barely waited a beat before following up with, "And his name was?"

"Joseph. Joseph Ember."

Remy's gaze met Colt's. He could clearly read the message in the other man's stare. Remy didn't believe for a moment that the name was real. Probably because of his own twisted past, Remy was all too ready to believe the father was the culprit. The one who'd stolen the necklace. Who'd brought such trouble chasing after Chelsea.

"We'll start a search on him," was all Remy said to Chelsea, though. He rubbed the bridge of his nose. "And now it's your turn, Colt. What's my lead? Or, rather, who is it?"

"Theodore Beasley. Retired jewel thief. And former client of Chelsea's."

"He wanted me to update his study," she murmured. "Gave me a fifty-thousand-dollar budget. Told me to wow him." A shake of her head. "He just seemed so nice."

"We always do." Remy rose. "Remember that. It's the nice ones you should worry about the most." With that, he strode toward the cockpit once more.

"I get to question him. That was the deal," Colt reminded him. A reminder that Remy shouldn't need.

Remy tossed him a smile. "I remember."

But do you care about the deal?

Remy turned away.

“This must be a really expensive plane,” Chelsea said.

Colt’s gaze was on Remy’s back. He knew the guy would try to discover as much as he could about Theodore Beasley. “It’s one of Eric’s private planes. And yeah, it’s probably stupid expensive.” He looked back at her.

Colt found her watching him with a careful, searching gaze. “What is it?” he asked.

“I thought you seemed incredibly nice when we first met.”

Fuck. Remy could be such a dick. “Nice doesn’t get the job done. A *nice* guy wouldn’t have been much help to you on the island.” Sometimes, you needed a guy who wasn’t afraid to get down and dirty and brutal.

He’d never been afraid to fight hard for what he wanted.

There was nothing—no one—he wanted more than her. “Don’t tell Remy about your night in the closet.”

Her lashes flickered. “I’ve never told anyone about that but you.”

Savage satisfaction filled him. *Good. That means you do trust me.* If he could just stop the bad guys, he might actually have a chance with her.

“But why don’t you want him knowing?”

Because he thought that night was tied to a whole hell of a lot. “I don’t trust him. I don’t trust Ty.”

“They’re CIA.”

“Exactly.”

“I don’t understand.”

"It means they're trained to lie and deceive. I don't have a full handle on what's happening, but I can tell you this...they are going to one hell of a lot of trouble for a stolen necklace."

Her hands twisted in her lap. "It's worth a *lot* of money. So much that a man is dead." She bit her lower lip. "I don't want anyone else dying."

"I know, baby."

"You're not going to die."

He reached for her hands. Caught one. Rubbed his finger along the top of her thumb. "Not for at least sixty more years."

"I'm serious."

"So am I. I have a lot of plans, and dying isn't on my agenda." His finger slid over her soft skin. "It's not on yours, either."

"You really think Mr. Theo will help us?"

Help? Not exactly. "I think you believed that your Mr. Theo was a nice man, and I think Remy isn't wrong about the people who seem nice." He cleared his throat. "Excluding your mother, of course." Now he was curious. "Just what did your mother look like?"

"Me." Her lips curled down. "I've been told that she looked almost exactly like me. I once saw a picture of her when she was my age. She was pregnant with me. And her face looked so much like mine that we could have been twins."

***

"Theodore is inside his house. We've had eyes on him ever since you made contact." Pierce Jennings slanted a glance toward a watchful

Remy. "Does your sister know you're stateside again?"

"Not yet." Remy didn't change expressions. "How many guards are on the home?"

They were in the back of a sleek limo. Chelsea hunched her shoulders as she perched on the leather seat. Everything seemed to be happening at super speed, and there was no control for her. When the plane had touched down, she'd immediately been whisked to the limo.

And she'd met Pierce. Handsome. Dangerous. And with a gun holstered at his side. Colt's partner had shaken her hand, and she'd felt his careful strength. Then Pierce and Remy had shared a weirdly intense look, one charged with secrets, and their group had piled into the limo.

Their group, *minus* Ty. He'd disappeared, and she wasn't exactly sure where he'd gone.

"Wilde agents are posted around the perimeter of the property."

With Pierce's response, Chelsea noted that he didn't say exactly how many agents were there.

"Like I said before," he continued, "Theodore is inside his home, and I figured you would want to have the pleasure of knocking on his door yourself," Pierce added with a wave of his hand toward Colt.

"Damn straight."

She shivered.

"I can take Chelsea to a secure location," Pierce offered with an incline of his head, "and after you've talked to Theodore—"

"No." She stopped hunching her shoulders. Instead, she straightened them. "No," Chelsea repeated. "I'm going to see Mr. Theo—Theodore." *He's not the friendly, harmless man you thought.* "I'm confronting him."

All three males immediately whipped their heads toward her. "Pardon?" Remy asked. "I think I misunderstood."

"I don't think you did." Her chin lifted. "I've been punched, kidnapped, and I had to swim through shark-infested waters in the middle of the night."

"Wait—shark what now?" Pierce queried. The soft illumination from the lights in the limo's floor let her see the furrow of his brow.

Colt cleared his throat. "There are technically always sharks in the water because they live there. But none attacked us so..."

She plowed on, "All of this has happened to *me*. Some crazy person out there thinks I have some million-dollar necklace—"

"The estimate is a million-point-four," Remy clarified.

She didn't need the clarification. "*I'm* the one they've been after, and I'm not about to just go and sit in a corner while the big confrontation goes down with Theodore." A confrontation without her? *No*. "I want to ask him what's happening. If he was acquainted with my mother, if he sent those people after me, *I* want to know."

Colt's fingers curled around her wrist. She felt his thumb trace her rapidly pounding pulse point. "I will find out for you."

She needed to do this. "*We* will find out. I'm not fading into the background. This is my life. I deserve to learn why all of this is happening to me."

"It's too dangerous." A dismissal from Remy.

"Dangerous." Yes, it was. Unfortunately, she was now familiar with dangerous situations. "As dangerous as everything else that's happened?"

The limo took a right turn.

Into the silence, she said, "I'll have Colt with me. He's proven to be more than adept at handling dangerous situations. We can go in together. Question Theodore together."

"Bad idea." Again, Remy was definitely not on board. "Theodore Beasley is an unknown quantity. You shouldn't be anywhere near him."

"I've been near him plenty of times before. He never tried to hurt me. If he wanted me hurt—if he wanted me dead—that could have easily happened by now. Even on the island, those men weren't trying to kill me."

"No, they just killed a cop," Remy growled.

Her stomach knotted. "He'll talk more to me. I *can* get him to talk." She was sure of it.

"I'm pretty good at interrogations." Colt released her wrist. "Kind of a forte of mine."

"He excels at playing bad cop," Pierce added.

She didn't want some intense bad cop scene. She just wanted the truth. She focused on Colt. "I need this."

"And I need you fucking safe," he growled back. "This is an unknown situation. When he's confronted, we don't know what the guy will do."

No, they didn't. "Then you *and* Remy come in with me. With both of you there, surely you can contain one retired jewel thief?" She glanced over at Pierce. His expression had turned pensive. "You did say that you had agents watching the house? With all of those people there, it seems like the risk should be minimal. I *need* to go in."

Remy stretched his legs out in the limo. Pulled out his phone. Sent a text. Then peered up at Colt. "Your call. I believe you wanted to, uh, run the show with Theodore? Or something to that effect. So you decide if she goes or gets benched."

She put her hand on Colt's shoulder. "I'm going in."

He stiffened beneath her touch. "At the first sign of trouble, you get the hell out."

Excitement churned within her. "Right. Sure."

A nod. "She's going in."

Soft laughter from Remy. "Somehow, I'm not surprised." A little salute. "She goes in, you guard her, and I will be your wingman."

***

"No one has made contact with him," Pierce said as the limo slowed in front of the horseshoe driveway. "We got eyes on him, and we made sure he was staying put. But he has no idea that our team is in position. We saved the big confrontation for you."

The limo stopped. Remy reached for the door, hesitated, and glanced over at Chelsea. "You sure you can play things cool?"

Her hands were already sweating. "I'm not sure cool is the word I'd use."

"Maybe follow my lead?" Remy suggested. "I'm great at cool."

"Great at being a dick," Pierce muttered when Remy slid out. Shaking his head, Pierce handed Colt a gun. Colt tucked it into the back waistband of his jeans.

"You good?" Pierce wanted to know.

"Good enough." Colt nodded. "Watch my six. You're the only wingman I trust."

"Back at you. Let's do this."

And Colt exited before her. She noticed he was scanning the scene. She reached for the door.

"He talks about you a lot." Low, from Pierce as he remained in the seat across from her. "And he's never talked about any woman before. You got to him."

Colt was reaching his hand back in the car toward her.

"Did he get to you?" Pierce asked.

She didn't answer him. She slipped outside of the limo. The sun was setting. The sky burned with a mix of deep reds and oranges that framed the imposing lines of the two-story home. A small balcony jutted above the entrance, a balcony supported by four thick, white columns. The landscaping around the home had been meticulously maintained. Not even a twig appeared out of place on the line of carefully pruned bushes and shrubs.

Remy headed straight for the black front door. A flickering gas lantern hung to the right of the door. He lifted his hand and pressed the doorbell. An old-fashioned doorbell, not one of the tech bells that so many people had these days—those equipped with tiny cameras.

"How are you going to start your questions?" Remy asked Colt. "Gonna play things nice at first or go straight for the jugular?"

The door opened. The light spilled over the gleaming, bald top of Theodore Beasley's head. He wore small glasses—he'd called them spectacles before—that covered his warm brown eyes. His black dress pants were held up by striped suspenders, and his crisp, white dress shirt contrasted with his warm, golden skin.

He frowned at Remy. "Can I help you?"

"I hope so," Chelsea said.

Theodore's head snapped toward her. "Chelsea! I didn't see you there!" He beamed at her. "What a surprise!"

Yes, she imagined the visit was a surprise.

"How can I help you and your friends?" Warmth seemed to pour from him. The same warmth that had always been there. He appeared so harmless. So friendly. So *nice*.

Her hands fisted. "You're a jewel thief."

Theodore sucked in a sharp breath. His left hand flew to his chest. The light caught the diamond ring that circled his pinky finger. His accusing gaze flew to Colt. "You told her?"

She could hear the rushing of her blood filling her ears.

"Retired," Theodore sniffed. Offered her his warmest smile. "A retired thief. A life that was so very long ago and—"

"You know me." Her hands unclenched. Fisted again.

"Well, of course, I do. You're my interior designer. And you did a wonderful job. I was thinking of hiring you again for additional work—"

"You *know* me. You sent those people after me, didn't you?"

Some of the warmth faded from his smile.

"We should take this inside," Remy directed quietly. "I also guess playing nice isn't an option. We'll just go straight for the jugular."

She stepped closer to Theodore. "I *liked* you." She *had*. "Men came to kidnap me! You sent them, didn't you? Why? Why would you—"

His face hardened. His brown eyes glinted. "Because it was either you or me, my dear, and I have a long history of choosing myself in these types of situations." He backed into the house. "I'm not in the mood for a visit now. Perhaps another time." He began to swing the door closed.

Colt shoved his foot over the threshold and stopped that swinging door. "Nope. Not how it works. The lady has questions, and you *will* give her answers."

Theodore sputtered. He also retreated. Colt and Remy advanced.

So did Chelsea. The door slammed behind her, and she faced off against the man who was staring at her with far too much familiarity in his eyes.

Theodore had done this to her. She'd been terrified, hunted, and it had all been because of this man. "Why would you lie? Why would you tell them I have a necklace like that?" She didn't even know who the mysterious "them" was, but she'd find out.

"I didn't lie." He stomped into the study. The study she'd painstaking decorated for him. The paintings she'd picked. The carpeting. The drapes. The colors. They all sort of blurred around her as Chelsea followed him. He grabbed a bottle of bourbon and splashed the drink into a glass. "You do have it."

"I *don't*." She was fiercely conscious of Colt and Remy watching the scene unfold.

Theodore whirled toward her. He stood near the massive floor to ceiling windows that were in the front of his house. "Your mother took that necklace! I know because I helped her do it!"

"Damn," Remy exclaimed. "Paydirt." He pulled out his phone. Quickly swiped his fingers over the screen.

"She took it, and she disappeared without giving me the fair share I was supposed to get." Theodore downed the drink. Tightened his hold on the glass. So tight that Chelsea feared it might shatter. "I couldn't find her. She *vanished*. And then one day I was walking down the street, and I saw you again." He shoved the glass down on a nearby, decorative table. An eighteenth-century piece that she'd selected to match—

I saw you again. His words registered and had her taking a sudden step back.

"No, no, not you." A hard, negative shake of his head. His spectacles slid down his nose. Theodore paced closer to the window but kept his eyes on her. Almost as if he couldn't look away. "You look just like her. Just like Mary. My beautiful Mary. God, she could lie and charm anyone. We all bought it—all thought she loved us—but Mary never loved anyone."

Chelsea shook her head. He was wrong. That wasn't her mother. He had no idea what he was saying. He was just wrong. *Wrong*.

"She was a user, through and through." His chin lowered toward his chest. "I was just the latest in a long line of fools who thought—"

"*Stop it.*" An angry cry from her. "Don't talk about my mother that way! Don't you dare!"

His nostrils flared as his gaze seemed to burn back at her.

"She was wonderful and caring and—" *Don't say nice, don't say—*"she loved me. She wasn't a thief. She wasn't a liar—"

A sniff from Theodore. "I'm sorry, but she was both. Beautiful, but devious. So deceitful. I was just another in a long line of men she tricked and betrayed."

"No." A hard shake of her head. She could feel Colt and Remy watching her. "You're wrong."

"I knew her. The real her." He jerked off his glasses. Gripped them in his left hand. Stared at her. Seemed harder. Younger. A different person?

Like Colt, taking off his glasses, pretending...

As her mother had pretended?

"*No.*" She advanced on Theodore. "I want the truth. The *real* truth." She had to get a handle on the situation. "Why did you hire me in the first place?"

"Because..." He turned his head and peered out the window. Shoved the filmy curtains even more to the side with his right hand, then those fingers fisted on the curtains. "Because I thought you had the necklace. When you were decorating my place, I was searching yours. I kept you busy here so I could take my time searching there."

Shock jolted her. "You broke into my condo?"

A rough laugh slipped from him. "Don't seem so shocked. And it would help if you dropped the innocent routine. You don't do it as well as she did."

Her back teeth ground together.

"While I was exploring at your home, your boyfriend was breaking into my place, too, and you're the one who gave him access."

"I did *not*."

His brows furrowed as his head swiveled back toward her. "Sounds like you mean it. Perhaps I was wrong. Maybe you can lie as well as Mary—"

"Her name was *Marilyn*. And I'm not lying!"

"Chelsea didn't know what I was doing." Colt's voice seemed so level and calm when hers had been high and breaking. "She thought you were a sweet, retired guy who wanted to update his house. She had no idea you were using her."

Theodore turned to better study Colt. "Or that you were? Did you tell her the full truth? That you threatened to arrest me if I didn't turn over the jewelry *you* were after? Such a small piece, barely worth twenty grand. Yet you had me dragged out of my house and I—"

"You reached an agreement with my client, don't make it more dramatic than it was. You gave back stolen property. And you kept your freedom."

Theodore sniffed. “I wasn’t the first to steal it. Did you know that? Were you told that particular detail before you invaded my life? Your client with *her* sticky fingers stole the piece first so I just—”

“*Ahem.*” Remy cleared his throat and waved when all eyes flew to him. His attention seemed locked on Theodore. “Hi. You don’t know me, and it’s really best to keep things that way. But I’d like to refocus and get you to tell me about the missing pearl necklace. You know, the one you believed Chelsea possessed? The one you just said you helped her mother to steal? The one that is worth one hell of a lot more than twenty grand?”

Theodore still gripped the curtains with his right fist. His hold seemed to tighten even more. A little more pressure, and she knew the expensive fabric would tear. “I haven’t seen that necklace in so long.” His voice softened. His grip didn’t. In his left hand, he held just as tightly to his glasses. “Once upon a time, it was supposed to buy me a new life.”

Remy glanced around. “Looks like you have a pretty cushy life to me.”

“You don’t know what I did for this life. Or the people I owe.” Once more, Theodore’s gaze shifted to Chelsea. “That’s why I had to tell them about you.” Mild regret. “Old debts that had to be repaid. I tried finding the necklace first. That was why I searched your place. I was going to take it. Give it back to the owner, but...”

“Oh, *now* you’re giving things back to the rightful owners,” Colt snapped in disgust. “How noble of you.”

Theodore ignored him. "I searched and couldn't find it. Then he came for me. After all this time, he'd found me..." His nostrils flared as he pointed at Colt. "Because of you. Because your company leaked my information. People realized who I was, and the debts came due. And I tried...*I tried, I swear...*" Tears glittered in his eyes as he let go of the curtain and took a step toward Chelsea. He gazed beseechingly at her. "I tried to find it. I was just going to take it, give it to him, but I couldn't. You'd hidden it too well, so I had to tell him who you were. There was no choice! If I hadn't told him, I-I think he would have killed me."

"I didn't hide *anything,"* she gritted. Why did he keep insisting that she had?

"Who is it?" Remy thundered. "Cut to the chase. Just tell us the person's name."

Theodore put his hand over his heart. "I loved her." His shoulders hunched forward. "Mary was my world, and then she was gone, and she never looked back."

"*Who did you tell?"* Colt this time. Surging forward. Demanding an answer.

"He loved her, too," Theodore whispered. "Loved her...until he hated her. That's what happens when you lie. Love turns to hate and then there's just nothing else left—"

Glass exploded. Shattered. A chunk flew into the air and sliced over Chelsea's cheek. She cried out in surprise but...

Theodore...his hand on his chest. Blood on his fingers. Blood pumping...

She grabbed for him, but Colt locked an arm around her waist and hauled her back. He dragged her away from Theodore even as she screamed.

Theodore's eyes flared wide. His glasses fell from his left hand and his right—his right was still covered with blood as his knees gave way, and he hit the floor.

"Shooter!" Remy shouted.

Her head whipped toward him.

A shooter? That was why the glass had shattered. Why Theodore was bleeding. He'd been shot. Theodore needed help, and instead of helping, Colt was pulling her away.

"No!" She struggled against Colt's hold. "Let me go!"

"The fuck I will." And he just lifted her up and ran out of the study with her.

CHAPTER FOURTEEN

Colt kept an unbreakable hold on Chelsea even as she squirmed and fought in his grasp. Let her go? Hell, no. Colt yanked open the door beneath the staircase. No windows. A safe enough space. He pushed her inside. "Stay here!" He'd help Theodore. He'd talk to Pierce and figure out how the hell a shooter had gotten past the Wilde team outside—

"No!" She grabbed his hand. Her nails dug into his skin. "Don't you *dare* leave me in a closet! No, *no!* I'm not staying here!"

Oh, fuck. What the hell was he thinking? He could see her fear. Feel it. The terror that had leached all of the color from her face. Her eyes were desperate, stark pools.

She'd told him that she'd been left in a closet. *Dammit.* What was he doing? He'd been reacting on instinct. Only wanting to protect her. "Chelsea..."

He heard the sound of shattering wood. He whipped to the side, looking toward the foyer even as he yanked up his gun and took aim.

Pierce burst through the broken door and aimed a gun back at him. Pierce and two other Wilde agents that Colt recognized—Casey Jones and Daphne Willow. Both Daphne and Casey were also armed.

"Are you hit?" Pierce thundered.

Colt shook his head. "In the study, to your right. Theodore is down."

Pierce jerked his head. Casey and Daphne both rushed toward the study.

"What in the hell happened?" Colt demanded as he kept his weapon at the ready. "How did a shooter get past our team?"

"That's damn well what I want to know." Pierce's stare swept over him. "Chelsea?"

Colt looked back. She stood in the open doorway of that little room beneath the stairs. A room that must have looked like hell to her. A trickle of blood slid down her delicate cheekbone.

He eased toward her. Carefully wiped away that blood.

She shuddered. "Theodore?"

The shot had gone into the man's back. And blood had pumped out his front. *The bullet went through him.*

"We've got agents searching the area. Keep Chelsea in here until it's clear," Pierce said before he bounded away.

It was supposed to be clear before. This shouldn't have happened.

But it had happened. He'd agreed to let Chelsea come into that house with him. He'd made the call.

And she'd been inches away from getting shot.

***

The flash of lights from the ambulance lit up the scene. The cops had arrived, they'd come just moments before the ambulance lurched to a stop at the house.

The shooter was gone. Chelsea knew the Wilde agents had searched, but they hadn't found him. She'd heard Pierce tell Colt that he believed the shooter had been in the house across the street. Second floor. That he'd been there and he'd waited for his shot. Then he'd raced away before the Wilde agents could get him.

The affluent street was lined with people who'd come out to gawk. A giant crowd, and Chelsea couldn't help but wonder...what if the shooter was somewhere in that crowd? What if it was someone who'd just blended with everyone else? Pierce believed he'd fled, but what if he'd hidden, stayed, and what if he was watching her right then?

She backed up and bumped into Remy.

"Easy." His hand closed around her shoulder, and she saw the blood on his fingertips. Her breath shuddered out as she jerked away from him.

"Clear a path!" A sharp cry that came just before the EMTs rushed from the house with Theodore strapped to a gurney.

He seemed smaller on that gurney. His expensive shirt had been ripped open, and she could see the blood that covered him. His head turned, and his eyes opened. His gaze seemed to lock on her as he passed.

His hand lifted. Reached out to her.

She stepped forward.

But the EMTs had already moved him on. They loaded him into the back of the ambulance. The doors closed.

The siren wailed as the ambulance took off.

"He's going to make it." Remy's calm voice. "Looked worse than it was. Nothing major was hit. An in-and-out shot, more to the shoulder area than chest. Of course, I'm no doctor, but I have seen my share of gunshot scenes."

Chelsea flinched.

"Guessing it's your first, hmm? You never forget your first."

She swung toward him. Only to find that, despite his causal tone, his expression was tense. Even suspicious.

"You never knew?" His head tilted. "Your mother never gave you any hints about what she was really like?"

"I know what she was really like. He's wrong about her." Wrong or he'd just been lying.

"The shooter stopped him before Theodore could provide a name for us. Unfortunate." Remy crossed his arms over his chest. "I'm guessing you don't have any insight to offer?"

"No. If I did, if I knew, I would have told you by now." Like she'd be protecting a killer.

"What happened to your mother's possessions?"

The question had her frowning.

"You strike me as the sentimental type. I don't see you just tossing away your dear mother's personal items. Not when she was the only family you had." He edged closer to her. "But Theodore said he searched your place. So, what did you do?

Get a storage unit? Did you hide her things there? Because I know you sold her house, not like the stuff could still be in that tiny town of Hollow, Georgia."

She had sold the house. As for her mother's personal items... "She wanted most of the stuff donated to charity. All of the furniture. Her clothes."

"Fuck. A real helper right to the end."

"*Stop it.*" Now she was the one to get closer to him. To stand toe-to-toe with him. "You don't know her. You don't know *me*. And Theodore—he sure didn't, either."

"She broke his heart. Cut out of their deal and left him high and dry. You can see where he would be bitter. When someone lies to you and betrays you, you get angry." His gaze shifted over her shoulder. "That's what happened with you and Colt, isn't it? He lied. He betrayed you. And you got so angry you left him."

She didn't look behind her. She didn't need to. She could feel Colt.

"Give me your fucking phone," Colt snapped.

That response from him *did* surprise her.

But Colt surged to her side in the next instant and shoved his hand toward Remy. "*Now*. Give me your phone, Remy."

"No 'please' with that request?" Remy made a tut-tut click with his tongue. "How disappointing. I thought you military brats were raised with better manners."

"Give him the phone." A snap from Pierce as he joined their little group. "We're not asking. We're ordering." He took up a position by

Chelsea's side. Colt was to her left, Pierce to her right, and tension rolled off both men.

"I'm with the CIA," Remy reminded them. "I don't take orders from Wilde agents. You're not exactly in my chain of command."

"Where's your partner?" A rapid-fire question from Colt. "The one you're supposed to be training? Where is he right now?"

"Ty had to check in with our boss. Don't worry. I'll update him about all the developments." Remy didn't make any move to surrender his phone.

Why did they want his phone?

"Right before Theodore was shot..." Colt's arm brushed against Chelsea as he glared at Remy. "I saw you send out a text."

"Yes. Is that a crime?"

"It's a crime if you told the shooter that Theodore was in position." Anger hummed in Colt's voice. "It's a crime if you were signaling him to fire before Theodore could tell us that your slippery ass was involved in this mess."

Remy laughed.

Colt and Pierce did not.

Remy's attention swung to Pierce. "Your partner isn't joking?"

Pierce just stared back at him.

"You're fucking in love with my sister." Low. Gritted from Remy. "You *know* me. You think I'd do that? Stage a killing right in front of you?"

"I do know you," Pierce agreed. "I know that you're dangerous. I know that you spent far too many years working with the wrong side of the law. You're a thief. Maybe this million-dollar payday was too good of an opportunity for you to pass up. Maybe you got personally involved. Certainly not the first time I've known of a CIA operative to go bad."

She could have sworn that pain flashed for just the briefest of moments on Remy's face before it was expertly masked. "Maybe I'm trying to go good," he muttered. "You ever think of that?" He shoved his hand into his pocket and hauled out his phone. He tossed it toward Colt.

Colt caught it easily. "Password."

Remy gave it to him. Flatly. Coldly.

Colt's fingers tapped on the screen. She looked toward him. The screen illuminated his features, and she caught the tensing of his jaw.

"See my text? Just a friendly note to my partner saying that Mary—correction, *Marilyn*—worked with Theodore to steal the necklace years ago. Confirmation that she was the original perp. No order of a hit."

Colt tossed the phone back to Remy.

"Your lack of trust is hurtful." Remy used his phone to point to both Colt and Pierce. "Deeply."

"Screw that," Colt snapped. "You're working an angle that you're not telling us about. You're holding back, and Chelsea's life is on the line. Tell me everything. Now."

Remy scanned the busy scene. The gawking neighbors. "Hardly the time or place. And I have a partner waiting. As well as a few leads I need to follow." He sent them a wide smile. "How about you take your precious Chelsea away from this scene? Get her someplace safe. Seeing as how her 'life is on the line' and all, you probably don't want to just stand out in the open with her for long periods of time."

Colt surged toward him. Chelsea grabbed his arm before he could attack Remy. "Stop!" The last thing she needed was those two going at it. "I do want to leave," she added quietly. "I want to get away from here."

She wanted to go home.

"Want some advice?" Remy asked.

Chelsea tossed a glare in his direction. Advice from him? Not particularly.

"Maybe don't go all in on Team Wilde. Got to say, I'm disappointed in their showing so far. My expectations were much higher." With that, he marched away.

She could feel the fierce tension in Colt's body. She knew he wanted to rush after Remy. Only that didn't seem like a good idea. A fight with the CIA?

"He gave up too easily," Pierce noted. "Like that shit isn't suspicious. I'm following him. I want to know what the hell he's up to." He pointed to the right. The limo waited. "I know you want to get her out of here. Our team is gonna keep searching and working with local law enforcement. When we learn more, I'll call you."

Colt was already pulling Chelsea against him, wrapping her tight even as he led her toward the limo.

"Wait." She dug in her heels. "Remy wanted to know what I did with my mother's possessions."

At her words, Pierce swung back toward them.

"I donated most of the items to charity. That was what she wanted."

Colt inclined his head. "Bet Remy is off to try and track down those donations—"

"But I didn't donate everything. There were a few books..." She made sure her voice was low and carried only to Colt and Pierce. "There were books from my childhood that I kept. Books we always read together." Those books didn't have anything to do with the theft, though. Right?

If you think that, then why are you mentioning them?

"Where are they?" Colt wanted to know.

"My place."

Colt urged her toward the limo. "We'll be making a pitstop there." He opened the back door, and she eased inside. "Be careful, buddy," she heard him call to Pierce, and then Colt was giving instructions to the driver. A man she realized was another Wilde agent.

They were all around her.

Maybe don't go all in on Team Wilde. Remy's warning.

Too late. She was all in.

Colt climbed in beside her. The door slammed shut.

***

Thirty minutes later...

"You're staying in the damn car." Savage.

Chelsea shook her head. "Colt, look, I get that the last scene was intense—"

Intense didn't cover things. She had a cut on her cheek from where the glass had bit into her skin. She'd been standing right beside Theodore Beasley. Instead of a small slice from the glass, she could have been shot. She could have been the one in the ambulance, or, heaven fucking forbid, she could have been the one on the floor and with a bullet in her heart.

"But this is my home," she continued doggedly. "And unless you've got some cuffs hidden somewhere on your person and you plan to cuff me to something in the back of this limo—I am going inside."

He leaned toward her. Tried to control the rage that pulsed through him. "You could have been shot."

"He wasn't aiming at me. The bad guys want me alive, remember?'

"That could change. Or maybe you get someone who is a shit shot and it doesn't matter. You get a bullet to the heart and you are *gone*, and I'm fucking wrecked."

Her hand pressed to his cheek. He could feel the tremble in her fingers.

I almost shoved her in a damn closet. Her own version of hell. I just wanted to get her somewhere safe. That was what he wanted most. Her safety. The way to guarantee that? Lock away the bastards after her. "The shooter is on the loose. We don't know where he is. You stay in the limo until I get back. It's bulletproof." She'd be safe if she stayed put. "Your building isn't secure."

"Colt..."

"I don't have cuffs, but I'm sure the driver does." Total bullshit. "Don't make me use them." A bluff.

She sucked in a sharp breath. "You wouldn't."

He leaned even closer. So close that his mouth almost took hers. "*Dare me.*"

"Dammit. This is my home. This is my life. This is—"

"And you are *mine*. If something happens to you on my watch, I'll lose my freaking mind. So stay in the limo. Stay here. I'll get the books, and I'll be right back." Then he'd get her to his place. His security was top-notch. Hell, he'd installed the security system himself. She'd be more secure there than she would be in any safe house in the area. "Stay here." This limo wasn't a closet. She could look out the windows—those bulletproof windows. She could get herself a damn drink from the bar, if she wanted.

"I don't like this."

He kissed her. Deep. Hard. A fast drive of his tongue to greedily taste the sweetness of her mouth. He was far too on edge. Far too angry. Desperate. As soon as he got her to his place...

His mouth pulled from hers. "I don't, either." Every time he looked at that small cut on her cheek...

Someone will pay.

"Th-the shelf in my bedroom. That's where the books are. Old fairy-tale books. The bindings are so old that my mom had to put tape on them to hold the books together. There are five of them—no, six."

He kissed her again. Softer, still desperate. He had the feeling that when it came to Chelsea, he might always be desperate.

"Be careful," she breathed against his mouth.

When he left the limo, he had his gun at the ready.

CHAPTER FIFTEEN

"What aren't you telling me?"

Remy paused when he heard the question. He'd known that he was being followed. Pierce might think he was some sort of super agent at Wilde, but Remy had been in the game for basically his whole life.

The game. The underworld. Dealing with criminals. Lying. Losing pieces of his soul bit by bit.

Pierce didn't get that shit. Because Pierce was one of those true-blue bastards who always did the right thing without hesitating. An annoying trait, but actually one of the reasons why Remy was glad the guy had wound up with his sister Iris. Iris deserved someone good. Someone who would walk through fire to protect her.

He knew that the true-blue bastard would burn in an instant if it meant keeping Iris safe.

Sometimes I miss her so much.

His secret. Not that he let it show. He loved his little sister—loved her more than anything else in the world—but in order to protect her, he'd had to walk away.

She'd thought he abandoned her.

I was trying to keep you safe.

Sometimes, being away from him was the safest place to be.

"Aren't you going to even look at me?" Pierce pushed.

"Why? I know what your face is like." But he turned around. Smiled. "I'm starting to think you just enjoy my company."

"What aren't you telling us?"

"A lot. Because you don't have CIA clearance." Remy thought that was a fine answer.

"I'm not sure you do, either. Can't decide if you're a criminal, a damn good con man, or some secret agent who is actually on the right side of the law."

Remy rocked back on his heels. "So many options. But, I do currently have a CIA identification card so let's choose lucky version number three."

Pierce put his hands on his hips. The flashing light from a nearby police cruiser swept over his face. "My partner cares about that woman."

"You don't say. I might have missed that tidbit when he was dragging her from the scene and using his own body as a human shield." When bullets started flying, that was when you could really tell a lot about a person.

Take Chelsea Ember...when she'd realized that Theodore had been shot, she'd immediately lunged for him. The man had lied to her, confessed to breaking into her place, and she'd still been fighting to help him even though the shooter could have fired again at any moment.

As for Colt Easton...ah, that tough sonofabitch had assessed things instantly, and he'd focused on his only priority. Shielding Chelsea. He'd dragged her out even as she fought him. He'd covered her, turned so that if any bullets hit, they'd have to go through him before they could reach her.

And Remy had fed the guy some BS outside. Chelsea hadn't been in danger when she stood outside after the authorities arrived. There had been a wall of police officers and Wilde agents at the scene. But Remy had rather enjoyed pushing Colt to see what he'd do in response.

If Chelsea hadn't stopped him, he would have punched me. Something told Remy that Colt packed a rather powerful punch.

Mental note. Let's not antagonize him again anytime soon. Where Chelsea was concerned, the man's control was too thin.

"You're not as much of an asshole as you want me to believe."

Great. Now Pierce thought he could be a good judge of character. "Are you sure about that? Maybe I'm even *more* of an asshole—"

"What are you holding back?" Pierce snarled.

"I'm just doing my job." A job that *should* have been over by now. He'd repaid his debt, too many times over. But just when he thought he was out, he'd be dragged back in because the people in charge sure liked to use his skills.

Correction, they liked to use him.

"What's the job?"

Easy enough to answer that question. "Retrieving the missing necklace. I thought you'd been briefed on the goal. Weren't you in the limo when we were all talking—"

"How were you supposed to retrieve it?"

He really had other places to be. “Didn’t your partner tell you? No briefing? Oh, well. The truth is that I was supposed to get close to Chelsea Ember. Learn all her secrets.” *Whoops.* He’d almost spilled too much right then. But he smiled to cover the slip. “Only Colt beat me to the punch. Lucky man. I can definitely see the temptation to cross the line with her. To stop playing a role and to see what it would be like to have her really care about you. Of course, she dumped Colt’s ass so I’m guessing things didn’t work out perfectly, but, hey, he got a second chance because of this mess, didn’t he?” Which, actually...*suspicious.* “If I were a less trusting individual, maybe I’d be looking a little harder at him.”

“What in the hell is that supposed to mean?” Instantly antagonistic.

“It means how else is a guy like him gonna get a second shot with a woman like her? He got to swoop in and play hero. How very lucky for him. Almost too lucky, some would say.”

“Colt isn’t like that.”

“I wouldn’t know. I don’t know him. I just know that Colt was originally supposed to retrieve some stolen jewelry. Wilde had a client—some mystery person that I can’t quite seem to identify—who hired Colt to get the piece back.” The unknown client raised more issues. He hated working blind. “Are we sure that client isn’t involved in what’s happening? Are we sure the client didn’t also recognize Chelsea? Because Theodore kept acting like Chelsea looked exactly like her mother.” With that in mind... “Maybe that client of yours *did* recognize her. Maybe the client told Colt about the mystery of the missing pearl necklace, and Colt decided that something so valuable was too good to pass up. He decided to get himself a not-so-little side hustle."

"You're saying the side hustle is Chelsea?" Hard disbelief underscored every word.

But Remy was saying all kinds of things in an attempt to throw off Pierce from his near slip earlier. "I'm saying why not kill two birds with one stone? Colt can get himself a million-dollar necklace, and he can get Chelsea, too. He can pretend to be her hero. Win, win." He was really warming to this version of events, and that gave him pause. *Hell. What if I'm right?* "And Wilde agents were all over the scene." A little slower. More considering. "Perhaps Colt simply had one of his friends shoot Theodore before the truth could come out."

"You're wrong."

"Oh, am I? Because Wilde agents haven't gone bad before?" He saw the hit. Nodded. "Maybe check out your own house before you start accusing me of doing bad things. Because believe it or not, I'm actually trying to do a little good these days." A teeny, tiny bit. "Now, if you'll excuse me, I have some business waiting." He swung away.

"You're going to try tracking down the donations."

If that was what Pierce wanted to believe...

"Do you have her real name?"

Now that is a much better question.

"I bet you do. I bet you know who Chelsea's mother was before she switched identities. Share the name with me. We can help each other."

Not yet, they couldn't. "I will keep that in mind for later. Tell my sister I said hello, will you?"

"Tell her your own damn self. Try picking up the phone and *calling* her. Better yet, go see her. Oh, and there's something you might like to know..."

He kept walking.

"She's pregnant."

Remy stumbled and almost fell straight onto his face.

***

The lock on her condo door had been smashed. Colt stiffened when he saw it. Theodore hadn't mentioned anything about kicking his way inside. He pictured Theodore being more the careful, stealthy type.

And if that was the case, then someone else had broken into Chelsea's home.

Plus Theodore said that he broke in when Chelsea was redecorating his place. That was months ago.

Some bastard had shattered her lock *recently*.

Colt's fingers brushed against the door as he pushed it open. Silently, he crept inside, and the rage within him grew stronger when he saw the wreckage that waited. This hadn't been some fast search. It had been thorough, brutal with its intensity. Her belongings had been smashed. Her picture frames broken. Her sofa cushions slashed. Fury was everywhere that he looked.

When the perp hadn't found what he wanted, he'd just gotten angrier and angrier...

I'm glad Chelsea is in the limo. I don't want her seeing this.

Room by room, he searched. Whoever had broken into her home was gone. Only the chaos remained. She'd been so meticulous with her home.

But her paintings had been sliced to ribbons.

Her delicate glass sculptures shattered.

And as for her bedroom...

The door was open. The mattresses thrown against the wall.

What the fuck did you think, asshole? That she'd actually hid a million-dollar necklace under her bed?

Her clothes had been dumped out of her drawers. Her closet looked like it had been hit by a tornado. Her bookshelf was on the floor, all of the books scattered and open.

Colt edged closer to those books. They'd been riffled through by the bastard. Colt could picture the perp lifting them, shaking each one. Getting pissed when nothing fell out. Not a slip of paper with a clue on it, not a key that would point him in the right direction.

But you weren't looking in the correct spot. That was your problem. Because the bastard didn't know Chelsea. He hadn't learned all of her secrets.

Colt bent and reached for the older books, the ones with faded print on the front. Fairy tales that

Chelsea had treasured from so long ago. The ones with spines that had been reinforced by her mother's hand—and by thick, sturdy, black tape.

Six books. He collected them. Stacked them up.

He found a bag on the floor of Chelsea's closet. One of those colorful bags that women liked to haul to the beach. The books fit perfectly inside, and he took them with him. He left the chaos behind him and hurried back to the limo.

The door opened and Chelsea was waiting for him.

Beautiful Chelsea. With her wide eyes and with the small cut on her delicate cheek.

They won't stop until they get what they want.

"You found the books." She bit her lip. "Was everything...okay?"

No, baby. It wasn't.

"Colt?"

"We'll call the cops. They will need to get a crime scene team to your place, though, honestly, Wilde will have a faster turnaround time for you. If any prints were left, they'll find them." He leaned forward. Tapped on the glass that separated him from the driver. When the privacy shield lowered, Colt told the agent to get them to his home.

Colt could feel Chelsea's eyes on him. He made sure the shield lifted once more, and then he settled back against the seat. He put the gun next to him. Pulled out the books. Ran his fingers down the spines one at a time. "Which one was your favorite?"

"Grimms' Fairy Tales. The blue one." Her fingers fluttered over his arm. "Why do we need a crime scene team at my place?"

He put down the other books. Pulled out the knife that he'd strapped to his ankle earlier. A knife that Pierce had given him when they'd met at the airport.

"Colt?" Alarm had her voice going breathy.

His gaze slid to her. He hated to tell her but, "It was searched."

"Theodore told us that he'd gone inside—"

"The way Theodore talked, he went in months ago, and he sure as hell didn't tell us that he'd trashed the place."

She flinched.

He should have been more tactful, but there was too much danger around to sugar coat things. "Your home was wrecked. I'm sorry, baby, but I'll get it fixed. After the crime scene techs are done, I'll get it cleaned up for you. I can buy new paintings and replace the glass sculpture work. I'll get a new couch that will be super comfortable, and any clothes that they cut will just be thrown away and—"

"They—they cut up my clothes? Someone...did all that?"

Someone with a whole lot of rage. He nodded.

Colt heard the soft catch of her breath before she asked, "What are you doing with the knife?"

"Ending this."

"I don't understand."

She would. "Your favorite book? This is it?" He held it up.

"Yes. Sh-she would always read me Hansel and Gretel and tell me that sometimes you had to follow breadcrumbs..."

Provided the damn birds didn't eat the breadcrumbs. "Consider this a very big breadcrumb." He sliced through the tape and spine of the book.

"Colt!" Alarm. "What are you doing? I don't have much left of her and that's not—"

A key fell into his hand. A key that had been hidden in the spine of the book.

"I don't...understand." Not breathless. Lost.

He put down the book and the knife. Lifted the key. Turned it over in his fingers. "Safe-deposit box key." Now it was just a matter of figuring out where the box was. The bank's routing number had been printed on the key bow, so getting the location would be a snap. "She left the key for you." Hidden it in Chelsea's favorite book because her mother had known the book was something Chelsea would always treasure.

But when he turned his head toward her, there was no relief on Chelsea's face. Instead, the soft lighting in the back of the limo revealed the pain in her expression, and he watched a tear slide down her cheek. A tear that stabbed him with the force of a knife.

"It's true," she said, voice thickening. "It's...the stuff Theodore said is true. She stole the necklace. It's not some terrible mistake. It's all true." Her lips trembled. "My only family, and I didn't really know her at all."

CHAPTER SIXTEEN

"Yeah, yeah, I've got her at my place. She's safe, and I won't let her out of my sight," Colt said into his phone. A new phone that had come to him courtesy of Wilde. Not like he'd keep using the one he'd gotten from Remy.

Colt had his eyes on Chelsea. She sat on his couch, about ten feet away from him, with her sandals on the floor in front of her and her legs curled under her body. She looked small and fragile and so beautiful he ached. All he wanted to do was take away her pain.

But I can't make a damn thing better for her.

Instead, he just seemed to be making everything worse.

"We'll work with the police and get our crime scene analysts in her condo," Pierce assured him. "Don't worry. If there is evidence left there that we can use, we'll find it."

"There could have been eyes on her building." A possibility he wouldn't overlook. "If so, then they know I left with something."

"Yeah, but they don't know you hit paydirt."

Paydirt in the form of a safe-deposit box key, a key that he'd discovered—with a little Wilde tech help that had traced the routing number—belonged to a small bank in Hollow, Georgia. The bank wouldn't open until nine a.m. the following day.

Colt had already planned for their road trip. "We don't have the necklace yet." But what else could be in that safe-deposit box? Had to be the one thing that everyone wanted.

Which meant they had to be very, very careful.

"Thought you might want to know that Theodore Beasley is going to be just fine," Pierce told him. "Checked at the hospital. Remy was right. Nothing vital hit, blood loss was controlled. Docs are just keeping him overnight for observation. That is one very, very lucky man."

"And the shooter?"

"The family who owned the home was gone on vacation. No clue on who entered the house, but he must have been there *before* the Wilde agents arrived. Guess he was just waiting for the perfect moment to strike."

Colt forced his back teeth to unclench. "Or he was waiting for Chelsea to show."

"Yeah, I was rather afraid that might have been his perfect moment. Then he took out Theodore—or tried to take him out—before the guy could name the bastard we're after."

Chelsea hadn't moved from her position on the couch. She was too still. Colt knew she could hear everything he said, but she showed no interest in the conversation.

"About our previous client..." Pierce's voice turned gruff. "Did the client ever meet your lady?"

"No."

"And you never mentioned Chelsea specifically to the individual?"

"No, there was no need. Before I could do anything more than search Theodore's place, the guy went to the client, and Theodore made the deal to return the jewelry. I got a call that the case was closed, and that was the end." But Pierce knew all of this. He'd been with Colt when the call came from headquarters. "What's this about?" Why the hell were they recapping?

"We looked at Theodore as a suspect. I'm thinking we need to look at the client, too."

"The client was vetted by Wilde." Which should have meant the person was as clean as a whistle. *Should* have meant...

"I know."

"She's a senator's wife. She wanted this case kept out of the papers because she didn't want to confess to cheating on her husband with a retired jewel thief." Apparently, Theodore could be quite the charmer.

"So you don't think we should investigate her—or her husband—at all?"

Investigate them? "I think we should tear their lives apart." He didn't want to leave any stone unturned.

Chelsea's gaze slid toward him.

"Because at this point, there are two people I trust," Colt added deliberately as he held her stare. "You're one of those people, Pierce."

"You know I always have your six," his friend replied.

"And Chelsea is the other."

She swiped at her cheek.

Dammit. Another tear? Those tears of hers wrecked him. "I want to talk to Theodore."

"Remy left a guard with him—that agent buddy of his, Ty."

Not surprising that the CIA had their hooks in Theodore. "We need to keep one of our team there, too. When he's clear to talk, I want to be in that room with Theodore." This time, a bullet wouldn't stop their conversation.

"Daphne is already on site. Gave her orders to call as soon as she saw he was conscious. Try to get a little rest meanwhile, would you? You and Chelsea are both probably dead on your feet."

Not quite.

But he hung up the phone. Put it down on the nearby table. Kept holding Chelsea's stare as he walked toward her. She tipped back her head when he reached the couch, and his hand slipped out. His fingertips caught the tear drop. Carefully wiped it away. "Baby, don't."

Her lashes fluttered.

"I can handle a whole lot of shit in this world." Could and had. Training to be a SEAL had been brutal, but that had just been the start. Then the missions had begun. The death... He swallowed. "But when you cry, it makes me crazy."

Her head turned. Her lips brushed over his hand. "I don't want you crazy."

What do you want? But he didn't ask that. Instead, Colt assured her, "We'll get the necklace. Do whatever you want with it tomorrow—"

"I don't want it." She stared up at him with the eyes that could bring him to his knees. "Give it to the CIA. They can keep it. Turn it back over to the person my mom stole it from—of course, that's provided she didn't kill the owner." She eased away. Rose to her feet. Paced a little, then turned back toward him. "It wasn't fireworks."

He didn't move.

"I realized that tonight when—when you were trying to push me in the closet."

Yeah, about that... "Baby..."

"It was gunshots, but you knew that all along, didn't you? Probably as soon as I told you the story. You realized that she'd put me in the closet, and she'd killed someone. And I was stupidly clinging to a belief that she'd fostered since I was a child. Fireworks..." Her lower lip trembled. "You knew—"

"*No.*"

Chelsea wrapped her arms around her waist. "No?"

His mind spun. "When the shot was fired at Theodore's, all I wanted to do was get you to a safe spot because I didn't know what the shooter would do next. I did that because—" *No. Not yet. She's not ready to hear that part yet.* He bit back the words he wanted to say. The words that kept wanting to spill out, but that would change everything between them. He had screwed up too many times before. Colt couldn't afford any other screwups. "I did that and your mother did the same thing because we wanted to protect you. She hid you *from* the gunfire. She was protecting you."

"You don't know that she wasn't the one firing."

"No, I don't. But I do know that you said she was a good person, and *I* know that she gave up everything that had been in her life before—before she had you. Whatever she'd done, whoever she'd been—it all changed when you were born. She was with you your whole life, sweetheart. Everything that happened during those years was real. Everything you experienced with her—none of that was a lie. It was all real. *She* was real. Don't ever let anyone tell you any different."

Her lashes lowered to shield her eyes. "I feel like everyone is lying to me."

Great. He was in that "everyone" category because he had lied. How could he fix this? How could he help her? "Truth or dare."

A negative shake of her head. "I don't want to play."

"Who said we're playing?"

Her lashes lifted. Hesitantly, her stare met his.

"Ask me anything. Anything in the world, and I'll give you the dead truth. There are no lies that I will tell you, not ever again. Understand that."

"Why? Why go all in with me?"

That was a question, so he'd give her the truth. "Because you're my end game, baby."

Her brow furrowed.

"When I look to the future, you're the only thing I see. The only person I want to see. I think I knew the truth when we first met, but everything else was wrong. Everything was wrong but you. I looked at you and knew you were right." The person he'd wanted, the one he'd been looking for when he hadn't even realized it. "Got another one?" With an effort, he kept his voice level. "Fire away."

"When we find the necklace, will you walk away from me?"

"Only if you don't want me." That would be the only way he'd go. If she told him they were done, fine. Otherwise... "End game, remember?"

She seemed to hug herself tighter. "You don't want the necklace?"

"I want to rip the thing apart and make sure it never can hurt you again."

Her eyes widened. "But it's worth so much money."

He stalked toward her. Slow, deliberate steps. Her head tipped back as he towered over her. "It's not worth you," Colt told her simply. "Nothing is."

Ask me more. Ask the question I can see in your eyes. Ask me...

Ask me if I love you.

Her chin lifted a little more. "I want a dare."

His jaw locked. "You can get whatever you want."

"That's you."

"You got me." Simple. Done.

But Chelsea shook her head. "I want you to-to let me do whatever I want *with* you." The faint stumble in her words gave away her nerves.

Intrigued, he waited for more.

She swiped her tongue over her lower lip. "You're always in control."

"Hardly." It was more like he walked a fine edge of losing his control with her.

"I want you to show that you trust me. I want you to let me be in control."

She didn't get it. The woman fucking had him wrapped around her little finger. He took her to damn interrogation scenes when he knew better. And she thought *he* had the control? But he'd go along because what sane man wouldn't? The woman of his dreams had just said she wanted him. *Take me, baby. All night long.* Colt motioned toward his body. "I'm yours."

"Promise?"

He might as well have her name tattooed across his heart. "Yes." But... "Only until you tell me to take over."

Her chest lifted and fell with the quickening of her breath. "You think I'll do that?"

"I'm counting on it." The conversation had derailed. His dick had shot to eager attention. He'd intended to comfort her. To take away her pain but, apparently, Chelsea had other plans.

If this is a distraction, I'm all for it. She could use his body all she wanted. He trusted her. They'd go up in flames together, and there would be no tears or pain for her. Only pleasure.

Only—

Her hands went to the front of his jeans. Colt jolted when her fingers brushed over his thick cock—through the denim—and he hissed out a breath.

"I wanted to taste you before." She released the snap. Slid down the zipper. He wasn't wearing underwear so his dick thrust straight into her hands. "This time, I will." She looked down at him.

He looked down, too. Saw her fingers stroking him. A silken touch when he felt burning hot. Her hands curled around him. Pumped him from base to tip. Over and over. His heels dug into the floor.

His knees locked. He'd survived torture before. He could do it again.

Only, this torture felt so good.

"Don't stop me." She lowered to her knees. "But if I don't do it just right, tell me, would you?"

Do it right? Like there was a way to do this wrong.

Her mouth opened. She took the tip of his cock inside.

Fuck. His hands clamped over her shoulders. His grip had to be too hard. Immediately, he tried to ease up.

Only to feel her tongue swiping along the sensitive head of his dick. Then she was sucking him in deeper. Taking more of him into her mouth, and his hips jerked against her.

She took more.

Licked.

Sucked.

His head tipped back. and his eyes squeezed closed. He was already so fucking close to coming. He could explode right in her mouth, but that wasn't what he wanted. He wanted her coming first. Wanting her screaming his name and raking her nails into his skin.

The visual made him even hotter. The image of her, locked in his arms. Riding his dick and urging him to go faster. Harder.

She released his cock.

He looked down. Her lips were red. Swollen. Wet.

"Tasting you makes me hot," she told him.

Every muscle seemed to have turned to stone.

She took him in again. His hips surged harder against her. *Control. She wants control. You don't get to take it. You don't get to lift her up, pin her against the wall, and plunge into her until she screams and comes apart around you.*

But he wanted that. He wanted in her so deep and far. Wanted nothing between them. He wanted her to know that she belonged to him, just as he belonged to her. Always.

Her hand was on him. Curled around the base of his dick. Her mouth was on the top. Licking. Stroking with her lips and tongue and he was about to go out of his mind. All he could do was growl and thrust his hips against her. His climax barreled toward him. He was about to explode—

She pulled back. Her hands flew behind her to brace her body as she stared up at him. "I want you." She yanked her blouse over her head. Revealed her bra. White. Lacy.

Had Remy fucking picked out that bra? How the hell had he even known Chelsea's size? Did he have a damn file on her?

Jealousy burned. Blazed. Mixed with the lust churning inside of Colt.

She blinked. "Colt?"

"You belong to me." He hauled her up. Pulled her into his arms. Held her easily. "Say it."

"You first."

He sucked in a breath. "Sweetheart, you fucking own me. Don't you realize that yet?"

Her lips parted. "I—"

"Let me take over."

Her hands curled around his shoulders. Colt felt the delicious bite of her nails. "Take me," she whispered. "Because I belong to you."

No control. No restraint. Nothing but a wave of primal desire and lust obliterating everything else. He shoved down her jeans, ripped away her underwear. Had her against the wall two seconds later, and he slammed as deep into her as he could go.

She gasped, then locked her legs around his hips. Her nails sank deeper into him. She was wet. Tight. So freaking hot. Nothing separated them. Her hot core clamped around him and—

No condom.

His gaze met hers. Colt could see the same knowledge in her eyes. He began to withdraw.

Her legs squeezed him. "I'm on birth control."

"Had a full fucking medical work up..." Talking was hard. He was mostly growling. "Less than a month ago. I'm good." There had been no one else since he met her.

There never will be.

"I'm good, too, I promise." Her words rushed out. "I want you like this. I want *you*. Don't stop..."

He didn't. He thrust back into her. Over and over. He pinned her to the wall because there was no way he'd make it to his bedroom even though he had fantasized about having her in his bed so many times. He locked her against that wall, curled his right hand around her waist, and his left pushed between their bodies so that he could stroke her clit. He knew exactly what she liked. He strummed her. She rode him.

There was no more talking.

Just need. Stronger and harder and hotter with every moment that passed.

Her inner muscles clamped greedily around him. Her body went bow tight as her release surged through her, and Colt could feel it. Every single second of her climax. She squeezed tighter around him, and his orgasm blasted through him. His cock surged harder into her once more. Twice.

His teeth snapped together so that he wouldn't say—

I fucking love you.

Her breath sawed in and out. Her body trembled.

He stared into her eyes.

"I belong to you," she whispered. "I feel like you are a part of me."

He carried her to the bedroom. Stayed inside of her the whole time because he was already getting hard again. And as he lowered her onto that bed, he began to thrust once more.

***

The phone on his nightstand gave a quick beep, then it vibrated across the surface. Colt cracked open one eye and glared at it. Vaguely, he remembered bringing the phone into the bedroom at some point. Some distant point in a lust-filled, pleasure-shaking night.

Truth be told, he'd been awake before the text arrived, but he'd just been enjoying his little slice of heaven far too much to move. Chelsea was in bed with him, curled around him, warm and soft, and he'd just wanted to savor her for a little while longer.

The phone beeped and vibrated again.

He reached out. Scooped it up. Read the text from Pierce.

Theodore is awake. Guy is grumbling and asking for a lawyer. He won't talk to the CIA, but maybe he will talk to you.

It was five a.m. If they hurried, they could hit the hospital, then be on the road to Hollow and make it to the bank by nine a.m.

Provided, of course, that Theodore would actually talk to them.

I think he might talk to Chelsea. His reply. Because Theodore had sure been talking plenty to her *before* the gunshot blast.

She stirred against him. Stretched. "What is it?" A sleep-husky voice that was ever so sexy.

"Theodore is awake. If we go now, we can talk to him before we head to—"

Chelsea had already jumped out of the bed before he could finish his sentence. Colt had a quick, awesome glimpse of her bare ass as she flew toward the door and darted out to collect the clothes they'd left scattered around his place.

"I will take that as a yes," he murmured. He typed back a quick message to Pierce. *On our way.*

But fifteen minutes later, when he opened his door so they could actually be on their way, Colt found someone blocking their path.

Remy smiled at him. "Morning, sunshine. Going somewhere?"

CHAPTER SEVENTEEN

Remy sauntered in, not waiting for an invitation. Since Colt hadn't planned on offering an invitation, the move wasn't particularly surprising. "Do you know what time it is?" Colt asked him.

"Five fifteen." Remy continued his saunter toward Colt's den.

Beside Colt, Chelsea shifted impatiently from her left foot to her right.

Remy headed straight for the brightly colored bag that Colt had taken from Chelsea's house. Again, the move wasn't particularly surprising. "A little birdie told me that you made a pitstop by Chelsea's place last night." He lifted the bag with two fingers. "And you left with this."

Colt shut the door because, for the moment, they weren't leaving. He flipped the lock. "Did that same birdie tell you that someone had trashed Chelsea's place?"

Remy peered into the bag. "Yes. How unfortunate."

Chelsea stiffened. "It's a lot more than unfortunate. Someone destroyed my possessions!"

"Not all of them, it would seem." Remy pulled a book out of the bag. "Because Colt brought these to you." He lifted an eyebrow. "Let me guess, sentimental value?"

"Yes," she hissed. She also strode across the room and pulled the book away from him. "Very sentimental."

He'd been holding *Grimms' Fairy Tales*.

"Couldn't help but notice..." Remy tilted his head. "The spine on that book has been slashed wide open."

"Her couch was also slashed open." Colt figured it was time to insert himself more into this conversation. Suspicion rode him hard because he did not trust Remy. In his experience, Remy had a tendency to look after himself first. Himself and his sister. But Iris wasn't part of the current equation, and Remy's buddy Constantine—the man who had once been the guy's shadow—had been nowhere to be seen on this case.

And a Remy on his own was a very dangerous and unpredictable beast.

"The person who trashed her house was searching for the necklace. He ripped and slashed everything in his path." Something that infuriated Colt. But he'd fix it. He'd repair or replace every item that had been destroyed.

Remy still held the bag. "And did he find the necklace during his search?"

"It wasn't there for him to find," Chelsea responded quickly. "I've told you before—I don't have it."

But we have the key to finding it now. Something told him that Remy suspected they'd had a new development since their last chat. "What happened to your leads?" he asked, trying to catch Remy off guard. "How'd those pan out for you? Pierce told me you were running down some things."

"Very well, thanks for asking." Remy put the bag back on the floor. "Thought you both might be interested to know that Marilyn Ember was once Mary Atkinson. A wealthy socialite who vacationed in Rome and lost her heart to a young and dashing suitor named Tommaso Bianchi. She fell in love, married him in a whirlwind romance, and then she took Tommaso home to meet her parents."

Chelsea had frozen. Her hands clutched the book to her chest.

"Mary's father was a wee bit suspicious of Tommaso," Remy continued his tale without any change of expression. "Because Mary's family had a great deal of money. He'd always feared that a fortune hunter would worm his way into Mary's heart." He glanced at the book Chelsea held. "It wasn't a fairy-tale ending."

"He—he was after her money?" Chelsea asked.

"No, turns out, Tommaso had plenty of his own money. Your grandfather discovered this fact, but, alas, he wasn't particularly pleased by the news because in the course of his research, he learned just how Tommaso had acquired said wealth."

And that was it. On that note, Remy just stopped. His hooded expression lingered on Chelsea.

"Don't leave me in suspense," she whispered.

His lips tightened. "Our fathers can be real assholes. They're supposed to be heroes, aren't they? Sometimes, they're not." Another pause. "You sure you'd rather just not know? Believe me, that can be better."

"I spent my whole life not really knowing. I want the truth, no matter how bad it is."

"I guess that's admirable." Remy rubbed a hand over his jaw. "Though I also think it's a mistake, but I suppose it's your mistake to make."

The guy needed to get to the fucking point. Time was ticking. Chelsea wanted the truth, and Remy had damn well better give it to her. "How had Tommaso made his wealth?"

"Gunrunning. Drugs. Prostitution. You name it, and Tommaso—and his father before him—had been involved in the crime. Mary's father revealed the news to her, and, of course, she was heartbroken. Felt utterly betrayed. Tommaso had lied to her about who he was. She'd fallen in love with a man who didn't exist."

A tremble slid over Chelsea's body.

Baby...

"She told Tommaso their relationship was over. She never wanted to see him again."

Fuck. The parallels were there, between Colt and Chelsea and her mother and Tommaso but...

I'm not a damn criminal. I'm not him, I would not—

"She went back to her family. She intended to never see Tommaso again." Remy watched Chelsea carefully. "Took some digging to turn up this information. Someone powerful wanted the past buried. A big red flag in my book. But I can be persistent, and I have sources that aren't all linked to the CIA. When the CIA stonewalled me, I ventured toward those other individuals."

"How did she wind up in Hollow?" Chelsea's voice was too soft. Too flat. "If she went back to her family—"

"This is the part where the story takes another turn. Again, no fairy-tale ending here. I'm honestly surprised she read you those stories at all." He reached for the book she held.

Chelsea jerked back and refused to give it to him.

Appearing unruffled, Remy explained, "She came home a week later after a night visiting friends—came back to what should have been a secure mansion—only to find both of her parents murdered and Tommaso waiting for her. He believed himself to be in love with her, though I have to say based on my experience, it seems more like an extremely unhealthy obsession. He told Mary that she could either run away with him or die with her parents."

Chelsea's breath sawed in and out.

"She chose to leave with him."

"No." A fierce denial from Chelsea. "Your sources are wrong. That's not what happened. She—"

"Tommaso hasn't been seen for almost twenty years. He took your mother back to Italy, but she disappeared on the one-year anniversary of their wedding. He searched and searched for her. I was told that he'd gotten a strong tip about her location at one point. He went after her—because, truly, some obsessions never die—only he didn't return from that trip. I suspect he's probably dead."

Chelsea turned her head toward Colt. Her green eyes swirled with pain and fear. And memories...

He could all but feel her memories in that moment.

Trapped in the closet.

Silent tears.

Fireworks.

Tommaso found his runaway bride. And she had someone she intended to protect. He wasn't going to kill any more of her family.

"Do you see what I just did?" Remy asked.

What he'd just done? Remy had fucking crushed Chelsea with his big reveal, that was what he'd done. Colt moved to stand in front of her. "Yeah, I damn well saw you." His hands had fisted, and all of him wanted to take a swing.

Remy seemed to realize that fact—and he wisely backed up a few steps. "What I did—I shared information that I had obtained. Very-difficult-to-discover information. I had to hit up lots of dark spaces and some rather unsavory characters to uncover that intel. But we actually have Theodore to thank for pointing me in the right direction. Once I had a little information from him, it was like unwinding a twisted ball of thread. You start slowly, then the ball will spin as it all comes undone."

Like he was supposed to buy this? "How do I know you didn't possess this intel all along?"

"Wouldn't I have told you?" He tried to peer around Colt so he could see Chelsea. "Wouldn't I have told her?"

Uh, no.

"I shared. Now it's your turn. What did you discover at Chelsea's house? What treasure did you take out along with the books? Something that everyone else missed, I bet." Remy refocused on Colt. "Everyone else, but not you. Because you got close to her. You charmed her. You learned all the secret parts that she kept hidden from everyone else."

Hell, yes. He'd be taking that swing. "I didn't charm her, you asshole. I fell in love with her." He leapt forward and—

Chelsea grabbed his arm. Just as she'd grabbed him before when she'd stopped him from charging at Remy when they'd been back at Theodore's house.

He looked at her. "Baby, come on. One hard hit. We will *both* feel so much better when you let me knock him on his ass." Because he truly thought Remy had known about Marilyn's past all along. That he was just revealing it now in order to rattle Chelsea. *And you don't get to hurt her.*

No one did.

But she tightened her hold. "You fell in love with me?"

Fuck. Not the way to tell her. He'd tried not to screw up with her, but he'd slipped in the heat of the moment. He could fix this. Maybe. He could—

"Do you love me?" Chelsea asked him. She let him go. Gazed at him with the deepest, greenest eyes in the world.

It wasn't a truth or dare game, and he only had the truth to give her. "Of course." Simple. "Why else would I have come to the island? Why would I have nearly compromised my original mission just so I could spend more time with you?"

"The original mission? But we...we hadn't even slept together back then!"

Her cheeks were dotted with red, and he was glad to see a little color returning to her too pale skin. "Didn't need the awesome sex to love you, though it is certainly a bonus." He caught a lock of her hair. Tucked it behind her ear. "Told you, remember? You're the end game."

"Colt..."

"Seriously? You two act like you're alone. You're not. I'm here." Impatience bled in Remy's voice. "And I was actually trying to help. I shared intel, and now it's your turn to do the same. I'm not leaving until I find out what you took from her home—"

"A key to a safe-deposit box in Hollow, Georgia." Chelsea didn't look his way. Her attention remained on Colt. "It was hidden in the spine of my book. Colt found it, and we're going to the bank to open the box at nine. I'll gladly give the CIA the necklace inside, and then this nightmare can be over. The people after me will know I don't have the necklace, so they won't hunt me any longer." She inched closer to Colt. "It will be over. Life can get back to normal."

I want a life with you. He didn't say that, not yet. He'd already revealed enough.

"I wouldn't be too sure of that," Remy muttered.

Colt glared at him. "And why not?"

"Sometimes, cases can take unexpected turns." He gave a little salute. "You understand that I will be there when the safe-deposit box is opened?"

"You can follow us every step of the way," Colt told him. He knew Remy would do that anyway. "She wants to get rid of the necklace. I want her safe. Once the CIA has the necklace, you talk to your unsavory characters in all those dark places that you know about, and you make them understand it's time to leave her the hell alone." He checked the time on the watch he'd slapped around his wrist. "If we're talking to Theodore, we need to move." His head lifted as he tossed a glare at Remy. "Unless you have more bombshells to reveal?"

"Theodore is awake?" A little edge entered his voice. "Ty didn't tell me that."

"Not my problem what your partner does or doesn't tell you." Colt caught Chelsea's hand. "You ready, sweetheart?"

A quick nod. "Colt, I—"

"I'll follow you," Remy affirmed. As if there had ever been any doubt. "Every step of the way."

"Great. Just what I wanted." No, what he wanted was Chelsea safe. He wanted to take away all of her pain and to discover if there was any way she might be able to love him one day.

But for now...

They had a million-dollar necklace waiting on them.

***

The hospital was eerily quiet. The tile had recently been mopped, and a triangular, yellow, *Wet Floor* sign sat in the middle of the long corridor.

Colt had driven them to the hospital in pretty much record time. Because it was so early, the normally busy streets had been empty. He'd parked out front, and in moments, they'd ridden the elevator up—with Remy—and were on the fifth floor.

As they headed down the hallway, Chelsea caught sight of Ty as he lounged near the door of hospital room 504. When he saw them approaching, he immediately straightened.

"Why the hell didn't you notify me that Theodore was awake?" Remy's first question.

Ty shrugged. "It's early. Was gonna call you soon." He slanted a glance at Colt and Chelsea. His features tightened. "Your Wilde agent friend has been here all night. Just got her to leave for coffee a few minutes ago."

"I didn't leave," a voice announced from the nearby nurses' station. "I just walked five feet to the right. Try being a wee bit more observant."

Chelsea turned and saw a redhead lifting a mug of coffee. "Daphne Willow," the woman said before taking a sip of coffee. "And I don't leave my post. Not unless I'm given a direct order to do so from a supervisor." She pointed to room 504. "Theodore is inside. No one is getting in or out of that room without me knowing."

"He's not talking," Ty announced in the next beat of time. "I tried to get him to cooperate, but the guy clammed up." He shrugged. "There's no point going in now. The CIA will transfer him to a secure facility when his doctor gives the all-clear. Until then, I suggest that you return to—"

"They know where the necklace is," Remy cut in quietly. "We're going to retrieve it, but first, Chelsea wants a word with the man who knew her mother. In exchange for that word, she's agreed to turn over the necklace to us without any issue."

She didn't frown. Didn't so much as twitch in surprise. Remy was making it sound like she'd worked out some sort of deal for this chat time with Theodore, but she hadn't. She had freely agreed to give the CIA the necklace, so what game was he playing?

"That's the price to get the necklace back?" Ty asked. "A few minutes with him?"

Remy nodded.

Ty moved to the side. "Have at it, then. But don't be disappointed when he says nothing. The man got scared by the shot. He's looking out for himself now. He knows that if he talks, hell, that might just be the last mistake he makes."

The words were odd. Almost...like a threat. But, surely, she was just imagining that tone. Ty was Remy's partner. Her gaze swept over him. His shoes weren't mismatching any longer. Both were black, polished. He wore black pants. A dress shirt. Not so disheveled, not like he'd been before they got stateside, even though he must have been at the hospital for hours.

His hair had been swept back. *Not at odd angles.* His gaze was sharp. Maybe a little too sharp as it lingered on her, and she could have sworn there was something about his gaze...something about the intent way he was looking at her...

"There something you want to share with the group?" Colt asked. "Or are you just enjoying the view?"

Ty whipped his stare off her and onto Colt. "I—"

"Yeah?" Colt growled. He stood right behind Chelsea.

Ty's phone rang before he could reply. He hauled it from his pocket. Glanced down at the screen. "That's the boss. He'll want an update."

"I'm sure he'll be thrilled to learn the necklace is coming his way," Remy noted smoothly. "I haven't told him that news yet. Thought you might want to do the big reveal to him yourself. Seeing as how you wanted to make a stellar impression on the gentleman." Remy pointed down the hallway. "Why don't you go take a private moment to chat? I'll stay with them and we'll see if Theodore has anything new to say."

Jerking his head in agreement, Ty scurried down the hallway.

"Don't mind me." Daphne leaned against a nearby desk. "The nurses are out making their rounds and I'm just here, holding down the fort." She sipped a little more coffee. "For the foreseeable future, I'll continue to be here watching for suspicious individuals—and making sure no one interrupts your talk."

"Thanks, Daphne," Colt replied. Then he was urging Chelsea inside room 504. His hand was warm against the base of Chelsea's back. Solid. Reassuring.

She opened the door. Stepped inside. And—

Frail.

Theodore had the covers pulled up to his chest. His head had turned toward her, and he seemed to barely be breathing. All of his vitality had drained away. His skin was as white as the bedding. And when she moved closer, his eyes opened, but he didn't appear to really *see* her at first.

"Theodore?" She hesitated near his bed. Talking with him had seemed so important before. Finding more pieces of the puzzle that was her mother but now...

He was in a hospital gown, but she could see the bulk of his bandage near his shoulder.

"Chelsea?" A croak. His hand flew out. Caught hers. "S-sorry, Chelsea."

They shouldn't have come. He needed more rest. Whatever else had happened in the past, he'd been shot hours before. This wasn't the time to—

"You look so much like her."

His unfocused gaze drifted over her. So very different from Ty's sharp stare.

"But you're not her, are you?" His breath rasped in and wheezed out. "S-sorry...should have...w-warned you..."

"Who did you tell about me?" Chelsea asked him. That was all they really needed to know. The name of the man they were after. If he'd tell her, they could leave. He could rest. Recover.

Theodore stiffened. Seemed to realize that they weren't alone.

Remy and Colt crowded closer to the bed.

"Don't...trust...what you see." Each word seemed to be a struggle for him.

Don't trust what? "We have the necklace."

He shuddered.

"Or...we'll have it soon. And I'm giving it to the CIA."

A hard shake of his head. "Chelsea—"

"Then this will be over. So whoever you told—he won't get the necklace. But the CIA can get him. If you will just tell me his name—"

"Can't..."

She leaned toward him. "You can't tell me?"

"Can't...get him..." So very low.

So low that she leaned ever closer.

"Can't..." His mouth was near her ear. Barely a breath. "When...he works...*with* them." The machines near him began to beep. Fast. Loud.

A nurse rushed inside. "Everyone out, now!"

But—

"Out!"

***

"That wasn't very beneficial," Remy huffed as they rode the elevator down to the bottom floor. "But, I did warn you it would be a waste of time."

Chelsea didn't speak. Her heart pounded so hard and echoed so loudly in her ears that she feared Remy and Colt could hear the frantic thuds.

"Next stop, Hollow, Georgia." Remy looked at the control panel. "Hopefully, that stop will be a whole lot more useful for us all."

Maybe.

She could feel Colt's gaze on her, but she didn't turn to look at him. She was afraid that if she looked at him, she'd give too much away with her expression.

The elevator dinged. The doors slid open. She hurried forward.

Remy put up his arm to block her exit. "Remember that I'll be watching every moment. I know you'll have Wilde agents with you, and your guard dog will be at your side." He flickered a glance toward Colt.

"Don't piss me off," Colt snapped back.

Remy's lips curled in a half-smile. One that vanished when he told Chelsea, "But I will be there every second. You don't have anything to fear."

Yes, she had plenty to fear, and she was very much afraid that she needed to fear Remy.

He stepped away. Motioned for her to exit first, and she practically flew out of the elevator. She didn't speak again, not until she and Colt were in his car. He cranked the engine. Pulled out of the parking space slowly. Checked his rearview.

She opened her mouth—

"Want to tell me what's terrifying you?" he asked mildly.

They were supposed to drive toward Hollow. Just a two-hour trip. A black delivery van had pulled out behind them. She glanced in the rearview mirror and saw Pierce driving the van.

Their procession had started. Remy would be following behind the van.

"Baby?"

"Theodore whispered something to me, right before the nurse came in."

"Yeah, I saw his mouth moving, but I couldn't hear him."

She tugged against the seatbelt she'd snapped into place moments before. "Theodore said the guy he told—Theodore said that he works with them."

"With who?"

"With Remy. With the CIA. The man who's been hunting me works with them." Or maybe he was one of them.

Remy.

Ty.

Agents who'd been tracking her.

Agents who knew exactly where she was going.

And she'd promised to just hand the necklace over to them.

CHAPTER EIGHTEEN

Mavis Higgins hummed as she pulled the safe-deposit box from its position on the top row. Her stylish pumps were a bright blue, a perfect match to the dress she wore. Mavis had been a fixture in Hollow for as long as Chelsea could remember. Married to the preacher, Mavis appeared at every potluck and every sporting event in the town. She cheered the loudest at the football games and sang the most in church. Everyone said she had the voice of an angel.

Her hair was in her trademark twist at the back of her head. And her heavy perfume filled the air around her.

"I kept wondering when you'd show up for the box." Mavis lowered it onto the table that waited in the middle of the vault. "Thought you'd be in after you sold the house, but you never showed. I did worry a bit."

Chelsea tried to muster up a weak smile.

"Then I realized it might just be too hard for you." Sympathy flashed on Mavis's face as she gave a soft pat to Chelsea's shoulder. "I know how close you and your mother were. And, please know, I thought the world of Marilyn. The world. Why, when I broke my right ankle ten years ago—you remember, we had that crazy snow that hit from nowhere and I slipped going down the back porch—your mother brought me breakfast and made fresh coffee for me every single day. She did my laundry, cleaned my house, why, she was just a saint." She winked. "Well, except for when we played cards. Then the woman was a shark." A sigh. "My dearest friend, and each day, I miss her." She pulled out a handkerchief. Dabbed at her eyes. "Well..." Another dab near her left eye. "I'll just give you a moment of privacy, shall I?"

"Thank you."

"Oh, wait, let's just unlock things first. Got your key?"

Chelsea handed her the key.

A moment later, the box was unlocked.

"Take all the time you need," Mavis encouraged. "I'll be right outside." Her attention shifted to Colt. "Nice to meet you."

"Likewise, ma'am."

"You're taking good care of our Chelsea, aren't you? Because she's very special to a lot of people in this town."

"Doing my best, ma'am, because she's very special to me, too."

Mavis beamed. "Good answer." She darted out the door.

The small room—vault—felt decidedly cold. It was a tight space, with safe-deposit boxes lining the walls, closing them in. Really, it was barely bigger than a closet...Chelsea shivered.

"Hey." The back of Colt's hand brushed over her cheek. "You okay, sweetheart? I get that you don't want to be here, but you're not alone. I will be with you the whole time."

Her gaze remained on the box. All she had to do was lift the lid, and this would be over.

"I'll always be with you," Colt promised.

His hand fell.

She turned toward him. "Why did you say that?"

He blinked. "Say that I'd be with you? Because I know this place is tight and you're scared and—"

"No. Why did you say that you fell in love with me?"

His eyes seemed to go even darker. "You're asking about that...*now?*"

Yes, now. Before she opened the box. Before the necklace came out. Before they saw the big, bad treasure that so many people wanted, but that she hated to touch. "Did you mean it?"

"I told you before, you don't get lies from me. That's done."

"Then why didn't you ask me how I felt?"

He leaned toward her. "What?"

"You didn't ask how I felt. Don't you care?"

"Fuck, yes." A growl. "But I thought if you wanted me to know, you'd tell me."

"I do want you to know." Chill bumps covered her skin. "I love you."

His mouth opened. He didn't speak.

So she said it again, "I love you. I loved you back when I thought you were Clark Kent."

"Uh, come again?"

"And it hurt because I didn't think you cared about me. I was in that mess alone—the tangled mess of emotions—and I tried to tell myself it was just attraction. Just need. It wasn't real. But it was. *You* were real. Then you came into my life again, and everything turned upside down." Her chest seemed tight, and she couldn't get her words out fast enough. "I don't want to be upside down any longer."

His fierce expression softened. "You don't have to be."

"I want to be with you. I don't want to be scared. I don't want to wonder what my life would be like without you. I want *you*." There. Done. Said.

She waited.

His arms wrapped around her. "You have me."

So simple. For a moment, Chelsea just savored being held by him. When she was in his arms, nothing seemed quite as scary. The walls weren't closing in. The world had steadied. She was safe.

She fit.

But she eased back. Gazed up at him.

"You're the mission," he told her. "The most important one of my life. My plans...Getting you back. Keeping you safe. Seeing if you could love me. You were it. You always were." A tender smile. "Now let's open that damn box, baby. Let's end this."

She didn't open the box. She shot onto her toes. Her hands locked around his neck. And she kissed him. Kissed him with a quick, wild abandon. With every bit of love that she had.

He kissed her the same way, and she wondered...why hadn't she realized it sooner? Why hadn't she seen the truth staring back at her?

We see what we want to see.

She wasn't afraid of the truth. Not any longer.

Not her feelings for Colt.

Not her mother's past.

It was time for the present. Time for her and Colt.

End this. She pulled away. Whirled back toward the little table. Yanked open the top of the safe-deposit box. Reached inside for the—

Photos?

Chelsea lifted the photos that were tied together with a little pink string. Her fingers shook as she untied that string. Her mother stared back at her in the top photo—her mother...her face so like Chelsea's when she'd been younger. Her mother was smiling. A big, wide grin that stretched across her face.

Smiling as she patted her pregnant belly. Only her mother wasn't alone in the picture. A man was with her. Broad shoulders. Tousled, dark hair. A slightly lopsided grin.

Her father?

But...but he didn't look like some sadistic killer. He was wearing a white t-shirt. Jeans. A baseball cap. And her mom seemed so happy. Not like she was being forced to stay with a man who had terrorized her and killed her parents.

Chelsea slid the photo to the side. Stared at another.

A picture of her mother in a hospital bed. Holding a baby.

Holding me.

For some reason, Chelsea found herself flipping over the photo of the baby—*me*. And on the back, in her mother's hand, she saw the words...

The day my new life began.

There were other photos in that stack. Photos of Chelsea riding a bike when she'd been a kid. Standing in front of a Christmas tree with a red bow on top of her head and a toothless grin on her face. A photo of Chelsea in her middle school cheerleading uniform...

A photo of Chelsea, Mavis, and her mom shooting off fireworks on the Fourth of July...

"She loved you very much," Colt said. "I wish I could have met her."

Tears filled her gaze, but Chelsea blinked them away. "My mother was good." She didn't care what Theodore had told her. His story hadn't matched up with Remy's. Maybe Remy had been lying. Maybe Theodore had been mistaken. Maybe no one knew the real truth but...

But I know her. Chelsea returned to the very first picture. The picture of her pregnant mother. The picture of her father?

She turned over the photo...

Her mother had written a note there, too.

Jo saved us.

But...Jo? Her mother had said that Joseph Ember was her father. Was this man Joseph? Was he her real father? What—

"Something else is inside, baby."

She wasn't looking at the box. She'd flipped the picture back over and was staring at the photo of the tall man with the broad shoulders. That lopsided smile. He looked so happy. As happy as her mother.

"It's a jewelry case." Colt scooped it out. "You want to do the honors?"

She didn't care about the necklace.

"Baby?"

Her gaze darted to him. "You open it."

He slowly opened the square-shaped case. The interior was black, to match the outside, but nestled *inside*...Pearls. Gorgeous, thick pearls...and a gleaming, diamond-filled clasp. Three strands of pearls, just as Remy had described. Absolutely breathtaking. A necklace worth over a million dollars. A necklace that someone had killed to possess.

She held the photos carefully, not wanting to wrinkle them, and Colt closed the lid on the case.

"That's it." Colt searched inside the safe-deposit box. Tapped the bottom. "Nothing else is inside."

The walls and the line of security boxes seemed to press in on her. "Let's go."

He nodded. He kept the necklace. She kept the photos. The image of Jo brushed through her mind as Colt opened the door that led back to the main section of the bank.

Mavis glanced up from her desk. Gave a cheery wave.

And Remy walked right through the front doors of the bank. He headed straight for Colt and Chelsea. He smiled, a smile that didn't reach his eyes. "I do believe you have something for me."

"Nope." Colt shook his head. "Not happening. No way I'm turning over a million-dollar necklace to a confessed thief."

"*What?*" A low cry of what sounded like real disbelief. "We had a deal—"

"Get your boss to meet me in person, and then we'll talk about a deal. Right now, I don't trust you. I don't trust your partner. And before you even think about making a move to physically try and take this necklace from me, I suggest you look around."

Remy glanced around.

"Wilde agents are everywhere. They knew about this location last night, so I had them get into position before I even entered the bank with Chelsea. You're outnumbered by about ten to one."

Remy's cheeks puffed out. "I'm with the CIA—"

"And I don't trust you."

Chelsea's attention jumped between the men.

"Theodore told Chelsea the man who was after her—he worked with the CIA." Colt's voice deepened with fury. "I will not risk her."

Something changed in Remy's eyes. A faint flicker. As if something had slid into place for him.

And that flicker made her uneasy. "Remy?"

His head turned toward her. Once more, he smiled. And, once more, the smile didn't reach his eyes. "I would never cause a physical altercation in a bank. How every undignified. Let's all walk outside and have a talk..." He looked toward the front door.

"How about...no," Colt replied. "Or rather, you go right out the front. We'll be heading out the back. Got a ride waiting out there. But thanks so much." He gave Chelsea a gentle push.

But she locked her feet in place. Following a hunch, she lifted the photo of her mother and Jo. She held it up for Remy. "Do you know this man?"

His lips parted.

That's a yes.

"You did your research on Tommaso. Is this him?"

Remy was suddenly glancing all around the bank as if he expected someone to attack him at any moment. "We need to get the hell out of here."

"That's my plan," a sharp retort from Colt.

She still didn't move. "Is this Tommaso?"

Remy moved his head in a quick, negative shake.

Her heart squeezed. "Then who is it?"

"You need to go," Remy ordered. He backed up. "Get her out, Colt! Go out the back door. Do whatever you need to do—just get her moving!"

"But—" Chelsea sputtered.

"Baby, I don't think Mavis will like it if I carry you out." Colt leaned in close. "She's already giving us suspicious glances, so how about we move? *Now.*"

Mavis was, indeed, sending them a worried look. And starting to close in as her heels tapped on the hardwood floor. So Chelsea unrooted herself from the spot and rushed toward the exit Colt indicated. A bank security guard was stationed near that door, but she knew him, and Rodney Wint just nodded toward her. As soon as they cleared that door—

"Chelsea!" Mavis called after her. "Wait! There's paperwork—"

The delivery van Pierce had driven was parked a few feet away. She rushed toward it and kept clutching her precious pictures.

"No." Ty walked from behind the van. He stepped from the shadows and aimed his weapon at her. "I can't let you run away with that necklace. That's not how this works."

She staggered to a stop. Behind her, Colt swore. She knew he didn't have a weapon on him. He hadn't been able to carry a gun into the bank.

"If you're looking for your Wilde friends, they're being detained." Ty jerked his head toward the van. "They're locked inside and being guarded by some of my fellow agents."

The CIA operatives who had been after her all along? The people Theodore had tried to warn her about?

"I can't let you run away with that necklace," Ty said again. His lips thinned. "I'd thought you were different. I'd wanted you to be different."

Different from what? "I'm not running away with the necklace!" That wasn't the plan.

"*I* have the necklace," Colt snarled. He curled his arm around her and tried to step in front of her. He was *always* doing that. Shielding her body every time a threat appeared, and she appreciated it—truly, but...

Not bulletproof. He could easily be hurt, and she didn't want that gun aimed at him.

"*Chelsea!*" Mavis burst from the bank. "You just cannot leave without—"

A hard arm flew around Mavis's neck and jerked her up against the body of the male who'd just sidled around the building. A man who hadn't made a sound. A man wearing a black ski mask.

Just like the one he wore when he broke into my hotel room. Because the man was the same height, same size, same—

"I'm going to need all the weapons on the ground, *now!*" he bellowed as he moved his own weapon—a gun—and pressed it to the side of Mavis's head.

Mavis let out a high, keening cry.

"Don't hurt her!" Chelsea surged toward him.

Colt grabbed her hand and jerked her right back. "Do not get near him."

"I don't see guns on the ground," the man in the ski mask barked. "So I guess I have to start shooting nice, small-town ladies..."

Chelsea heard Ty swear, right before he dropped his gun.

"Excellent decision," the man praised him. He jerked his head toward Colt. "And you?"

She could see his eyes—blue eyes. Blue eyes peeking out from the holes in his ski mask. Chelsea knew those eyes. She knew him. *Brian.* The man she'd first spotted on the beach. "I wish I had never seen you."

He laughed. "Don't worry, soon enough, I'll be out of your life."

"I don't have a gun on me," Colt said. His tone was low. Steady. Not the least bit scared.

"No? Ah, right, couldn't take it inside, could you?" A laugh. "That would be why I stayed out. Stayed out and waited for my moment. Nothing personal about this but..." He yanked the gun away from Mavis. Aimed it at Colt. "You're in the way."

He was going to fire.

"No!" Chelsea screamed. She shoved her body against Colt as hard as she could. The gun thundered and—

Fire.

Along her back. It blazed and burned deep, and she fell to the ground, tumbling on top of Colt.

"Fuck!" the shooter cried.

"Baby?" Colt stared up at her with horror on his face. "What did you do?"

Mavis screamed. Chelsea wanted to turn and look at her, but her body felt funny.

And then...

Something pressed to her temple.

"That's my gun." The masked shooter—*Brian, I know it's Brian*—snapped. "If I don't get the necklace in the next five seconds, I will be pulling the trigger. Her brains will explode all over you."

She could only look straight at Colt. Her body sprawled on top of his, and in his gaze, she read the mix of flashing emotions. Fear. Worry.

Rage.

He lifted his hand. Held out the jewelry case. "You are a dead man."

Brian snatched the case from him. "Thank you, and now, hate to do it, but when the boss gives an order..."

The gun still pressed to her temple.

Somewhere nearby, Mavis was crying. Chelsea could hear the sound of her tears.

"You have to obey. The bastard has a long memory, and he never forgets any slight." The gun lifted from her temple. Aimed at Colt. Because she was still on top of him, he couldn't fight. Brian was going to pull that trigger. He'd shoot Colt right in front of her.

I'm sorry. She'd been trying to save him. Her body felt so heavy and sluggish and—

"Hey, asshole, over here!"

Remy?

Then...then someone was slamming into Brian's body. Tackling him. The gun flew to the side, and Colt rolled with Chelsea. Pain burst through her at the movement, but she bit her lip to hold back her cry.

"Do not *move,*" Colt ordered. Then he launched his own attack. She could see Remy and Brian—Brian's ski mask had come off—they were rolling on the ground. Colt jumped into the fray. He drove his fist into Brian's jaw. Once, twice. Then delivered a powerful blow to Brian's nose.

She heard bones crunch.

"Chelsea!" Ty touched her cheek. "Are you okay? For a minute there, I thought you'd been hit!"

She had been hit. But she was lying on her back, and she didn't think anyone could see the blood. She could feel it, though. Soaking her shirt. Wetting the ground beneath her. "Help..."

"I will help you, don't worry. Come on, let's get you up—"

Where in the hell were the other CIA operatives? The Wilde agents? Why wasn't there—

"You're dead." Colt's voice. Low and lethal.

She realized there wasn't a need for the cavalry to rush in. Colt and Remy had subdued Brian. Remy held Brian's arms pinned behind his back, and Colt aimed a gun dead-center on Brian's forehead.

"Hell!" Ty whirled to face them. "Don't do it! Don't pull that trigger. Stand down!"

Colt didn't. He smiled at Brian. "You should have never, ever touched her. You just wouldn't stop, would you? But I'm going to make you stop!"

Brian spat blood on the ground. Blood from his busted nose? His lip?

Chelsea tried to sit up, but pain burned through her, so intense that, this time, she couldn't stop her quick cry.

Colt's head whipped toward her. He frowned. "Baby?"

Brian slammed his head back into Remy's face. Remy's hold eased, for just a moment, and Brian broke loose. He flew toward Colt.

Bam.

One shot. Right to the chest. Brian stopped, his body seemingly half-frozen. "Not... personal..."

"No, it fucking was," Colt assured him grimly. "Very personal."

Brian fell onto his side.

"Secure him!" Ty yelled.

Remy swiped a hand under his own bloody nose. "I'm pretty sure he's dead—or damn near dead—and that seems secure enough to me." But he bent and brushed his hands over Brian's prone body.

The back of the van burst open. Two men that Chelsea had never seen before leapt out. Men in black suits. Men with guns. Men who—

"Get the Wilde agents out!" Ty ordered the men. "Uncuff them!"

Uncuff them?

"The perp is down," he blasted. "Search the area. Make sure he didn't have backup!"

Ty was shouting out orders as if he was in charge. But she'd thought that Remy had been training him. Once more, she tried to rise, but...

Something is wrong.

Her body just wasn't responding correctly, and Chelsea realized that the pain she'd felt before was gone. She'd didn't feel any fire along her back. The fire had been replaced with an icy numbness.

"Chelsea." Colt fell to his knees before her. Anger deepened his voice as he growled, "Baby, we fucking talked about this. You were never supposed to get between me and a gun. You could have been hit—"

"I...was..." Slurred. Weak.

He jolted. "What?"

But his gaze slid to the ground. "Is that blood? *Your* blood?"

Probably. But she couldn't tell him that. Couldn't say anything else because she'd started to shake and shudder.

"Chelsea!" A roar. Or maybe it was a whisper. She could see his mouth moving. Horror filled his face. A sort of desperate terror. He reached for her. Pulled her up.

Pierce hit his knees beside Colt. A handcuff dangled from one of Pierce's wrists. "Don't move her! Dammit, man, you know better! Don't—"

I love you. She wanted to say those words to Colt. Needed to say them. She was cold and everything seemed to be getting dark, and she was afraid that she was going to lose him.

Or maybe he's losing me.

Because she'd been shot. There was so much blood. She was so very, very afraid. But not as afraid as Colt. His fear twisted his face. Broke her heart. And she—

"Chelsea!"

This time, she was sure he roared her name. It was the last thing she heard.

CHAPTER NINETEEN

"The CIA swarmed us." Pierce sat with his hands dangling between his legs. The waiting room held a few Wilde agents, and one very somber-looking CIA operative.

Ty Crenshaw huddled in the corner.

"Bastards came at the van, said that we were under arrest. They slapped the cuffs on us. Then sealed us in the van." He swore. "I'm fucking tired of BS arrest scenes from government assholes." He tossed a glare at Ty. "The next thing I knew, I heard a gunshot."

The shot that had been meant for him. The shot that Chelsea had taken. "I didn't realize she'd been hit." He'd just...pushed her to the side. Yelled at her to stay down. She'd had a bullet in her, and he'd left her in the dirt.

Fucking hell. He put his balled hands to his eyes. His eyes burned. Grief wanted to choke him. Grief and pain and terror. They'd had to airlift her to this hospital for treatment. He'd ridden with her, and she'd been out the whole time. He hadn't been able to take his gaze off her. He'd prayed over and over.

She hadn't made a sound. She'd looked so weak and broken.

I left her in the dirt.

"She is my whole fucking world," he rasped.

"You're hers."

His head snapped toward Pierce.

"Why else would she take the bullet?" Pierce asked him.

The words didn't give him any comfort. They just made Colt hurt even more. What in the hell was he supposed to do now? How in the hell was he supposed to—

The waiting room doors burst open. Remy filled the entrance. Fear was stamped on his face. He bounded toward Colt. "Any word?"

Colt could only shake his head. She was in surgery. She had to be okay. The doctors had to fix her. She *had* to be okay.

"Where did she get the pictures?" A quiet question. Hesitant.

Colt, Remy, and Pierce all looked to the left—toward Ty.

Ty lifted the pictures he gripped in his left hand. Chelsea's pictures. Pictures stained with her blood. "Where did she get them?"

"This is your damn fault," Remy accused. He stalked across the room. "Who the hell gave you the authority to lock up Wilde agents? They were supposed to be Colt's backup. I *knew* they were out there, why the fuck do you think I let him go out that way? Why the hell did you interfere—"

"My...my dad gave me the order." He looked down at the pictures. "Where did she get them?"

"You're pulling freaking amateur hour," Remy spat. "I don't give a shit who your dad is or how powerful, I am about to kick your ass—"

And I will help him.

Colt jumped to his feet.

"Shit," Pierce muttered. "So much for sanity." He motioned toward the quiet Wilde agents in the room. "Might need some help over here."

Fuck help. Colt lunged at Ty.

"Where did she get a picture of my dad?"

Colt froze.

Ty lifted the blood-stained picture. The picture of Chelsea's mom and the man in the white shirt. "Where?"

"Such a clusterfuck," Remy muttered.

Colt looked at the picture. Then at Ty. "The photos were in the safe-deposit box. Along with the necklace."

Remy yanked out the necklace from his pocket. "Got this from the dead man." He threw the necklace toward Ty. "Choke on it. Tell your old man—I'm done. You're both bastards, and I am *out*."

Ty had caught the necklace. He held it, but didn't even glance at the pearls. "The photos...were with it?" He stared at the picture...*of his father?* "That's why he sent me after her. Why he wanted her secrets..." His head tipped back. Tears glistened in his eyes. "That's why, and I didn't realize...I talked to her, I had the chance to know her, and I fucking got her *shot!*"

Once more, the waiting room door opened. Only it didn't fly open this time. It opened slowly. Softly. But even at the faint *swish* of sound, Colt whirled.

A man in green scrubs smiled wearily at him. "Are you her fiancé?"

A lie he'd given. So what? He would be her fiancé. Eventually. When she was better. She *had* to get better. "Yes."

"She's going to make it. We removed the bullet and stabilized her..." The doctor kept talking, but all Colt could hear was...

She's going to make it.

She's going to make it.

Hell, yes...*she's going to make it.*

***

"I'm angry."

She opened her eyes. Blinked a few times so things could come into focus.

"Did you hear me, baby? I'm mad. Fucking pissed."

Colt.

"You knew the rules, and you broke them. You nearly died, I wanted to rip the world apart...and that shit can't happen again. It *won't*. You don't get to break your word to me, but, more than that..." His hand brushed over her wrist. "You don't get to be hurt. When you're hurt, everything goes dark. I can't *breathe*. I can't function. I want to destroy and rip apart everything around me because you're hurt. Because I want to hurt someone back. Because I need—"

Her head turned toward him, and Colt stopped talking.

"Baby?"

She swallowed. Her throat ached.

"You...you with me for real this time? Or are you about to fade out again? Because you come in and out, and each time I think you're back with me but—"

"I...heard you."

"You're back. You didn't talk before." He jumped out of his chair. Lunged toward her. Pressed a kiss to her cheek. "You *terrified* me."

She hadn't meant to scare him. She'd only wanted to protect him.

"Never again. Never. Got it? Repeat after me...I will never, ever put myself between Colt and a—"

"Love...you," she said instead. Because she vaguely remembered wanting to say that before. So she said it now. Her voice came out raspy and a little croaky, but that was better than not being able to say anything at all.

His head lifted. His eyes blazed with dark fire. "You are my world. I love you more than anything else, and I always, *always* will."

That sounded good. Better than good. "Am I...okay?" She was afraid to find out—

"You're perfect, just like always. You need time to heal, and you're going to take things extra slow, but you are going to fully recover. Before you know it, you will be drinking margaritas on the beach with me."

That made her smile. "Not so...sure about that..." She might be staying away from beaches for a while. Tentatively, hesitantly, she wiggled her fingers. Her toes. Moved her legs.

Everything works.

"Fine. We don't have to go to the beach for our honeymoon. We can go anywhere you want."

Honeymoon? Just what had she missed?

"Too fast. Right." A nod. "I'll slow down. But just know, I'm planning for it all. The ring. The proposal on one knee. Having you walk down the aisle in whatever dress you want while your friends clap and cheer and I swear to love you forever in front of everyone." An exhale. "A life with you. That's what I want. I'll do anything to have that life."

That life sounded pretty good to her. No, not good—great—to her. But first... "Brian?"

His features darkened. "He's dead."

She'd thought so but... "His boss?"

The door opened. Footsteps shuffled toward the bed.

"Is she..." A voice cracking with hope. "She's awake? Really awake this time?"

Her head rolled on the pillow. Ty stood just inside the doorway. He had a bouquet of flowers gripped in his hands. A few of the petals dropped to the floor because he was shaking those flowers—a nervous shake.

"I'm...awake," Chelsea answered. She frowned at him. Squinted a little. "Aren't we...mad at you?'"

He'd locked up the Wilde agents. Some things were a little fuzzy, but that part wasn't. She remembered him doing that and she also remembered...

Someone stood just behind Ty. An older man. Just as tall. With wide shoulders. And when she looked at him, his lips curved into a slightly...lopsided smile.

OhGod.

Colt threaded his fingers with hers. "I learned a few new things while you were recovering."

Ty and the man behind him made no move toward the bed. They seemed to be waiting for her.

"We identified the man in the picture," Colt explained. "He is Tyler Lawrence Crenshaw. Goes by Law. Currently, he's a very highly ranked operative at the CIA. One might even say he's second in command."

Currently, he was standing behind Ty. And the haziness she'd felt moments before had vanished. Her body seemed hyperaware.

"But back in the day," Colt kept talking, "when your mother met him and he was working undercover, he went by the name of—"

"Jo," the stranger behind Ty finished. "Back then, I was just Jo. Tommaso believed I was a pilot, but I was working undercover."

A dull ringing filled her ears. She...she wasn't ready for this.

Colt's grip tightened on her. "Want me to make them leave?"

Her head turned on the pillow, rolling back toward him.

"Baby..." His face hardened. "We've talked about what happens when you cry." His right hand kept holding hers. His left carefully brushed away her tears. "Don't. I'll send them out. If you don't ever want to talk to them again, you don't have to. I care about the present. Your future. You can forget the past, if that's what you want."

She'd just woken up. Her upper back, near her left shoulder, felt sore. Tight. Her mouth was bone dry, and tears kept leaking from her eyes. No, she wasn't ready to handle the men in the doorway and what they might mean to her. Not now, not on top of everything else—

"I fell in love with your mother right after I met her." The gruff voice from the man in her doorway. "I had thought that I might be able to get close to her. To get her to help me bring Tommaso down..."

She was staring straight at Colt, so she saw his flinch.

"But she got to me, instead. Soon all I wanted was to get her away from him. To get her to safety. She knew what he was, and she feared that Tommaso would never let her go. He'd already made her life hell. Sweet Mary...her smile could light up a whole room." Not gruff. More ragged. "It lit up my life."

"It's time for you to leave," Colt directed. "She just woke up. She was fucking *shot*. And she doesn't need this crap added right now—"

"I'm sorry." From Ty. "Sorry for everything that happened. I-I was supposed to—"

"My fault." Jo—or Law—or whoever he was spoke quickly. "I asked my son to go on this mission because I saw a picture of you, and I remembered the woman who walked away. The woman I *loved*. I thought of your mother a million times, but Tommaso was watching, and my enemies grew over the years, and I just wanted to protect her."

She found herself looking toward him once more.

Tears gleamed in his eyes. "I didn't tell Ty who you were to me. Or rather, who I thought you were." His Adam's apple bobbed as he swallowed. "Being my child puts a target on you." A jerk of his chin toward Ty. "He knows that's true. And you already had enough targets on you. Tommaso has been in the wind for years. I've hunted and hunted, but he's gone to ground so well..."

Oh, I think he's gone to ground, all right. More like, gone in the ground.

"Then one day, I got intel about the necklace." He swallowed. "Mary's necklace."

"That's enough," Colt said. "She's fucking *tired*. You—"

"She...stole the necklace from Tommaso?" Chelsea asked as she tried to put everything together.

A negative shake of his head. "That necklace was hers. Always, hers. Belonged to her mother, been in Mary's family for years. But Tommaso took it. Like he took so much from her. And the night I got her out—the night we fled—she wanted to take a part of her life with her. She got Theodore to help her. Hell, back then, he had a different name, too. Guess we all did. He broke into Tommaso's safe, got the necklace for her, and I took care of getting her flown out of there." His lips pressed together. "She was pregnant with you. I-I thought you were Tommaso's. Thought she wanted to get you away from him before he could hurt you like he'd hurt her."

Colt's lips brushed over her cheek. "I need you to stop crying. Please."

She couldn't.

Law kept talking. Revealing the past bit by bit. "I pulled strings. Got her a new identity. When we landed in the US, Marshals were waiting for us. She kissed me goodbye and thanked me for saving her." His head sagged forward. "She saved *me*. My wife had died three years before. I was a fucking ghost of a man, but she brought me back. I knew I had to stop Tommaso. I couldn't let him hurt her, but the sonofabitch had so much power. When I got back to Italy, he'd learned that I betrayed him. He knew I'd helped her escape..." He stopped.

Ty finished, "He shot my father. Dad wound up in a hospital for six months. He was in a coma for three of those months. Took him a long time to remember everything that had happened. Hell, he didn't even remember me at first." A glance back toward his dad, before his gaze darted to Chelsea. "And it was only later that he'd remember your mother and you."

Remember.

"Mary had a lot of secrets," a rumble from Law. "One of the biggest was you. You don't look a fucking thing like Tommaso. But you do have my mother's eyes. The greenest eyes I've ever seen. When I saw a picture of you...when I learned about Mary's necklace and the hunt for it and I saw a picture of you with those eyes..."

Her breath shuddered in and out. Too hard. Too fast.

"Enough." A growl from Colt. He let her go. Stormed toward the two men. "What part of *she-was-just-fucking-shot* do you not understand? You don't dump life-altering shit on her now. I don't give a damn if you do run the CIA. Get the hell out. When she's stronger, when she wants to talk to you, we'll come to *you*." He jabbed his finger into the older man's chest. "And when—if—we do, then you had better have one damn fine explanation as to why you didn't get in her life sooner, asshole. Because you don't abandon—"

"I thought she was his! And I thought she was safe. Until I saw..." He ran a shaking hand over his face. "I didn't know the truth until after Mary died. My life was one damn mission after another. Over and over." His eyes glittered. "I was a shit father to my son, and I wasn't there for you, Chelsea. I didn't know...I didn't *know*. But I'm here now. For you both. And just...maybe it's not too late?"

Her hands twisted against the sheets.

"Out the door," Colt ordered. "Now."

Ty put down the flowers. Sat them on the little table near the door. "I didn't know what kind you liked." His hand shoved into the back of his jeans. He rocked forward. "I'd like to find out. I'd like to find out everything about you. And perhaps you'll want to know some stuff about me?"

Dazed, she could only stare at him. What they were saying...

The man with the desperate eyes—he was her father?

And Ty was her brother?

A fist tapped against the door. "What in the hell is going on in here?" Remy called as he poked his head inside the room. "A party, and no one invited me?" He shouldered past the two men who gazed so desperately at Chelsea.

He peered at everyone. Noted Colt's stiff shoulders and clenched fists, then shot a glance Chelsea's way. He smiled at her. "Hi. Glad to see you're back with us." Casually, he made his way to the bed. Ignored everyone else. "Do you know how absolutely freaked Colt was? Totally thought the man was about to rip the hospital apart with his bare hands if they didn't let him see you. Oh, and you're his fiancée, in case anyone asks. He told them that because you didn't have any next of kin—"

Both Ty and his father—*my father?*—flinched.

Remy smirked a little, a quick flash, and she realized he knew the truth. He'd just been making a dig at the silent men. "So Colt made sure you had someone to claim you." He took the seat Colt had vacated. "But between us, you and I both know he's probably actually already carrying around a ring and waiting for the right moment to propose." He cleared his throat. Raised his voice. "FYI for the people in the room, the right moment for big bombshells is *not* after a woman first wakes up from being shot and needing surgery to remove the bullet. That is not the perfect time to drop big deals on her. Anyone with a lick of tact would know that."

"I was scared." Her father. His identity was slowly sinking in. Gruffly, he added, "If you want to talk...*When*...I'll be waiting." He turned away.

After one last look at her, Ty turned away, too.

"One thing..." Remy called. "Before you go."

Both men stiffened.

"Did everyone notice how I gallantly turned over the necklace? How I didn't run with it?"

They glanced back at him.

"Shouldn't I get a 'job well done' for that? It would have been so easy to take it and vanish. But here I am." A long exhale. "Who knew being good was so exhausting?"

"You're done, Remy." From...*her father*. Still felt weird. Crazy. "Consider all debts paid." He reached for the door. He and Ty filed out.

She could pull in deep breaths again. A lot of breaths that didn't help to steady her nerves.

Colt hurried back to the bed. "Sweetheart, look, you don't have to see them ever again—"

"I...want to."

A line appeared between his brows. "You do? You're sure?"

"I want to talk to them. Both of them." *Family*. Twisted, secretive...family. "I want to learn more." *Because my mother looked so happy. Because she said he saved us.* "About them both." When she was stronger. When she wasn't in a hospital bed. When she hadn't just woken up. When the tears would freaking stop.

Colt gently wiped them away for her again. "Then you will. I'll make sure of it."

"*Ahem*."

Colt didn't look Remy's way. He kept his stare on Chelsea. "I want to be alone with my *fiancée*. I nearly lost my mind, and I'd like some time to just be with her without the whole freaking world busting in and stressing her out." His tone was flat. But his smile for Chelsea was ever so tender. "Get out, Remy."

"Sure. Sure. Definitely will be getting out. But first, I was wondering...just when are you going to tell the big CIA boss that Chelsea's mother killed the infamous Tommaso?"

CHAPTER TWENTY

She surged up. Winced in pain.

"No." Colt gently pushed her back. "No way, baby. Enough. You take it easy. I've already lost at least ten years of my life because I was so scared. You don't get to go ripping open stitches." Now he did glare at Remy. "Can you stop being an asshole for five whole minutes?"

"Look, I'll admit, that was just a guess on my part, but her reaction confirmed it. From what I learned, Tommaso wasn't ever going to stop hunting Mary—correction, Marilyn. And she'd found a safe spot. A life she loved. One that gave her a place for her daughter."

Chelsea didn't speak.

"Wonder who helped her get rid of the body," Remy mused as he tapped his chin.

"Leave," Colt directed. "Out the door. Now."

"You know, this might sound crazy but, my money is on Mavis." A nod. "She was your mom's close friend, wasn't she? Mavis also knew about the safe-deposit box. I bet she knew a few other secrets that she never told you, too. The kind of secrets that a best friend normally takes to the grave."

Mavis?

"Maybe you should have a talk with her. Or maybe not." He rose from the chair. "Because it'd be awfully unfortunate for a preacher's wife like her to be sent to jail for covering up a murder so long ago. Especially when the dead man was a total bastard who deserved what he got." Another smile toward her. "Just my two cents." He rolled back his shoulders. Inclined his head toward Colt. "And don't worry. I might not be CIA official any longer, but I will find out where Theodore went. You have my word. The case doesn't end for me until we locate him."

"Theodore?" What was he talking about?

Colt grabbed Remy by the shoulder. Pushed him toward the door. "You're as bad as they are," he snarled. "*Just woke up*. No more bombshells."

"And you want alone time with her, got it," Remy replied as he was shoved forward. "But I was worried, too. I like her. So I wanted to check in." He fired a glance over his shoulder at Chelsea. "I mean 'like' not in a romantic sense, of course, because Colt would want to fight me then—"

"I want to fight you now," Colt groused as he yanked open the door.

Remy winked at her. "Glad you're awake. We'll talk more later about—"

Colt slammed the door shut on him. Kept his hand pressed to the door for just a moment. His strong back remained to her.

"I don't...I don't think I want more bombshells."

His back stiffened.

Oh, no.

"I'm sorry, baby, but there's gonna be one more. I can't leave you in the dark. Fuck it." He straightened. Turned toward her.

She grabbed the remote for the bed. Pressed the button that would angle her up because she needed to be higher to feel better and more in control. A quick stab of pain slid through her. She ignored it. "Just tell me so we can get back to you holding me and saying you love me and that everything is going to be all right."

With slow, but certain steps, he returned to the bed. Sat down beside her. Tucked a lock of her hair behind her ear. "I love you."

Her breath whispered out. The world steadied. "I love you."

His hand took hers. "I will hold you forever."

That sounded nice.

"And everything will be all right, I promise you that. I will work the rest of my life to make sure that you are safe and happy and protected."

She'd do the same for him. Didn't he understand? He might be furious because she'd taken that bullet but...She loved him. She wanted to protect him. She wanted Colt safe and happy and protected, too.

"Theodore Beasley escaped from the hospital in Atlanta."

Escaped. An odd word choice.

"Daphne was stationed outside of his room. He didn't exit that way. He climbed out the fifth-floor window and shimmied down with a rope he'd made by tying sheets together."

She laughed. Nervously. Shook her head—

"He's not in his eighties. Apparently, that's one of his many lies. The man was quite the gymnast back in the day, one of the reasons he made such a good thief. He was great at getting in and out of places. A habit he's maintained." His jaw tightened.

"He ran...because he was afraid of being charged with..." Chelsea floundered. With what? "My break-in? Or stealing the jewelry from your client—"

"Murder."

"What?"

"Brian Lambert was a hired mercenary. When the CIA got his phone, they traced his calls—they went back to Theodore. Theodore was the man who hired Brian. Brian and several others. Theodore wanted the necklace. Felt like he was owed it, according to the texts we've recovered, and he was going to do whatever it took in order to get it back."

"But he was shot!" Right in front of her. In his own home. "By someone in the house across..." *Oh.* Damn. "Someone else he'd hired?" she guessed.

"That's what we think. That's how the shooter knew to be in position before the Wilde agents ever arrived. Think about the scene in the study. Theodore tugged the curtains open a little before the shot was fired. He gave the signal and positioned himself. The shot hit nothing vital, and he was able to be whisked away from the scene. Suddenly, he became the victim. No one suspected him, and he was able to slip from the hospital—"

"While he sent Brian to collect the necklace." Anger blasted inside of her, giving her some much needed strength. "That bastard!"

"He's in the wind, but Wilde is looking for him and so is the CIA. He won't escape. We will get him, I swear it."

The door swung open—

"Dammit, I just kicked you out!" Colt blasted as he turned and...

The nurse shot him a quelling frown. "No one kicks me out. I am here to check on my patient. *You* need to step outside."

A muscle jerked along Colt's jaw.

"No, I want him to stay. Please." Chelsea needed him.

"Apologies on the yell," Colt said stiffly, and his cheeks held a tint of pink. "I thought you were someone else."

The nurse lifted a brow. "Mind if I check on my patient?"

"I...go ahead."

Shaking her head, the nurse reviewed Chelsea's vitals. "Someone's heart rate is up," she noted.

Yes, but that had nothing to do with her injury. It had a whole lot more to do with learning her father's identity. Discovering she had a brother. Realizing that Theodore had been behind the attacks all along. And knowing—

"Just so you know," the nurse said as she checked on Chelsea, "your fiancé has been the bane of this hospital from the moment you arrived. I think he's terrified the doctors. Threatened them if they didn't get you in absolute perfect condition. He and his mini army that has been filling the hallway and waiting rooms...I thought they'd storm the recovery room when word reached them that you were out of surgery." But she gave Chelsea a small smile. "A lot of people must care a great deal about you."

She'd thought she was alone. After she'd lost her mother, it had just been her.

"Does everything look okay?" Colt's soft question. One laced with worry.

"She is healing nicely. Told you that about twenty times already—you know, all those other times I came in and you *didn't* yell at me." The nurse turned away, but pointed sternly at Colt. "Don't stress my patient. No more racing heart rates." She made her way to the door.

Chelsea gazed up at Colt. "My heart races a lot when I'm with you," she confessed.

He closed the distance between them and put his forehead against hers. "I fucking love you. Don't ever get shot again. Ever."

She inhaled his crisp, masculine scent. Pulled in his warmth. Felt surrounded by his strength. "It is not on my agenda."

His head lifted. "What is?"

"Loving you."

He kissed her. And she knew that everything would be all right.

"Oh, by the way," Colt murmured against her lips. "That necklace is legally yours...so what do you want to do with one-point-four-million dollars?"

When she gasped, he drank up the sound...and kissed her again.

CHAPTER TWENTY-ONE

Four months later...

Theodore Beasley squinted at the annoying man in front of him. He'd been relaxing in his chaise lounge, listening to the beautiful thunder of the waves, and enjoying some warmth from the amazing Mediterranean sun. He was on a tiny Greek isle, a million miles away from those fools at the CIA, and...

This asshole had just appeared. An asshole who was blocking his sun and his view.

Behind the lenses of his sunglasses, Theodore glared. He also straightened. "You're in my way."

The man kept gazing out at the waves. His broad back was to Theodore.

Growing angrier, Theodore bolted out of his comfy chaise and stood up. "Did you hear me?" he demanded. "You're in my way. There is plenty of space on this beach. There is no need for you to be right in front of—"

The man turned toward him. Smiled.

Shit.

"There's plenty of need," Colt Easton told him. "Because I'm pretty fucking pissed at you. You hunted the woman I love. She was shot."

"I-I—" Fuck. Screw this. He turned. Started to run back toward the hotel.

A large beach umbrella slammed into his stomach. The surprise of the blow had him stumbling back. Tripping. Falling onto the sand.

"That was for lying to me," Chelsea announced. She came closer. Glared down at him as she still held the umbrella.

He blinked up at her—and Colt. Fear thundered through him. They'd found him. But...but they could work out a deal. Surely—

"I kept trying to figure out what I could give to my wife as a wedding present." Colt stared down at him. Colt wore sunglasses, and Theodore's own desperate reflection peered back at him from the dark lenses of those glasses. "Then I realized, hey, let me gift wrap the bastard who made her life hell. Let me hunt him down and get my CIA buddies to toss him in a cell for the rest of his life. Perfect present."

"Perfect," Chelsea agreed.

This couldn't happen. "No, no, look, I have money—lots of it! And connections. And, and—"

"And I have a prison cell waiting for you." Another head joined and stared down at Theodore as he sprawled in the sand.

"Did you ever meet CIA operative Ty Crenshaw?" Colt asked. "No? Probably were too busy doing other things...like staging your own shooting, ransacking Chelsea's place, or, hell, maybe even climbing down the side of a hospital building."

Theodore pushed up to his elbows. "You...you..."

Ty told him, "Theodore Beasley—or whatever alias you're using these days—you are under arrest."

When Theodore screamed in rage and flew upright, when he barreled forward determined to get the hell away or to take them down or to—

Chelsea hit him with her umbrella again.

His body sagged on the sand.

***

"That was an amazing wedding present," Chelsea told Colt as she watched her brother lead away a cuffed Theodore. "Thank you."

"Well, I know it wasn't on the registry." He settled on the chaise lounge beside her. "But it seemed like something you would enjoy."

She more than enjoyed it. Their lounge chairs were positioned right next to each other. The waves crashed and rolled nearby.

"I wasn't going to stop until I found him," he added, and Colt's voice had gone hard. "No way that bastard was staying on the loose. No one hurts you and gets away. *No one.*"

She pulled her gaze from Theodore. Found Colt looking at her. His expression was so fierce, but his eyes held such tenderness. That was her Colt. Tough and scary with the rest of the world, but with her, softer.

Because he loves me.

"I know you weren't wild about a beach honeymoon, so how about we fly out of here..." He suggested. "We can hit the slopes in Switzerland, we can—"

She leaned toward him. Her hand pressed to the stubble on his cheek. The man was so sexy. "All I want to hit is the nearest bed, and I want to hit it with you."

He surged out of his chair. "That can be arranged." He grabbed her hand. Pulled her up. Scooped her into his arms.

"Colt!" Laughter spilled from her. Not her nervous laugh. A happy, free laugh. One of absolute joy. Because she *was* happy. She had a family—a father she was slowly getting to know. A brother who had plenty of his own secrets, but seemed to love spending time with her. And, best of all...

Colt.

She had a husband who put her above everything else in his life. One who loved her, protected her...

And who had given her the best wedding present of all time.

With Colt, she would have a wonderful life. One filled with great memories, adventures, and the most phenomenal sex a woman could want.

Her mouth slid toward his ear. "Want to play some truth or dare?"

His hold tightened. He double-timed it across the sand.

And she laughed once more.

THE END

A NOTE FROM THE AUTHOR

Thank you so much for taking the time to read EX MARKS THE PERFECT SPOT! I love writing second chance romances, and I hope that you enjoyed Colt and Chelsea's story. I can't believe that EX MARKS THE PERFECT SPOT is Book 16 in my "Wilde Ways" series. It has been such a wonderful experience writing these books! All of my "Wilde" books are complete, stand-alone reads—with guaranteed happy endings. Because we can all use some happiness now and then.

If you'd like to stay updated on my releases and sales, please join my newsletter list.

https://cynthiaeden.com/newsletter/

Again, thank you for reading EX MARKS THE PERFECT SPOT.

Best,
Cynthia Eden
cynthiaeden.com

ABOUT THE AUTHOR

Cynthia Eden is a *New York Times*, *USA Today*, *Digital Book World*, and *IndieReader* best-seller.

Cynthia writes sexy tales of contemporary romance, romantic suspense, and paranormal romance. Since she began writing full-time in 2005, Cynthia has written over one hundred novels and novellas.

Cynthia lives along the Alabama Gulf Coast. She loves romance novels, horror movies, and chocolate.

For More Information

- *cynthiaeden.com*
- *facebook.com/cynthiaedenfanpage*

HER OTHER WORKS

Ice Breaker Cold Case Romance

- Frozen In Ice (Book 1)
- Falling For The Ice Queen (Book 2)
- Ice Cold Saint (Book 3)

Phoenix Fury

- Hot Enough To Burn (Book 1)
- Slow Burn (Book 2)
- Burn It Down (Book 3)

Trouble For Hire

- No Escape From War (Book 1)
- Don't Play With Odin (Book 2)
- Jinx, You're It (Book 3)
- Remember Ramsey (Book 4)

Death and Moonlight Mystery

- Step Into My Web (Book 1)
- Save Me From The Dark (Book 2)

Wilde Ways

- Protecting Piper (Book 1)
- Guarding Gwen (Book 2)
- Before Ben (Book 3)
- The Heart You Break (Book 4)
- Fighting For Her (Book 5)
- Ghost Of A Chance (Book 6)
- Crossing The Line (Book 7)

- Counting On Cole (Book 8)
- Chase After Me (Book 9)
- Say I Do (Book 10)
- Roman Will Fall (Book 11)
- The One Who Got Away (Book 12)
- Pretend You Want Me (Book 13)
- Cross My Heart (Book 14)
- The Bodyguard Next Door (Book 15)

Dark Sins

- Don't Trust A Killer (Book 1)
- Don't Love A Liar (Book 2)

Lazarus Rising

- Never Let Go (Book One)
- Keep Me Close (Book Two)
- Stay With Me (Book Three)
- Run To Me (Book Four)
- Lie Close To Me (Book Five)
- Hold On Tight (Book Six)

Dark Obsession Series

- Watch Me (Book 1)
- Want Me (Book 2)
- Need Me (Book 3)
- Beware Of Me (Book 4)
- Only For Me (Books 1 to 4)

Mine Series

- Mine To Take (Book 1)
- Mine To Keep (Book 2)
- Mine To Hold (Book 3)
- Mine To Crave (Book 4)
- Mine To Have (Book 5)

- Mine To Protect (Book 6)
- Mine Box Set Volume 1 (Books 1-3)
- Mine Box Set Volume 2 (Books 4-6)

Bad Things

- The Devil In Disguise (Book 1)
- On The Prowl (Book 2)
- Undead Or Alive (Book 3)
- Broken Angel (Book 4)
- Heart Of Stone (Book 5)
- Tempted By Fate (Book 6)
- Wicked And Wild (Book 7)
- Saint Or Sinner (Book 8)
- Bad Things Volume One (Books 1 to 3)
- Bad Things Volume Two (Books 4 to 6)
- Bad Things Deluxe Box Set (Books 1 to 6)

Bite Series

- Forbidden Bite (Bite Book 1)
- Mating Bite (Bite Book 2)

Blood and Moonlight Series

- Bite The Dust (Book 1)
- Better Off Undead (Book 2)
- Bitter Blood (Book 3)
- Blood and Moonlight (The Complete Series)

Purgatory Series

- The Wolf Within (Book 1)
- Marked By The Vampire (Book 2)
- Charming The Beast (Book 3)
- Deal with the Devil (Book 4)

- The Beasts Inside (Books 1 to 4)

Bound Series

- Bound By Blood (Book 1)
- Bound In Darkness (Book 2)
- Bound In Sin (Book 3)
- Bound By The Night (Book 4)
- Bound in Death (Book 5)
- Forever Bound (Books 1 to 4)

Stand-Alone Romantic Suspense

- It's A Wonderful Werewolf
- Never Cry Werewolf
- Immortal Danger
- Deck The Halls
- Come Back To Me
- Put A Spell On Me
- Never Gonna Happen
- One Hot Holiday
- Slay All Day
- Midnight Bite
- Secret Admirer
- Christmas With A Spy
- Femme Fatale
- Until Death
- Sinful Secrets
- First Taste of Darkness
- A Vampire's Christmas Carol

Printed in Great Britain
by Amazon